SPARCUS
BROKEN WORLDS

BOOK I

GIUGI CARMINATI

*To Alejandro, Lorenzo, Raphael, Fernando,
Federico & Giuliana*

PROLOGUE

Forty-seven years ago, on June 14, 2198, Earth was contacted by the people of the twin planets Astarte and Qetesh: the Sparcus. Soon after Contact Day, or C-Day, as it had become known, eight other civilizations made themselves known to Earth as well. Their alliance—acquaintance was a more correct term—was tenuous at best. From C-Day to December 21, 2200, all ten civilizations had tried to get along, but simply been unable to. Most of the resentment came from the inability of seeing each other as anything other than "alien" and, consequently, a threat. Inevitably, as some would say, on December 21, 2200 war broke out and lasted fifteen bloody, inexorable, and painful years. The battles raged from planet to planet. No surface was left unscathed, no civilization untouched or uninvolved. Alliances had formed, disintegrated, re-formed, shifted, and been altered by the changing tides and strategic motivations of their leaders. Human colonies on Mars and on an Earth twin called Earth 2—named either for lack of a better moniker or insufficient imagination—were Earth's meager outposts in a war where its forces eternally played catch-up. Despite numerous attempts to end the violence, whether by diplomacy or brute force, the conflict raged on, with no end in sight. That is, until it became apparent that brute force — Sparcus brute force, to be precise — could finally end it all. The Sparcus's dominance became undeniable and terrifying. Sparcus armies began sweeping across the galaxy, bringing every other civilization but the Bar'aat (the consummate arms dealers) to their knees. To the subjugated civilizations, it was all but inevitable that the Bar'aat would agree to a ceasefire and supply the Sparcus with enough weapons to make their victory permanent. And time was running out.

Unsurprisingly, in the year 2200 the other eight planetary systems finally agreed on something: the Sparcus had to be stopped. And Earth had the solution: Project Geno. The concept was simple, devastating, and elegantly brutal: distribute a sterilizing agent that targeted the Sparcus men throughout the galaxies, using the already-existing distribution routes. Over the preceding fifteen years, weapons and technology had stretched far and wide. The Sparcus controlled and operated most of the network. The toxin could be released in the air, the water, and the food, infecting every Sparcus that came in contact with it. It only affected Sparcus men, but women needed to be inoculated too in order to ensure the sterilization of any gestating fetuses. The Bar'aat agreed it would be in their interest to cooperate, seeing the Sparcus as a soon-to-be-defeated side of the conflict.

Project Geno was implemented in mere days. Within a month, Earth assured its newfound allies that distribution was complete. By the time the Sparcus received official news that they had been the targets of a slow-progression genocide, they had already become aware that something was wrong. Their usually very high rate of pregnancy had plummeted. Medical tests on the males confirmed they — and not their mates — were the source of the problem. The inability to reproduce made it impossible for the Sparcus to keep fighting. Every lost soldier would never be replaced. The Sparcus capitulated and had no choice but to acquiesce to the other civilizations' demands. The Great Conflict ended in 2215, leaving Sparcus the sole loser in the first intergalactic battle involving Earth.

BOOK I
CHAPTER 1

Wes stepped into the warm New York night. He had been on Earth for an entire twelve years, but still missed the orange skies and purple moons of his home planet, Nash'amir. For the son of a human, he was strangely uncomfortable being on what was supposed to be his "home" planet. He walked away from the restaurant, leaving a frustrated date to finish her meal alone. As soon as his IPP communicator had gone off, he had bolted up and quickly excused himself. As he had anticipated, the call was urgent. He had to get to IPP headquarters immediately. The warm lights of the romantic setting glowed behind him, reflecting in the water on the pavement. The rain had just stopped. Wes pondered his new assignment as he picked up the pace. He had asked for an assignment as a human handler to a Sparcus covert agent, and his request had been granted. She was supposedly a handful and particularly hateful of humans. Now, without even meeting her, they had been assigned to investigate a murder. He felt both anticipation and trepidation at the idea of being so close to a Sparcus again. Something about their presence was comforting, although they certainly never viewed it that way. The agent probably would have preferred to see him dead than anywhere near her.

The fact was, Wes mused, the Sparcus *were* tougher, faster, stronger, supremely well trained, and both their women and their men participated in combat equally, which automatically doubled their fighting power. In fact, the women were usually in leadership positions. The Sparcus also had unimaginable esprit de corps. They left nobody behind and took no prisoners. It was them against the galaxy, no matter what, no matter how. These thoughts led Wes to ponder the Great Conflict, which always brought back memories of his mother, teaching him the lessons of the past. Her black waist-length hair stroking his face as he placed his head against her chest, listening to her tales of battle. Her voice always dropped to a soft, measured, but tense cadence when she got to describing the Slaughter. It was this part of their history where she most tried to seem collected although the atrocity tore both her and Wes's father to their core.

Wes's thoughts returned to the present: the thought of Project Geno always made his skin crawl. An act of genocide, even if committed by his father's people—humans—and even in the name of interplanetary salvation, was still an act of genocide. This was the legacy Wes brought with him as he prepared to meet his new Sparcus covert agent. This was the legacy every human brought into the room when they met a Sparcus.

Wes walked toward IPP headquarters at a brisk pace. He knew he was in for a long night, but he hoped he could make it home before dawn. The IPP, or Interplanetary Police, was the product of futile attempts to create a peace commission. As a child, he remembered the Peace Patrol sending its "forces," the Peacers, throughout the galaxy, trying to make sure the cease fire was respected and that the Sparcus—or anyone else—didn't try to reignite war. Peacers wore distinctive purple sashes to distinguish themselves from every other organized force. But constant fights, riots, ghettos, and discrimination made it impossible for them to do their jobs. Conflict was everywhere. Public sentiment eventually turned against the Peacers, who were viewed as ineffective and useless. Indeed, nobody ever used the term Peacers, preferring the derogatory moniker Beauty Queens, both because the sashes made the Peacers look like contestants in a pageant and—in most people's estimation—because they were just as effective at bringing about "world peace." Eventually the Peace Patrol—and with it the Peacers—was eliminated and the IPP took its place. First, with nothing more than armed soldiers keeping people subdued, then with an ever-growing infrastructure that included intelligence officers, covert and overt agents, and informants of all races. Of course, the "handler" system Wes was so used to. The IPP recruited agents from every planet, including Sparcus. Every covert agent had an overt handler, and the two were never of the same race. The idea was to create alliances across species, making it harder and harder for war to break out. It seemed a good idea in theory. In practice, it created tensions throughout the IPP. Bringing civilizations together by force did nothing to actually unite them.

Wes reached the glass IPP door. The building was completely lit both inside and out. This was truly the agency that never slept. Officers worked twenty-four hours a day, seven days a week. Around the clock they processed data, debriefed informants, and designed missions—all in an effort to stay a step ahead of those threatening the tenuous peace. At least, that was the official policy. Wes wondered how much good they were really doing.

He walked through the lobby, which resembled a cathedral of some sort. Large, white tiles laid in a singular pattern across the reflective floor. Barely noticeable sensors and cameras mounted along the walls began scanning him. Upon recognition, he was given access to the rest of the building. He reached a large red sign seated above two large, heavy sealed doors that read, "Unauthorized Personnel Will Be Shot." Indeed, security guards were a thing of the past. Two single-barrel dart guns and two rapid-fire laser guns protruded from the walls, pointed inward, ready to maim or kill any unauthorized person who attempted to venture any further. The heavy silver rifles were set to fire tranquilizers, while the machine guns were less innocuous.

Wes took a left following the mandatory checkpoint. He opened a door and stepped into a darkened briefing room. Streetlights filtered through the shades, which gave the four floor-to-ceiling windows a slight glow. The only other light source in the room came from the projections on the oval conference room. Photos from a crime scene flittered across the room. The four people at the table were moving the images around with their fingers, flipping back and forth from one to the next and back. One of them brought a photo from the autopsy into the foreground. There was low muttering of a barely audible conversation. Wes's eyes grew accustomed to the low lighting immediately and he saw her: Sarza — the Sparcus — his covert IPP agent. She had found the only place in the room where the shadows were so dark he could barely see her.

"Wes Venta, IPP." Wes uttered mechanically, nominally, to the humans at the table. He didn't take his eyes off Sarza as he spoke. She wore knee-high black leather boots with flat soles. Her black velcra leggings hugged her perfect athletic figure, while her two holsters hung by her side, strapped to her thighs. Her black turtleneck and jacket, also velcra, covered everything up to her neck. Her face was made up of beautifully sharp features: light lips, large eyes, long eyelashes, and a strong jawbone. Her long black hair hung to mid-torso. Velcra was the material of choice for the Sparcus. It was laser resistant (although not laser proof), easy to move in, able to neutralize all odors, and adaptable to all weather conditions. Velcra had interesting physical properties as well, hardening when hit with a high-velocity impact over a small surface but moving almost like liquid when spread out across large surfaces – the way a limb moves inside clothes. Most importantly, it was painful to the touch for any non-Sparcus. Sarza's two hands wore black half-gloves that left her fingers exposed. Each glove had a small silver circle in the middle of it, in the center of the palm, which reacted to extended pressure (for example against an enemy's head). Her arms and hands hung relaxed on the sides of her body. Her fingers curled gently against her thighs, always in between a fist and an open hand, ready to either punch or liquefy her opponent's brain with a single touch from her native hand-worn weapon. Either one of those gloves, the Sparcus Gloves, could produce a pulse so powerful, that Wes's brain would turn to liquid in just seconds. Very few Sparcus were allowed to wear their native weapons. The interdiction on weaponization was the punishment the others had imposed on the Sparcus after the Great Conflict. As an IPP agent, Sarza was one of the trusted few.

As Wes took in Sarza, she did the same to him. She noticed he was tall with olive-toned skin, wearing an unbuttoned freshly pressed white collared shirt, along with black suit pants. His eyes were green, his hair dark brown, and his masculine jaw covered with an inviting five o'clock shadow purposefully left there for effect (she was sure). Many would have considered his figure striking: tall and muscular, with wide shoulders and visibly strong arms. He obviously worked at maintaining his physique. Sarza knew he'd been on a date. She could smell the expensive red wine on his breath from across the room, although it was a very faint odor. He'd had just a glass, maybe two. Sarza also detected some female perfume of some sort. The smell resembled that of a sweet vanilla flavor. Wes finally looked very briefly at the three individuals sitting at the table, then up again toward Sarza. Gazing straight toward her, as she still stood at the back of the room, his glare surprised her. She stared back, knowing full well he couldn't see her eyes. He looked back at the people flipping through the photos. They looked up at him.

Sarza had entered the room after the people at the table had already taken their places. She stood in the back, watching them. They knew she was there, she could sense it, but none of them would turn around. None of them would look at her, let alone acknowledge her presence. She could smell the stink of their fear dripping off of them.

Now that Wes was in the room, they were talking to him and still ignoring her. One of them, a young, skinny, eager-looking blonde obviously impressed by Wes stood up, "Valerie Bloom." The two of them shook hands. She continued trying to make the same point that she had tried to make a few times before. Sarza moved imperceptibly to listen to what she was saying.

Valerie turned back to the photos, trying to pull Wes's attention to the images she'd been focusing on. "He's nobody we know, but that doesn't mean he's a nobody. We are not familiar with the power structures in each of the other civilizations. It could be nothing, but it could be anything." Valerie's words had fallen flat in the room multiple times before. The other two weren't listening to her. *Why would they? She's a woman*, Sarza remarked to herself, noting the usual Earth inter-gender warfare. Just then, Wes took her by surprise and acknowledged to the blonde, looking her straight in the eye and nodding.

The two men in the room already knew him, apparently, because they dispensed with introductions. "Sit down Wes. We want to go through the file with you before we hand it off to. . ." Sarza could feel their attention flash to her. They wouldn't dare speak the name of her breed. The attention moved back to Wes. Wes looked up at Sarza again, and looking straight at her, said, "She'll brief me."

"We . . . we haven't talked to her yet," they tried to interject.

"How long have you been in the room?" The question was directed at her, although Wes didn't look at her when he said it, his attention fixated on highlighted portions of the medical examiner's report.

"Forty-five minutes." It was the first time Sarza had spoken since she had slipped into the room from a window. Wes looked back at Valerie and the other two. Pressing his fingers on the table, he simply said, "She can brief me then. She has what she needs from this. You can leave now." The three of them stood up and walked out. They had brought in nothing, and they left with nothing. The images were still splattered across the white plastic table. The door closed quietly behind them. The room was still dark and filled with disturbing images.

He slipped his hands in his pants pockets and walked slowly toward her. He was relaxing, easing into the conversation. He was making it harder to defend himself by keeping his hands so remote. Sarza noted that he was either clueless or actually didn't fear her as much that others did. Then she noticed that although he had moved closer, he hadn't allowed himself to get too close. At least three meters still separated the two of them, indicating to her that he was totally aware of the potential danger she posed, but that he was not imminently worried about it.

"I'm your handler." He stepped forward some more until his upper thighs tapped against the table.

Sarza thought he must have done something very stupid or he had pissed someone off to be assigned as her handler. Or he was suicidal, or perhaps both. Being in the same room as a Sparcus was usually left to the rookies, who were not allowed to refuse. Or it was done as punishment. Being assigned as a handler was usually considered a suicide mission. Despite a Sparcus never — directly — harming a handler, tensions still ran high.

"Do you understand your assignment?"

"Yes."

"Do you understand the parameters?"

"Yes."

"I'm going to repeat them."

Silence.

"You cannot be detected. You cannot tell anyone IPP is investigating this murder. If questions come up, you say you are from NYPD Earth. You do whatever it takes to get this resolved. Time is not on our side. The Arapesh are accusing the Carlans, the Carlans are accusing the Corsini, the Corsini are accusing the Velins, the Velins are accusing the Braxians, the Braxians are accusing Earth, and any one of those planets would be more than happy to have a pretext to start a war, which will undoubtedly happen if you don't figure this out, and fast." Wes's tone was even as he covered the protocol. No emotion about any of those planets reflected in his face, not even Earth. *He has admirable self-control*, Sarza thought. She was a little bit impressed, despite her best efforts not to be, not to mention her general condescension and disgust for anything remotely human.

She stood in silence; she knew all of this already.

Sarza thought it remarkable that he was talking to her so directly, and that he was doing so while looking directly at her. Slowly, she confidently moved out of the room's shadows. Her purple eyes leveled on his. He didn't look away.

She could tell he was a little aroused, but not scared. Humans were so confused in many ways — sexually, emotionally, politically. She found them all so inferior. Arousal was usually mixed with fear, which she found repulsive. But this one wasn't scared. *Interesting*, she thought to herself.

"Do you have any questions for me?"

"Money?"

"You ask me," he answered.

"Guns?"

"You ask me."

"Permission to kill?"

"Given."

Permission to kill was usually given on a case-by-case basis, unless an immediate threat to life was present. Apparently IPP was serious about catching the killer. An all-go blanket okay meant this was coming from very high up.

"Partners?" That was a giveaway. Nobody ever partnered with one of them. The handler/handlee relationship was not a partnership. It was a forced hierarchy.

"Only me. Nobody else." Self-identifying as a partner to her was defiant, and dangerously so. He was baiting her. Saying they were somehow equals. That he would watch out for her, thereby belittling the suffering of her people at the hands of his.

"I volunteered," he added. "I know what happened to your last handler." That was a concession. Bad cop, nice cop in less than a sentence.

"Good. Maybe you learned something." *She doubted it.*

"Also, I want a weekly debrief. I want to know what you know. We will do it in person. Wherever you want to meet up, I'll show." He was still looking at her. The female perfume and wine had dissipated. He still didn't smell like fear, even after being in the room with her for this long. And she sensed a lingering . . . familiarity maybe? Sarza couldn't quite tell, but it was like she'd smelled him before. Her eyes moved to his clothes, down his torso, hovering for a moment, then moving down, hovering again, taking her time assessing the target. It was involuntary. Both genetically bred for and culturally engrained to assess all males and females. No exceptions. He seemed like a suitable candidate for intercourse. *Sarza! What are you doing?* Her conscious mind was trying to throw up barricades to her instinctive review of Wes a male subject. *He's human!* But no sooner had that voice resonated through her head than she heard another one. *Not bad for an Earthling.* And she had to admit, he certainly was among the better specimens she had had the opportunity to assess. He was a little taller than she was, which was surprising. Sparcus women were usually taller than men from most all other species — Sparcus men even more so, although now that didn't matter anymore. Height was only an interesting attribute if it could be passed on to future generations. That was out of the question for the Sparcus. Sarza tugged her conscious mind from that thought. Wes was still looking at her, waiting for her to be done. Still no fear, still no discomfort on his part, and still, she could sense that slight arousal.

"Our first briefing is *now* Sarza." Hearing her name from his mouth was surprising. No member of any other race addressed the Sparcus by proper names, finding them too monstrous to deserve such denominations.

Wes's voice was stern. "What do you know?"

Sarza moved closer to the table, still scanning him and the room. "Male, Braxian, approximately forty-two Standard years old, found dead in somebody's apartment on Sulpuro. Stab wounds across his arms, his chest, his face, and his legs. They were all inflicted while he was dying, but none of them killed him."

Wes was listening closely while his fingers, in midair, flipped through three-dimensional images of the dead man projected from the deskrock. Deskrocks were Bar'aat computing machines. They looked like rocks, which was deceptive. The interior was anything but primitive, containing hundreds of millions of circuits that worked at lightning speed. The man in the photos had pale blue skin and fan-like extensions protruding from his forehead. He had the typical Braxian gills found one inch under his jawline. His eyes were closed, and his elongated mouth ran mid-cheek to mid-cheek. His nose consisted of two partially closed holes.

While he continued to flip through the images, Sarza noticed Wes's long and strong fingers. The thought of what they could do to her, how they could please her, flashed through her mind. The hair at her nape started turning blue. She sensed it, but nobody would notice. It was a Sparcus irony that having been bred for strength, agility, resistance to pain, speed, and fertility, the Sparcus were still unable to eliminate such a weakness: hair that changed color with mood. Blue for arousal, green for climax, red for anger, white for sorrow. And it only happened to the Sparcus women, which, for Sarza, was even more maddening.

She continued, "He was killed using poison from Vedic." Wes looked up at her.

"But not administered in the Arapesh way," she added. The Arapesh civilization inhabited the planet Vedic. She wasn't going to explain, but he nodded, indicating he understood. The Arapesh were highly ceremonial beings that only administered poisons in political murders or honor suicides. But it was always ingested. The male Braxian had been injected.

"No defensive wounds. So he was either incapacitated or restrained."

"You can't tell from the report?" Wes asked.

"No photos of his wrists or ankles." She had already made a mental note to go find the body.

"There were ropes tied with Corsini knots lying next to the bed. They had no epithelials on them. And the ropes came from Earth."

"Set up? Make it look like the Corsini did it?"

"Maybe."

"His name?"

"Unknown. And irrelevant at this point."

Sarza noted Wes's disapproval of that last statement. She was being arrogant by dismissing information as irrelevant so early in the game, but he kept quiet.

"Who is he?"

"Earth says he's nobody. And nobody is saying he's anybody. So he is very likely somebody."

Wes kept looking at the photos. He paused, and then looked up at her. "Figure it out Sarza."

Wes pulled his other hand out of his pocket and walked toward the door. Sarza was gone, disappearing through the window she had used to get into the building, before his hand could wave in front of the black sensor, signaling the door to open.

Leaving the conference room, he exhaled slowly. Everything his mother had taught him through painful hours of training would get him through the first round. But there would be many more, and he had to make sure he would keep his cool. Being in the same room as a Sparcus was both very difficult and exhausting. He felt the similarities and some of their pain, which was exactly why he had volunteered for this assignment in the first place. It was senseless to pair Sparcus with handlers who either hated them, feared them uncontrollably, or both. The feeling of hatred was always mutual. He walked down the narrow hall that led to the elevators. Valerie, the blond NYPD officer, was sitting on a bench next to the doors. She stood up quickly as he approached.

"I wanted to make sure you were okay." She looked eager enough.

"I'm fine. Thanks. You can go home now." He pulled out his personal communicator. It was a small stone-like object, oval, programmed to shine a display in front of him that only he could see. Each one of these gadgets was programmed specifically to its owner. The woman he had left at the restaurant had sent him several messages—most of them very inviting. After this encounter though, he certainly was not in the mood. He rubbed his face as the many thoughts ran through his mind.

"Long night?" Valerie was standing there trying to be nice.

"Yes." She was still there, and the elevator was taking forever to show up. "Do you need something?"

"No." Following the sound of a bell, the elevator had finally arrived. He stepped in, and so did she. He punched the button for the bottom floor. Valerie was looking at the floor. "Why are we using *them*?"

"The Sparcus?"

"Yes. They would slaughter us in our sleep if they could."

Do you blame them? If Wes had expressed such thoughts or even alluded to Project Geno, he would lose his job, and probably become a pariah among law enforcement agencies. "They're good at what they do," he answered instead.

"What is it that they do, exactly? I had never heard of Earth, or any other planet, relying on them for anything until tonight." That showed just how green she was. IPP used Sparcus — a lot — and usually for the dirtier jobs.

"They investigate. They see and detect smells better than we do. They are faster, stronger, they don't get tired as easily, and they are capable of single-minded determination." Wes knew all those statements were accurate.

"They have no emotions," she snorted.

Wes exhaled slowly, trying to make it seem innocuous. "It makes them capable of doing whatever it takes to achieve their goals, or, in this case, ours." Wes stepped out. He was not interested in continuing this pointless conversation.

"Why does our government trust her?"

"That's beyond your pay grade, officer." Wes walked away. Valerie took a few hesitant steps at his pace, but then stopped. She had finally gotten the hint. Wes continued down a white corridor, and took a right into a barely visible white door that blended in perfectly with the walls. Two women were waiting for him. The room was brightly lit in fluorescent lighting. The floor was decorated in boring grey linoleum, and the walls were painted the color of ugly brick red. There were empty desks along every edge of the room, facing the walls; each one of them with a deskrock flashing a password prompt across their projected screens. The two women were standing in the middle of the room. One of them was holding a file.

"Good evening, Wes."

"Hi Mary." He looked over at the other woman and nodded. "Captain." His tone was respectful and professional, acknowledging her presence, but no more.

"Venta," she answered in the same tone. "Did you make contact with the agent?"

"Yes. She debriefed me already."

"Any incidents?" Mary looked a little concerned.

"No. No incidents. The other agents were there, but I didn't talk to them. They were still messing around with the file."

The Captain started walking back toward the door and said, "Let's go to my office." Wes and Mary followed closely behind her, keeping up with her fast clicking heels. Mary handed Wes the file she was holding. "This is what we have on the Sparcus agent. I'm sorry I couldn't get it to you before you met with her." The file was old school. It was kept in a handheld screen with a touch-interface. Each agent file was kept on an individual tablet of the sort. Wes took the tablet in his hand but didn't have time to read up the details. The Captain's voice reached over her shoulders. "As I told you earlier, she is a highly valued Sparcus agent. She's been working for us since her mid-teens. Nobody has ever seen anything like her."

Wes was a little startled. "Since her mid-teens? When did we hire her? At sixteen?" There was a little humor in his voice. He couldn't imagine them actually hiring children to do their work.

"You can read the details in her file, but her first mission for the IPP was a few months after she turned fifteen. She's been working for us thirteen years." Sarza was his age, twenty-eight. Which meant she was born in 2215, just before the end of the Great Conflict. This also meant she was one of the last children of her race. There would be no others after her.

Wes opened the file, and Mary, who was walking alongside him, pointed to the tab containing the mission entry. Mary, lowering her voice, explained, "She seduced the son of a Velin rebel leader. The son invited her into his home. She slaughtered him, his father, and three guards."

"What was her mission?" Wes was a little taken aback. He was very familiar with the legendary warrior training and the importance of seduction in Sparcus culture, but this seemed extreme. And he couldn't understand why the IPP would be using teenagers to fulfill missions.

The Captain interjected, "To do just that." They had reached the Captain's office. Wes closed the file and walked in, followed by Mary.

The Captain's office looked the same as the rest of the building. Red brick-colored walls, grey linoleum, and a white desk. She had, however, upgraded to a personal projector much like the one in his personal communicator. A long, smooth, sausage-shaped black deskrock sat on her desk. These were the contributions of the Bar'aat people. Although the Bar'aat looked like little more than the mythical yetis, down to the immaculate white hair and heights ranging from two to two-and-a-half meters—some of them being as tall as three—they were also one of the most technologically advanced civilizations humans had encountered so far. They sold weapons and technology far and wide. Even during the Great Conflict, they had sold to everyone. The neutrality of commerce was somehow the most respected one. An image flashed above the object. All three of them looked at the display.

The Captain pulled up Sarza's photo and agent file.

"Venta," she began. Wes sat down across from her, while Mary stood at the door. "This Braxian is somebody's agent.

I don't know whose yet, but he was working for one of the planet agencies. That's just chatter from our informants. I can't get anything better and I can't get any collateral on the rumors."

"Without collateral, they're just unsubstantiated rumors. You know informants and double-agents spread those all the time to create static." Counterintelligence was one thing, but many times Wes had to sort through plain inaccurate information. Not every lead was reliable. In fact, quite the opposite. A good agent knew the difference.

"I know. But that's what I have so far. Also, I need you to keep an eye on Sarza." The Captain looked up. Her blond hair was held up in a tight bun, which matched her crisp white suit and flawless posture. Wes had never been impressed by her looks, although she and many of her male subordinates were. The Captain looked at Mary. "You can leave now."

"Yes Ma'am." Wes didn't turn around, but he felt Mary exit the room. He sensed her disappointment at being asked to leave.

"She doesn't need to hear about this." The Captain leaned back and said, "Sarza may be a double-agent." Wes's eyes opened wider, registering surprise. "We've known for a long time there was a possibility. Hell, the fact she's a Sparcus makes it likely in and of itself. But I need you to be very careful."

"Double agent for who? For what?"

"For Sparcus covert intelligence."

"You mean Sparcus police?"

"No." the Captain paused and looked off to the side for a moment. She readjusted her shoulders as though giving herself courage and continued. "She could be part of a Sparcus covert intelligence agency."

Wes sat back, a puzzled expression across his face. "There is *no* such thing Captain. With all due respect, everyone in the galaxy has been over this. We have kept our ears to the ground for this for twenty-eight years. You and I and the rest of the intelligence community know there is no 'Sparcus Intelligence.'" This was ludicrous.

"Well . . . I don't know more than that. But there has been chatter. And I ask that you keep it to yourself. We don't want to spook her. We might be onto something big here."

"Do we have collateral?"

"No."

Wes dismissed the rumor instantly. He wouldn't tell his Captain as much, but it would be too easy for people to make themselves appear more valuable than they were by making up rumors about non-existent Sparcus agencies. Then, Wes thought back to images of Sarza's previous handler, his throat slit, lying on the cold dark pavement of Vedic. "Did she have something to do with Agent Bent's death?"

"No, not at all. He overplayed his hand and put her in a compromising position. He nearly blew the mission. She could have saved him, undoubtedly, but she didn't have to. So, she let him get killed. They don't take prisoners. Nor do they save any."

"So why the suspicion she's doubling?" Wes was still somewhat curious.

"Someone saw her on Sulpuro when she had no business being there. She could have been passing through, but normally she doesn't leave Astarte-Qetesh unless she's on a mission."

"So, you think she's betraying us because she took a vacation somewhere?" Wes wasn't buying it.

"Venta, just take the information and be careful." Her tone hardened as her eyes stared at Wes with seriousness and concern. She wasn't going to discuss this any further.

"Understood." Wes wasn't going to press the point. He stood up.

"I want you to investigate this case just like it was a regular IPP case. You run interference between the various agencies, keep tempers level, make it look like all the regular channels are engaged. The less information you disclose, the better. While you do that, Sarza investigates in her own way."

"Why the smoke screen?"

"As long as everyone thinks this is being investigated, we can control the tension. And whoever did this will get the impression they can monitor a highly visible investigation. They'll be easier to catch." Wes nodded.

"Can you tell me if something in particular is causing tension?"

The Captain snorted. "The same things as usual. That humans don't care about other races. Well . . . it's that every race doesn't care about any other race but their own. A Braxian killed on Sulpuro just adds to the mix." She paused, looked at Wes, and then abruptly added, "You're excused."

"Thank you Captain." Wes stood up. He walked out of the office, down the endless white corridors, and back into the lobby. He took a brief look back at the barrels hanging in the lobby and walked back into the street. He still had Sarza's file in hand, the cold metal of the tablet pressing against his hand. It was three in the morning, and the city was reaching its coldest. He would head home in hopes of getting a few hours of sleep. Tomorrow he would go to Sulpuro and talk to the Velin authorities. He was sure Sarza was already on her way there.

From a windowsill, Sarza watched as Wes walked along the sidewalk. She hung to the wall, jumped onto a window ledge, and then caught on another wall. This effortless dance had become very familiar to her. She wanted to know where he would go next. She knew he was IPP, but his file was completely blank prior to his eighteenth birthday. Someone had made great efforts to erase his past. And if there was something she trusted less than a human, it was a human with secrets. He took a right at the end of the block, then a left. He was going straight home. He wasn't going to give away anything she didn't know already. Not tonight. She climbed up onto the rooftop terrace of a restaurant. It was empty. She crouched, feeling the arousal spread through her, as her hair started to turn into a shade of telltale blue in response.

For her to find an Earthling so objectively suitable for sex was near impossible. To feel arousal for him was altogether disturbing. The Sparcus ability to effortlessly assess all individuals for sexual and reproductive compatibility was one of the staples of their culture. Every Sparcus was taught to grade and to assess. The visible markers on people were innumerable and so subtle that only a Sparcus mind could detect them. But after years of doing it, the Sparcus simply processed the information and came up with an assessment. Sarza was a carefully programmed being, designed through generations of careful breeding to only react to good genetic matches, which would provide the best quality offspring. A human and a Sparcus could not reproduce. It was biologically impossible. So her body's reaction was an aberration, like the result of some static interference in radio communications. Cautiously, she stood up straight and walked across the terrace. The best place to start looking into her assignment would be the morgue on Sulpuro, if the body was still there. She would have to get to her pod quickly to leave undetected.

As Wes approached his apartment building, his thoughts wandered, despite the noise from the busy roads filled with passing hovercraft. Sarza had no way of knowing he had noticed her hair stirring. The idea of Sarza straddling him in ecstasy, her hair glowing green, flashed through Wes's mind. His loins stirred. He pushed the idea aside and kept walking. It would be better to fantasize about someone else altogether.

He got to his empty apartment a while later. It was dark. He had hoped to come back to it with his date from just hours before, but his mind was somewhere else.

As he walked through the living room without turning on the lights, he detected a very faint smell. Despite the Velcra, his nose was still able to detect her: Sarza had definitely been in that room. He wondered if she was still there. He waved his hand, folding his fingers into his palm, and the lights turned on. Nothing was disturbed, and he was alone in the room. He walked toward the bedroom, his senses on alert. He repeated the hand gesture in the bedroom, but he could see it was also empty. He relaxed a little and moved through the apartment. She was gone.

* * *

As Wes walked through his home, Sarza crouched outside, on his windowsill. She heard Wes walk in and saw the lights turn on in the living room, then in the bedroom. There had been nothing out of the ordinary about his apartment. She had visited it moments after he left it earlier that evening, and she was glad she had done so. She didn't trust a human who didn't fear her.

She jumped down onto a balcony, then onto a lower one, catching herself on the emergency ladder, then swung down to the ground. She started a brisk run toward the outskirts of the city. She couldn't understand what was so familiar about him. Why did he arouse her, and why didn't he fear her? The humans had decimated her people, and yet, they feared them so much they couldn't stand to be in the same room as them. True, a Sparcus could kill a human with incredible speed, precision, and an utter lack of empathy. There were few enemies the Sparcus couldn't defeat, and even fewer that they would fear. But Earth's Slaughter had been a brilliant plan, depriving the Sparcus of their natural advantages. Her people were still alive, but they were dying—a slow, inexorable, maddening death that nobody could or would stop. The thought of it made the bitterness and anger roil inside of her. She hated them. She hated every last one of them. Her hair, moving in the wind and in rhythm with her running body, turned red violently.

Sarza's thoughts were interrupted by the sight of New York City's outskirts. Even though the innermost core of the city still had very tall buildings and streets, the area was more desolate the further one traveled. She had seen photos of the sprawling city before the Great Conflict. She knew it used to be far larger, with many more inhabitants then it currently had. Fifteen years of war had taken a toll on all of the planets, including the victorious ones.

Although she would have preferred taking off vertically from inside the city, traveling by pod or by transporter at night would have violated curfew, and she would certainly have gotten noticed. Being on foot until the Spaceport and using other methods of transportation from there was certainly the more advisable avenue. It was a good thing that as a Sparcus she could go long distances without tiring. Finally, as she finished her run, she reached her Nego-Pod, waiting for her on a launch pad at the Spaceport. There were at least two-hundred of them lined up in rows of tens, each of them hovering thirty centimeters above the ground on a circular disc, just waiting to be launched, looking like human-sized grains of rice, standing upright. Nego-Pods were a Sparcus invention. Sarza looked around the Spaceport. Every mode of space travel there was *not* from Earth. Humans weren't quite primitive, but their inability to focus on intergalactic travel was nonetheless puzzling to her, and their ineptitude at developing adequate reusable launch vehicles dumbfounding.

She approached her Nego-Pod and laid a hand on its outer shell. The soft grey material contoured to the shape of her fingers. Once the hybrid material was done reading her biological markers, it opened up, allowing her to enter. She stepped in, crossing her hands over her stomach. The pod was just big enough to fit around her, wrapping her entire body when it closed.

The Nego-Pod was an ingenious invention. It employed the same technology as other spacecrafts, enabling passengers to move faster than the speed of light while eliminating the physical stresses of traveling at such speeds — but it did so with a craft that was not much larger than a person. It was fast, efficient, compact, and stealthy, the ideal covert agent mode of transportation. The technology consisted in emitting negative energy, which distorted the space-time continuum. This created a bubble around the spacecraft — in this case the Nego-Pod. Inside the bubble, time and space continued to exist as they normally would. Outside the bubble, space-time was modified in such a way as to allow "faster-than-light" travel. In fact, it wasn't really traveling faster than the speed of light, but rather warping space-time around it, propelling the craft across a dramatically reduced surface area. But even warping alone would have been insufficient for travel from one planet to another in meaningful periods of time. A wormhole network, The Network, which predated all of the races' recorded memory, solved the latter problem. Each planet had a wormhole about a half a day's travel from its surface. Each wormhole ended at a wormhole central, usually called "the Hub." The Hub was a circle of wormholes, each leading to a different planet. Everyone knew that a force field kept the wormholes from collapsing into each other and allowed them to stay stable, but nobody knew how the force field had been created, or by whom.

Sarza felt the gel at the back of her neck warm up, allowing the pod to read her instructions. She closed her eyes and let her thoughts wander. She would let the pod work its magic, putting her in a suspended state. But it wasn't restful sleep and it didn't make up for the lack of rest. She would have to take a break on Sulpuro.

BOOK I
CHAPTER 2

The landing on Sulpuro was soft. Sarza's Nego-Pod had been traveling eight Standard hours (the equivalent of twelve Earth hours, or 19.2 Sparcus hours). Every planet was a day's travel from any other planet, so a day was always defined as sixteen Standard hours. The Standard hour, as well as the Standard minute and the Standard day, had been a necessity for interplanetary coordination. It would have been impossible to organize travel, communications, and even war efforts without a unified system of time. Sarza woke up as she entered the planet's atmosphere — just in time to watch the landing. The planet was as beautiful as it was inhospitable. The yellow air created a constant sheen, amplifying the sunlight, and making the planet look like it was early morning all day long. Numerous pods were falling down to the planet alongside Sarza. Traffic was at a peak. She and the other Nego-Pods looked like small flecks descending to the surface like ethereal wombs. Space travel rarely looked this amazing.

Sulpuro air had high amounts of sulfur. In fact, nobody other than the Arapesh and the Velins could move around it without nasal cleansers—small, clear clips placed at the base of a the nose that allowed visitors to breathe. Sarza put hers in. However, this didn't do anything to decrease the spoiled smell, and extensive exposure to the outdoors could cause skin and tissue damage to just about any non-native being.

The pod landed at the Varenna Spaceport, near Varenna, one of the largest cities on Sulpuro. A slit appeared along the length of the Nego-Pod. It opened a little. Sarza pushed her hands and then her arms through it, widening the opening. As she stepped out, feeling the Earth-like gravity settle her legs and body into an easy stance, a Velin attendant approached her. His large, semi-transparent yellowish glob of a body oozed toward her. He had no legs and no feet. Two small beaded eyes looked at her from the mass. The top of his head reached just below her waist. As soon as he was close enough to see her, he stopped and retreated a little. As he reversed slightly in his path, he left a little yellow slime where he had stood. He looked at the floor and stepped further away from her as she walked past him. He finally mustered the courage to stammer, "Gre-ee-tings." The Velins communicated using gurgling sounds with varying pitches, lengths, and tones. It was all they could do given their bodies. Sarza actually understood the Velin language. But, when she joined IPP, she had also received a linguistic transposer—a small, flat capsule inserted along her auditory canal, just before her tympanic membrane. It translated every language. Sarza hated the thing. She was already conversant in every language, but she couldn't turn the preming thing off, which meant she had spent the first few months after implantation distracted by the fact that she could hear everything in double, all the time. To make things worse, she often disagreed with the inelegant or plainly inaccurate translations. But removing it was not an option. It was IPP standard procedure. If there was one thing IPP believed in, it was standard procedure.

Sarza didn't speak a word, and instead just kept walking. Her pod closed behind her, and the outer shell turned hard, making it impossible to use by anyone other than herself. She reached the edge of the Spaceport and caught one of the available shuttles into Varenna. As she boarded, her hair turned a deep shade of black. When her hair was this color, some people could confuse her for a human, as long as she covered the Velcra outfit with her cloak. Further, most members of the population weren't intimately familiar with the sartorial details of the IPP uniforms. But if any emotion was betrayed by changes in color, which it was bound to do, then she was immediately recognizable as a Sparcus.

Velin merchants were selling silk, jewelry, opulent furniture, and countless Bar'aat gadgets. Money changed hands fast, negotiations were heated, and the noise was continuous. The yellow sulfuric air created a toxic haze that hung in the air like a constant veil. The earth itself was light yellow under the slime. Crowds of people from all planets pushed and jostled each other down the hoverways. Varenna was an ode to the Velin way of life. From the sky, the cities looked as though someone had taken a pen and neatly drawn diamonds and triangles, with large circles at each end. Large avenues crisscrossed each other, meeting in elaborate plazas decorated with ornate statues made of precious metals. Velin police forces spent more time protecting the opulent buildings than the people of Sulpuro. Truth is, Sarza thought, it was probably time better spent. She had rarely met a Velin worth knowing, let alone protecting. There was no vegetation. Velin plant forms were small, close to the ground, and — according to the Velins — inadequate to decorate cities. Instead, the Velins used holograms, synthetic replicas, and a few unfortunate foreign plant samples to create the semblance of flora. A whole department of the Velin government was dedicated to maintaining and improving this particular aspect of the city. Their work usually entailed clearing out the non-Velin plants that died rapidly due to the air and soil sulfur content and replacing them with identical and just-as-doomed plants.

The Velin enjoyed all things opulent: food, money, clothes, spices, technology, buildings, weapons — the more difficult to obtain, the more they wanted it. Which partly explained their obsession with exotic plants. The more it gave pleasure, the more they sought it. Regardless of whether it actually gave *them* pleasure. Sarza mused at the dumbfounding irony that a population so hell-bent on all things pleasurable was unable to glean any from sex and reproduction. Velins reproduced by coming together, mixing their bodies, and separating, leaving behind a small Velin formed from both of them. The process took an hour, and was devoid of enjoyment. In stark contrast, the Sparcus, who embraced a simple, harsh, warrior way of life also indulged in every aspect of the pleasures of the flesh. Sparcus Bashbathars — "warrior orgies" as labeled by the humans — were nights of sensual pleasure between Sparcus men and women warriors. This tradition strengthened the bonds between them and made them equals. The respect and acceptance of each other's pleasure, desire, and physical needs brought them together and made all of them feel so alive that they were willing to die for each other. The hair at Sarza's nape turned blue and started humming, lifting itself from her skin and hovering. This would certainly attract attention, which is something she didn't want. She stopped thinking about it, with some regret. She hadn't been to one in months, and there would be no opportunity until she solved this murder. These thoughts quickly brought her back to her mission.

The Varenna morgue was a salmon-colored building without any stairs. Instead, the only way to move from one floor to the other was by elevators or ramps, also covered in slime. Sarza stood on the other side of the hoverpath upon exiting the shuttle. Security was light. In fact, she didn't see a single armed individual or stationary guns set up to stop people from going in. She crossed the hoverpath and looked at the entry. There weren't doors, but a pressure plate lifted a metal curtain to let people enter. Anyone could stand on the plate to open the door.

"Prem!" She swore under her breath as she saw cameras sweeping the doorway from the inside of the building. Prem was a human word for "love." The Sparcus had quickly—and gleefully—adopted it as a swearword. They found human love a ridiculous concept that made no sense and only enslaved people into relationships doomed to failure. Sarza reflected on her options. Just walking in wouldn't be possible. Her instructions were to keep a low profile. The less she was caught on recordings or photos and the less she interacted with other creatures, the better. Her only alternative was to come back later, during the night hours, but not through the front entrance. Some of the passersby—Velins, Bar'aats, Ishtars, Arapesh, Kerouacs, Corsini, Carlans, people from all over the galaxy—were already starting to look at her with curiosity. Sarza reached into her pocket for a small black cord. She twisted each end in opposite directions, and the cord turned into a black visor. She covered her eyes with it. Although Sparcus were allowed to travel from one planet to the other, they usually attracted attention. The less she got noticed, the better and easier it would be. She shrugged her ankle-length black mantel around her body and pulled her hood over her forehead. Dressed like this, there was nothing to differentiate her from a tall human or a dressed Ishtar woman. She started walking away from the morgue. The Braxian would have to wait for nightfall. In the meantime, she would try to find a place to sleep.

Sarza lost herself in the crowd. She was transported in the sea of bodies slipping in and out of streams of people. Finally, she disappeared into a small avenue off to the left. It was barely a shoulder-width space between two yellowish mud buildings. The light sand from the walls dusted her black cloak. She kept walking until she reached a large heavy metal door. As she approached, she let her hood fall back and gently tapped two fingers on the top left above her eye to her visor. It disappeared, leaving the black cord between her thumb and index. She tucked it deep into her cloak and tilted her face toward the camera above the doorway. The door opened for her to walk in, and then closed behind her as quickly and as quietly as it had opened.

The inside of the hostel was well lit. A Velin attendant stood behind a short counter. He looked at Sarza as she approached.

"Marmar. You rascal. Still here doing . . . nothing," Sarza said, nearly showing a faint grin.

"Sarza! Welcome back to Sulpuro." He knew her, had helped her several times in the past, and had earned the right to use her first name. Marmar's globulous body oozed from his worn, dark red satin armchair. Even in this hostel, the walls were covered in jarring gold velour drapes.

"Thank you Marmar. I need a room for the night."

"Same as usual?" Marmar slid a square piece of red glass across the counter, serving as a bio-recognizing key plate. She placed her hand on the device, leaving little gaps of space from one finger to the next. The template recognized her biological form right away as it began to read her markers. Although resembling the human form, the markings on her skin were unmistakably that of a Sparcus. A few moments later, once confirmed, she made her way to her room.

The Varenna morgue was supposed to keep the body for two days. The Braxian had been found yesterday, so his lifeless body should still be there, Sarza thought to herself.

Upon entering the narrow doorway to her private room, Sarza decided she would get some rest while she still could. Remaining completely dressed with her boots on, she lay on the white bed, which was made up of a soft mixture of cotton and silk. It was just a mattress on a low rectangular box, obviously made for a biped like herself. There were no covers and no pillow. Sarza kept her half-finger gloves on her hands, her weapons still resting by her sides. She quickly fell fast asleep.

She was awakened by a loud thud. Her first reaction was to unsheathe both weapons, aiming them directly in front of her without even opening her eyes. After the noise passed, Sarza remained poised on her back, in the pitch black, her weapons still outstretched in each hand. Technically, Sarza was not supposed to be carrying weapons. She obtained dispensation when the IPP hired her. The guns that extended from each of her arms were Bar'aat radiating guns. One click of the trigger and they would deliver very high energy beams made up of tiny particles that could literally shred holes through the enemy at the receiving end.

The room continued to remain in a palpable, near-unbearable silence. Was someone else in her room? No, she was alone. She decided to get up, repositioning her guns back into her thigh holsters as she quickly stood up from the bed. Pulling out a small object that resembled a visor, she placed the item in front of her face. It altered the shade of her eyes, turning them from her usual purple color to a deep shade of blue. The color-changing would fade in a day or two. But by then, she would be long gone. And for the time being, the more of her features she could alter, the harder it was for anyone to describe or trace her. Now adequately disguised, she was ready to make her way to the morgue.

Leaving her room, Marmar was nowhere to be found. Sarza reached deep into her cloak, pulling out a yellow card — Velin currency. Swiping the card under a blue light on the counter, Sarza instantly paid her balance for the room. She dropped the card back into her cloak, and left the Inn.

Sarza began retracing her steps toward the morgue, but instantly had a feeling that someone was following her. She couldn't detect from where or from whom, however, and it could have been simply that the streets were so packed with people that it was throwing her off. Sarza blamed the crowd and shrugged it off. She pulled the cloak closer to her body, pulled her hood over her head as much as possible, and stepped into the moving crowd.

She noticed that the day's markets were now replaced with Velin nightlife. Some were dining, while others were prancing around showing off their expensive clothing, which invariably got soaked in ooze. The blasting music of loud parties echoed from one building to the next. At these events, Velins showed off their various expensive gadgets—as though that was a measurement for one Velin being better than another. Peering through the windows of the city nightlife, Sarza watched them indulge in various inebriants. Although Velins were not able to get a high off of chemicals themselves—for the same reasons they could not enjoy sex—they would ingest large amounts of liquors and stimulants as a sign of wealth. If others were doing it, then they wanted to do it as well.

Approaching the morgue, Sarza cautiously checked around to make sure no one was there. She noticed a back window and decided to slip in that way. Upon entering, she saw within the large room that the massive walls were covered in small cubicles, acting as desk drawers that would pull open, and slide back closed. Fifty rows up and two hundred rows across, almost every single one filled with once-alive bodies. Sarza recalled the autopsy report, which contained the cubicle number of the victim. Her eyes scrolled the walls until she found lucky number 3-6-9. The Braxian body should be in there.

Slowly opening the cubicle, Sarza saw nothing but a large empty metal tray shining as though it had been purposely made spotless. The body was gone. Glancing around, she caught sight of a workstation area with an interface on a table, along with a chair. Maybe she would find something in there.

As she waved her hand over the deskrock, a projected screen lit up her face. She used her fingertips to enter her standard IPP credentials, and the office's information came alive under her hands. She easily retrieved the autopsy report, which mirrored the original. Sarza scanned the screen and noticed that, again, there were no photos of the extremities to be found within the report. Someone had either never taken them — which stood in breach of protocol — or destroyed them. Sarza kept flipping through the report until she found the signature line: Merx Caragan, Necrological Reviewer.

Sarza, making a mental note of the name, proceeded to pull his personnel file. After finding his address, she continued to shuffle through additional documents, hoping to find something more. Aside from the surprisingly high number of Sparcus employees embedded in the morgue, Sarza could find nothing suspicious. She closed down every file, record, and document, ensuring her presence would not be detected. Leaving the room as she had found it, Sarza left the same way she came in.

She slipped out of the window and ran into the morning light of Sulpuro's three suns, which were slowly beginning to pop up over the horizon. The planet's purple moons were slowly moving in the sky. On the planet of Sulpuro, the sky stayed orange because of all the yellow powder from the planet's surface, and its two purple moons remained visible in the sky during all hours of the day. Sulpuro days were fifteen Standard hours long — or forty-five Sulpuro hours. It made them feel better that their days were "so much longer" than everyone else's. Walking the quiet streets that were not long ago filled with nightlife, Sarza found a public hovercraft and started traveling toward Merx Caragan's home. Maybe he could shed some light on where the body had gone, or why there were no photos of the Braxian's extremities. Any information would help.

A few blocks from the house, Sarza decided to get off the hovercraft. Trying to be as discrete as possible, she walked casually toward his home. She noticed that the neighborhood was elaborately decorated. Ridiculous adornments filled the yards, and all was manicured. *At least it's quiet and there is nobody on the streets*, she thought to herself.

Sarza saw Merx Caragan's house number posted above the entryway to his home. The tall, cylindrical building was laid out like a series of patio homes, with each unit including a rectangular yard with a cylindrical living unit in the middle. The Velin homes resembled upright white tubes. Not sure on how to proceed, Sarza approached the home the old-fashioned way: she stood in front of the door expecting automatic chimes to go off inside. Door chimes were typical of Earth but the Velins had adopted the measure, finding it "adorably quaint." The door opened. Sarza's heart jumped into her throat and she swallowed hard. Wes—in IPP uniform and fully armed—stood in front of her. He looked striking in the tight long-sleeved dark red shirt and multi-pocket vest. A gun hung on each side of his waist, and a long-barrel shooter was strapped to his back. His shoulders were massive, far more noticeable in the uniform than they had been in the white shirt that he'd been wearing last night. His pants hung lose, in semi-stiff cloth, also dark red. Sarza was trying to regain composure. Although she knew her face wouldn't betray her, her hair could. Any minute now. Without saying a word, she stepped in, expecting him to move. He didn't. She found herself very close to him, their chests nearly touching in the narrow hall. Sarza felt Wes's breath brush her face, and strands of her hair immediately turned bright blue, leaving no doubt as to how she felt about the proximity. Sensing the visibility of her arousal, she became angry—which led contradictory red streaks to appear alongside the blue ones. She resented that a human could make her feel this way. It felt transgressive. And she *never* experienced her sexuality as transgressive. It was a fundamental contradiction of terms.

And more than that, her body was betraying everything that she was. Sparcus sexual desire and sexual compatibility were important matters. As a consequence, these reactions could not merely be dismissed as momentary bouts of lust. Sparcus women were *not* attracted to people wholly incompatible and who would not satisfy them. Her attraction said just as much about how she felt about him as it did about what they could do to each other. Wes watched her, enjoying a similar feeling, but he didn't smile. Standing this close to her, and given the red in her hair, she would likely kill him.

Sarza uttered through clenched teeth, "Venta?"

"Sarza. I expected you would end up here."

Silence.

"Come in." He turned away and walked into the house. "Unfortunately, your trip is for nothing." Sarza followed him in. The bottom floor was obviously a living space. It had a large ornate purple couch with gold flecks. Most of the couches were flat, with no arms or back rests, which would have been superfluous for a Velin.

Wes stood behind her. "Caragan is dead."

Sarza stopped and turned around sharply in surprise. The mood fell from attraction to seriousness. Whatever electricity they had between them was put out and dampened — although not eliminated — by the news.

"This means someone is a step ahead of us."

"Yes." Wes walked toward the living room, passing Sarza. "Someone is a step ahead of both of us. I figure you've been to the morgue?"

"Yes. The body's gone."

"I got here this morning and found him dead."

"Where is he?"

"The body?" Wes raised his eyebrows.

"Yes. I need to look at it."

"Upstairs."

He gestured toward the ramp. Sarza started moving in its direction, but Wes hesitated for a moment, then followed suit. "Don't touch anything."

He knew the moment the words came out of his mouth that he would regret them. Sarza didn't answer, but simply shook her head in disappointment. She was appalled that this human would presume to tell her how to treat a crime scene. The anger in her body began to boil to the surface, fueled by his impertinence. The hair wasn't red . . . yet.

She stopped at the door, barely able to contain herself. In a low and steady voice, she whispered, "You've probably seen my file?" Wes nodded, unsure what was coming next. "Then you know I've created and examined more crime scenes than there are years in your life. Just shut your mouth." Wes clenched his jaw. He did not want to be talked to like this, and between the arousal, the irritation at her demeanor, and her proximity, he had half a mind to push her against the wall right there. And, he wasn't sure what he would do to her next — whether to reprimand her or have sex with her. He caught himself. She was pushing all sorts of buttons, simultaneously. He regained his composure. That's not the man he was. And she would probably kill him if he dared to carry out his thought. He exhaled through his nose and just walked into the bedroom.

A puddle of ooze covered the bed and slowly dripped onto the floor. Two eyes floated in the puddle, looking blankly at the ceiling. This was a disgusting sight, even for Sarza. She exhaled, "Cause of death is always such a preming mess with Velins . . ." Their bodies didn't really have "markings," they just fell apart, and quickly. She looked at Wes.

"Beats me, Sarza. I came in this morning and found him like this." He wanted to add that he'd also detected a faint odor of Sparcus in the air, but he was afraid the information would alarm her. Sarza looked at the scene carefully. Only one weapon could cause such liquefaction, and she was wearing it: the Sparcus Glove. Contact with a person's head—or in this case an amoeba-like body—combined with pressure made the power disk in each of the palms emit high intensity vibrations that liquefied brain matter and most internal organs. The thought of that sent shivers down her spine. Chasing a murderer was one thing. Chasing a Sparcus was another task altogether, one she didn't want to be a part of. Her people were her people, no matter what. She doubted that she would even be able to bring them to justice. And if anyone found out that she had, her cover would be blown. Thirteen years of helping the idiotic humans would all go to waste, and she would never get close to uncovering Project Genesis.

"Let's go before the investigators get here." She walked out of the room quickly, following closely behind Wes. They crossed the living room and found themselves back onto the street in seconds.

"Where do we go from here?" Wes asked her.

"*We* don't go anywhere. I'm going somewhere and I will report to you in a week for my de-briefing."

"Sarza." She turned to face Wes as he continued, "I'm staying here. If anyone asks, I was alone the whole time. I found him like this, called the investigators, and waited for them—alone. Understood?"

"Understood."

Wes walked back toward the house, while Sarza began walking to the nearest hover transport to take her back into town. From there, she would get back into her pod. Where she would go from there was unclear. She was without a lead and with significant suspicions that her people were behind this, at least to some degree.

Back in Caragan's home, Wes was alerted by two beeps in his ear. His internal communication device signaled he was getting a call. The cochlear implant served the purpose of displaying information to IPP agents. It was mandatory for all IPP overt agents. The two-part system included an ear-piece and a retinal implant that could either be kept in the eye for good, or removed when desired. This allowed the user — the IPP agent — to see who was making contact. The implant allowed Wes to communicate easily. The two beeps indicated Wes was receiving an IPP call. He pressed on his ear to pick up. The Captain appeared in his eye, while her voice was transmitted into his ear. He knew there was significant delay between the Captain uttering words and his perception of them. The same was true of the image. Relaying satellites were located both at each of the wormhole entrances and in orbit around each of the planets, as well as between the wormholes and the orbiting satellites. The Bar'aat had also created an accelerator that moved information faster than the speed of light. They claimed this was a technology of national security, so nobody knew how it worked. Regardless, the delay was close to a tenth of a Standard minute.

"Wes. I got your call. What's going on?"

"The Necrological Reviewer that examined the Braxian is dead." A quarter of a Standard minute went by.

"Shit. Shit." The Captain was irritated. "This is turning into a shit storm."

Now Wes was irritated. Wasting time on the coms to swear and complain rubbed him the wrong way. "Yes Captain."

"I just got chewed up by the Braxian IPP saying we're not doing enough to investigate *their* people's death. It's the usual us versus them bullshit."

"Captain . . ." he was speaking out of turn. "Why is the Earth IPP investigating a Braxian murder on Sulpuro?" Another pause while the message hurtled through space and the response hurtled back.

"None of the other governments trust each other."

"And they trust *us*?" Wes found it hard to believe that *every* other species would trust Earth.

"They mistrust us the least. The instruction to assign you, well . . ." He heard the hesitation in the Captain's voice. "To assign Earth IPP came directly from the IP Council. Not IPP."

The IP Council (Interplanetary Council) was the political body that governed relations among the civilizations. Leaders from each civilization represented their civilization's interest to the others, and all diplomacy took place through it. The IPP Council, on the other hand, was solely responsible for interplanetary police affairs. The two communicated often, but remained separate bodies. Wes sighed. Assignment of murder cases should not be this political.

"Why is this one so important? It's just another murder."

"I don't think it is Wes. I think it's an IPP covert and they don't want to tell us that. But that's between you and me. The IP Council was adamant that someone neutral enough to investigate had to be assigned. So Earth was picked."

"Okay Captain."

"How is the Sparcus helping you?" She was changing subject.

"Fine. She's doing her part. We talked."

"Good. Anything I should know?"

"No. She's just doing her job."

"Good."

"Is she with you?"

"Not right now."

"Make sure she uses the cover that she's NYPD police."

"I will," Wes paused, "It seems though—"

"What?" Captain was irritated again. He could see her features tensing.

"It seems odd for a Sparcus to use an Earth cover. She could just be an IPP agent." This could be insubordination on his part. "It would make more sense than saying she works *for* humans."

"That's not for you to think about, Agent Venta." Clearly, he'd touched a nerve.

"Yes Captain."

The Sulpuro stench was starting to nauseate him. He exhaled, trying to rid himself of the smell. The Captain continued, "I don't want any more bodies, Venta. Stay ahead of this."

"Yes, Captain." The display disappeared, and his earpiece went dead as she disconnected the call. Wes looked down the street. The Sulpuro IPP division was approaching in marked, square, light grey hovercrafts. One came to a stop directly in front of him.

Three Velins oozed out and stood face-to-face with him. Their IPP jackets seemed farcical on their constantly jiggling yellow bodies. One of them reached out with a hand. It—literally—extended to Wes. "Agent Berks, Sulpuro IPP. And this is Agent Barks." This particular Velin had invested in a voice synthesizer that changed his gurgles into any language of his choosing. The black box made of a carbon-fiber material sat where a mouth would have been, had it been normal for him to have one. It had a small speaker made of vertical slats. The voice was surprisingly natural.

"Did they pair you on purpose?" Wes smiled. Neither of them seemed amused. Wes stopped smiling. Obviously humor wasn't going to get him very far.

"What's going on here?" the Velin continued.

"There is a dead Necrological Reviewer inside."

"Why are *you* here?" Wes noted the suspicion.

"He was a potential witness in an investigation I am conducting for a murder that took place here."

"Why are *you* investigating a murder on Sulpuro?" Apparently, the Velin felt the need to interrogate him, right then and there. Suspicion was on the menu today!

Wes shrugged. "I don't choose the assignments buddy. I just do my job. Like you." Agent Berks uttered a gurgle from somewhere on his body that Wes recognized as a Velin chuckle. If there was something that united people, it was to complain about their common employer.

"I hear you, Agent . . .?"

"Venta. Sorry. Agent Venta. Earth IPP." Wes realized he hadn't even introduced himself yet.

"Very well. Shall we go inside?"

"Absolutely."

"Have you been inside yet?"

Wes hesitated, "Yes. I didn't touch anything." He reassured the local. "I was trying to find him." He started walking toward the home. The two Velin agents followed behind him. Soon the yard and the home filled with local and IPP Sulpuro agents processing the crime scene. Wes watched as they got to work. They quickly began taking samples, scanning the room, detecting foreign presences. Finally, after several hours, Agent Barks slimed his way over to Wes. "We're all done, Agent Venta." Wes had waited patiently outside, as was protocol, trying to glean information from conversations. But nothing had transpired. And he was reaching a state of contained impatience.

"Can I see the rapid results?"

"Hum . . . I need to check with HQ." Wes always wondered why a single organization needed internal authorization to share information across offices. They were all supposed to be working together.

Agent Barks disappeared into the house and then came back again. "I am sorry, Agent Venta. But it seems that all reports related to your investigation have to go to HQ first."

"Excuse me?" Wes was incredulous. The fact he had to ask for permission was standard. But for permission to be denied was out of left field.

"All reports have to go to HQ because they are related to your investigation." Agent Barks repeated his superior's orders — obviously to the letter. He was like a broken record, repeating himself over and over.

"I'll call my superiors about this." Wes knew this was futile. Agent Barks had orders and he had to obey them.

"Yes, Agent Venta."

Wes pressed his earpiece and muttered the Captain's contact information. "Earth-New York City-IPP-Captain-Office." There was silence, and then the Captain's image appeared.

"Yes Wes? What else do we have to talk about?"

"Captain. I would like authorization to get rapid results on this scene. Sulpuro HQ just prohibited me from getting any information."

"I know Wes. That's the way it is for this investigation."

"What?" Now he was pissed off. "What on earth does that mean? How am I supposed to figure this thing out if I can't get the information I need?"

"You're at the scene aren't you? Get what you need."

"I'm not a crime scene detector. And protocol requires us to step aside while local law enforcement does its thing!" He was furious. He wouldn't raise his voice, but he was seething. Hampering him with ridiculous rules, and then refusing to assist him was typical of IPP. And made no sense from a practical point of view.

"Agent Venta. You'd better check your tone of voice. The IPP council was concerned with local bias and agent tampering. So all test results are sent, unprocessed, to IPP HQ here on Earth."

This is fucking bullshit, he thought. "Captain . . ." Thank goodness there were filters between thoughts and words.

"Agent Venta. If you need information, ask the people there. Do your job."

"Yes, Captain." He hung up before she could say anything else. This was ridiculous. He had never heard of IPP investigators being denied access to processed rapid results. For some reason, a lot of people were very worried about the conduct of this investigation. It just seemed like useless layers of politics and paranoia. Wes started walking away from the scene. His next step would be going back to Earth. He would try to get access to the report from there. If that failed, he would wait for Sarza to come back — from wherever she had gone.

BOOK I
CHAPTER 3

Sarza's Nego-Pod trip to Maka took the inescapable Standard day: all sixteen Standard hours of it. As she landed at the Maka Spaceport, Sarza noticed just how busy it was. Multi-person Nego-Pods, each equipped with added storage capacity at the bottom, lined infite criss-crossing roads scattered around the scenery. Sparcus didn't mind traveling so close, their bodies pressed against each other. Other species' (the humans, really) found it "inappropriate." The Maka Spaceport was filled with transporters of all shapes and sizes, and with them people from every planet buying and selling guns. Bar'aats were directing traffic on their home world, loading and unloading boxes that no doubt contained weapons. The Bar'aats were the foremost merchants of weapons and technology. Indeed, it was because of their critical role during the Great Conflict that the Standard hour was based on the Bar'aat hour. The Bar'aat had easily convinced the other planets that if they wanted their weapons to arrive on time, it was best to adopt the number one manufacturer's time measurement scheme. Everyone else just had to adapt.

The Nego-Pod opened, and Sarza stepped out. She felt herself relax for the first time in days. Bar'aat was a very comfortable place for the Sparcus. Although the planets had not always been on the same side of every conflict, the Bar'aat were highly egalitarian, which pleased the Sparcus. Both civilizations thrived on war—but did so with honor. They also both placed great emphasis on the importance of being a warrior while adhering to a code of conduct. Another welcome similarity.

As Sarza's pod closed behind her, a male Bar'aat named Car-ahic approached her. Immediately she recognized him and gave a half-moon smile. His hair, perfectly white, was one of the distinguishing characteristics of his race. Standing nearly nearly three meters tall, his very large hands and feet were covered in brown hairless leather-like skin. Car-ahic had dark brown eyes. His nose was wide and flat. Sarza had once seen a picture of a yeti on Earth and remembered musing about how similar they were to Bar'aats. Sarza was happy to see him. They hugged, patting each other on the back.

"Sarza, old friend. I have missed you." He let go and stood in front of her.

Sarza, who seldom warmed to anyone, answered, "It has been a while." Not only did Sarza feel the warmth of an old friend's presence, but she was reassured by the weaponry and the general strength of the Bar'aat people. She relaxed. She was among friends.

"So, what are you doing here?" Car-ahic asked.

"I have to track down a lead for IPP."

The two friends had known each other since Sarza was a young teenager, freshly admitted to the IPP, chasing down targets and—usually—killing them. Car-ahic had taken a liking to the abrasive and proud young woman. Early on, shortly after turning sixteen, she had been on a mission on Maka. She was supposed to set up a sale of illegal weapons and catch the merchant in the act. She had presented herself as the young warrior mistress of an undisclosed (and non-existent) human mercenary. It had worked. The Bar'aat had agreed to sell them crates of weapons without reporting them to IPP. But, at the time of IPP intervention and arrest, the Bar'aat had taken Sarza hostage. The IPP agent in charge of the operation decided they would bomb the entire Bar'aat compound, killing Sarza and the criminal in one swoop. Car-ahic—then a member of Bar'aat police—had advocated saving Sarza. It violated his sense of justice to simply kill an agent because the enemy had caught her. And—although he would not have admitted to this—he also still viewed her very much as a child. Which doubled his outrage at the Bar'aat decision to simply label her as collateral damage. Disobeying his superior's orders, he had taken a team of five, broken into the compound, killed the Bar'aat arms dealer, and let Sarza go free. Since then, he had become well aware of Sarza's work for IPP. And his actions had irreversibly gained her trust. She had been able tell him mostly anything having to do with her missions. When she withheld information, he knew, it was usually for his own protection.

"What is your cover exactly this time?"

"NYPD Earth." She winced.

Car-ahic raised his eyebrows and smirked.

Sarza understood his expression and grunted, "I don't *make* the covers, I just live with them."

Car-ahic sighed. "Well, is there anything I can do to help you?"

"Actually, yes. There is. I am looking for someone who is selling SG-33s." She raised her glove toward him: the Sparcus Glove, thirty-third generation, or SG-33.

Car-ahic's face turned concerned with a frown. "Those are usually bought and sold on the black market by people who will kill for money. You know that!" She could tell her request was highly distasteful to him.

"I know, I know. I understand, but I need to find out where they are sold. I'm not here to buy one. I don't need to, Car-ahic." She wasn't going to tell him the rest of her thought: that someone had probably used it to kill a Velin, and that someone was also involved in the murder of a Braxian.

His frown started to loosen. "Okay. Just as long as it's not for you. You should start with the Bar'aat in the Old Town. It's a small village on the outskirts of the capital. He sells Sparcus wares."

"How will I know which one it is?"

"You'll know. It's hard to miss." Car-ahic had a knowing smile.

"Thank you." Sarza paused. "Hum . . ." She looked around. "Do you have something I can borrow to get there?"

Car-ahic pointed off to the right toward a gorgeous open-cabined red and white single-person transporter that resembled a flying motorcycle. The bottom was shaped like a skirt rimmed with blue lights. In addition to looking attractive, the lights emitted energy that lifted the machine off the ground. It was perfect for Sarza to get around.

Sarza whistled in admiration. "A GS-4322 . . . very nice." She was delighted. This was exactly the kind of thing she loved to ride. "I will get it back to you in one piece."

Car-ahic laughed, a loud booming laughter that came out of his massive frame and rolled out with surprising humor. "Sarza, don't make promises you can't keep." Sarza nodded and shrugged. He was right. Car-ahic hesitated, then added, "And Sarza?"

"Yes?"

"Expect a fight. He doesn't like visitors."

"I didn't think he would."

After one last farewell, Sarza hopped on the GS-4322 and flew off. Lights along the floor guided the hovercraft, making sure traffic followed orderly routes. Sarza spoke into the navigator, "Old Village," hoping the machine had been there before or was programmed to recognize the direction. A beep told her the message had been received and understood. The GS-4322 got itself on the right path. Sarza could enjoy the ride. As she headed toward her destination, Sarza took in the scenes of Maka. Rainforests interspersed with extremely advanced cities. As the planet's plains turned into very tall mountains, the green of the rainforests gave way to year-round snow as white as Bar'aat hair. But despite appearances, the Bar'aat rarely ventured away from the warm and humid plains. Ironically, although they were mostly covered in fur, they also hated cold temperatures.

Hours went by, and Sarza was still traveling toward her destination. She was getting tired. Aside from the few hours on Sulpuro, it had been days since she had really rested. But she wasn't going to let up until she talked to this black market arms dealer. Hopefully the lead would bring her to something other than a dead end.

Finally, Sarza approached the capital. The Old Village would lie just beyond that. Some Sparcus on foot were negotiating with Bar'aats. She didn't see IPP uniforms anywhere. This told her the conversations were very likely illegal. Sparcus were not allowed to purchase weapons directly. It had to go through the IPP. In fact, only Sparcus IPP were authorized to purchase weapons. The Sparcus people themselves, including the government, were under a strict prohibition. They could not buy, build, rent, or borrow weapons. The memory of Sparcus warrior brutality during the Great Conflict had left a lasting impression on everyone. After the Great Conflict, the other planets had agreed that the best way to keep the Sparcus threat at bay would be to prohibit them from ever acquiring anything that could even be called a weapon. The Sparcus joked that it was a good thing they didn't use silverware to eat, because the planets would have taken their knives and forks too.

But human intervention notwithstanding, Maka was an unspoken safe zone. Even the IPP looked the other way, partly because the Bar'aat had tremendous leverage and didn't want to be meddled with. Regardless of the various embargoes and the general restrictions on Sparcus movement and ownership of weapons, Sparcus were rarely bothered on Maka.

The capital was orderly. The buildings were made of metal and smooth, black rock—much like the rock used for deskrocks. Most of the money generated from the galaxy's legal and illegal weapons trading ended up on Maka—as did the money generated by interplanetary technology sales. Although it was night, the hustle and bustle of business wasn't showing signs of slowing down. In fact, business was good around the clock. Sarza kept flying until the metropolis was behind her. She felt the exhaustion sinking in. The moon shone on her as she pushed on.

It took another Sparcus hour (0.4167 of a Maka hour), but finally she was able to slow the GS-4322 down. She was in the Old Village. Now came the difficult part. The Old Village was comprised of somewhere between twenty and thirty rectangular buildings, each two to three stories high. They were spread out in circles around a central cluster. The buildings on the outskirts were homes. The central cluster was probably businesses. Sarza looked around, trying to understand what Car-ahic had meant when he said she would know which one was the right home. A building toward the back of the cluster lit up with massive white strobes facing outward when she passed in front of it. Two Bar'aats stood guard outside. Three more sat playing some game with metal chips the corner. This was the place. The GS-4322 touched the ground. Sarza parked and stepped off. Stealth was obviously no longer an option.

She walked toward the two Bar'aat guards, her hips swaying in the tight velcra leggings. Her knee-high boots crushed the ground underneath her. She nonchalantly rested her right hand on the butt of her gun. If she had to kill them, she would have to make that decision fast—and execute it even faster. They watched her approach, neither one of them moving for their weapons. They would probably wait until she was closer. Small red lights along the top of the doorframe were beeping. She noted some cameras that were probably busy identifying her. Whoever was inside would tell the guards what to do within seconds. She slowed down, taking very deliberate steps, her eyes scanning the two guards as well as the three playing Bar'aats. Suddenly, one of the three off to the side fired a shot from a gun concealed in his lap. She jumped up. Gravity on Maka was higher than on Earth but still less than on Astarte and Qetesh. Movement was easier for her than for the natives. As she jumped forward, the other two guards started shooting at her. She landed behind one of them and used him as a shield while she pressed her gloved hands against each side of his head. The SG-33s did their job quickly and efficiently. Brain matter flowed out of the Bar'aats ears and nose as his burn-riddled body collapsed. She reached down for her gun, pulled it out, and while running toward the second guard—who was no more than a few steps from her at this point—shot him point blank in the forehead. The Sparcus fought up close, hand to hand, body to body. And they moved much faster than the Bar'aat ever could.

The three Bar'aats who had been feigning disinterest were now standing and shooting at her. Sarza looked up, then jumped up in the weaker gravity, grabbed onto a ledge on the building, and pulled herself up onto the roof. The Bar'aats ceased fire as soon as they realized that shooting at her would also mean shooting at their boss's building. Sarza ran across the roof until she stood directly above the three Bar'aat. They were looking up, trying to see her past the bright lights that ran along the roof. She jumped as far out over them as she could, landing behind the furthest one of the three. Standing behind him, she fired her gun over his shoulder. With the other hand, she grabbed the nape of the Bar'aat's neck. This method of execution was slower. It destroyed the spinal column at the nape, killing prey by interrupting signals for breathing. The Bar'aat stopped moving in her grip. She couldn't see where her shots were landing but from the thud, she guessed one of them had been hit. She let go of the Bar'aat's nape and, as he collapsed, heaving, she crossed the axes of her body with her gun and shot the third Bar'aat in the abdomen. Though clearly wounded, he was still trying to operate his weapon. She walked over to him, watched his breathing slow down, and took one final aim at his head.

It was only then that she realized she was panting from the exertion. She stood there, watching the bodies strewn over the ground, catching her breath.

She was not welcome here. Interrogating the Bar'aat inside would not be a social visit.

At that moment, she heard the front door open on its own. Nobody was there. Sarza unsheathed her second gun from her thigh holster, but she didn't raise it. Both hands and their respective guns hung by her side. Passing several nondescript white doors along the way, Sarza entered the building and walked down a narrow corridor that ended with yet another door. This one was a bright, fire red. The door opened quickly, swinging away from her, revealing a Bar'aat seated behind a large hover desk. He was obviously waiting for her.

Two Sparcus soldiers, one woman and one man, were standing in front of the desk with their backs to the Bar'aat. They were relaxed, leaning against the table, but the tension in the room was palpable.

"Welcome." The Bar'aat's voice reached her loud and clear. "Don't make yourself comfortable." He leaned back. "Why are you here?"

Sarza needed to know what he knew. However, with the other Sparcus there, she wasn't sure how to approach the subject. She didn't know how much *they* knew, and she didn't want to divulge anything herself. Further, the fact that Sparcus were mysteriously involved in the murders made it even more important that she keep this from her people. She didn't like the thought of having to hide something from her own people, but investigating this murder was her job—and part of a carefully crafted cover in service to her people's greater good—so she would have to do whatever it took. Any lack of enthusiasm or diligence toward fulfilling her IPP missions would probably raise suspicions. This would have jeopardized thirteen years of undercover work and her efforts to uncover Project Genesis. Sarza decided that cutting to the chase would be the best approach. It was clear the two Sparcus were not leaving any time soon.

Sarza swallowed. "I need to know if you sold Sparcus Gloves in the past few months. And if yes, to whom?"

The Bar'aat sat back in his chair. "If I told you, I would have to kill you."

"If you don't, I'll kill *you.*"

He laughed. It wasn't Car-ahic's booming, warm laugh. It was cruel, dishonest, and honorless. Sarza's grip tightened on her weapon as it hung by her side. The Bar'aat and the Sparcus could see her weaponws too, although they weren't looking *at* them. The not-so-veiled threat infuriated her. Nobody challenged a Sparcus and got away with it. The other two Sparcus stayed motionless and emotionless. She didn't know how they fit in this situation yet. *Why aren't they talking?* She asked herself, irritated.

Slowly, almost in slow motion, the Bar'aat waved his right, white, fur-covered hand, and Sarza glimpsed a barrel coming out of the ceiling in front of her, just above the Bar'aat's head, aiming her way. She jumped on the desk, raising her guns. Using the table as a platform, she jumped up and over the Bar'aat, landing behind him. Both of her guns were pressed against the Bar'aat's skull. Where she had stood just moments before, the floor was damaged and wisps of black smoke filled the room. The barely noticed barrel had fired a laser beam. One more second and she would have been history.

The two Sparcus raised their weapons at her. Despite years of a mercenary life, the idea of having to shoot two Sparcus made her blood freeze. She was glad there was no hair color for fear.

"I need to know if you sold SG-33s. *Now.*" She nudged the guns against his head. The Bar'aat lifted his hands in the air. His head was bent forward. He was looking at the two Sparcus. They were still silent, as if they were watching the scene unfold but weren't actually involved.

She sensed the Bar'aat wanted to talk, but he looked at the Sparcus again and went silent. He stared at the desk, saying nothing. All of them stood in the room, as though suspended, waiting for one of them to make the next move. Sarza looked at both Sparcus soldiers and she finally understood. She lifted the guns off the Bar'aat's head and pointed one at each of the Sparcus. She was going to throw up. She had never, in her entire life, aimed a loaded gun at a Sparcus. And now she had to. They both looked alarmed. This was outside the realm of the imaginable. Sarza's heart was pounding through her chest and into her throat. The back of her head was turning white. She was terrified and, most importantly, heartbroken.

The Bar'aat lifted his head and turned it to look at Sarza. She saw what she had expected—fear. But not at her or the guns in her hands. Fear of the two other people in the room. She asked again, "Who did you sell a SG-33 to?"

The Bar'aat started talking fast, "I sold one to—"

"*Quiet!*" The Sparcus woman pointed a laser bow and arrow at the Bar'aat. Sarza was still aiming at each of the two Sparcus.

Sarza, talking to the Sparcus woman, said, "I need this information. I need this information, and I will get it from him."

The tension in the room was palpable. Sarza was going against years of training, centuries of conditioning. She was

54

pointing her weapons at her own people. The disgusting feeling in the pit of her stomach growing sickeningly stronger.

"We can't let you do that Sarza."

"Why not? And how do you know my name?"

"We can't let you do that. For the greater good, that is information you cannot know. This is not part of your mission."

Those words had weight. It meant they knew her, they knew why she was there, they knew why she worked for IPP, and they had instructions for her. This lead would have to go unused. Sarza relaxed, glad there was some sense of normalcy restored to her. They were on her side. She started breathing easier. They *had* to be on her side. The Sparcus woman had lowered her bow and arrow.

Sarza breathed in deeply and exhaled slowly. The Bar'aat was looking at her. She looked at him briefly and then back at the smoldering spot in the middle of the room. "Why did you try to kill me?"

"I don't like cops, snoops, snitches, and people who ask about other customers," he grunted. He was lying. He had another reason to kill her.

The prostrated body of the Bar'aat merchant suddenly lurched forward, his head hit the desk, his brain matter spilling onto the otherwise immaculate metal surface before him. Sarza stood behind the Bar'aat facing the Sparcus. The Sparcus man had shot the Bar'aat in the head. Sarza looked at the Sparcus, uneasy, unsure about the Bar'aat's killing. It felt like an execution. "He was reaching for a gun." The Sparcus man's explanation sounded flat, forced, and definitely untrue. He put his gun away. Sarza looked back up at the two Sparcus. The white hair on the Bar'aat's body was soaking up the blood, turning the fur pink, and making him look like a tie-dyed ape. Silence deadened the room.

Sarza was trying to process the events. Too many pieces of the puzzle didn't fit. And she didn't have enough information to make any deductions. "Who the prem are you? And why are you here?" Sarza was getting impatient.

"SparIntel." The Sparcus intelligence agency, or covert activities, or whatever it was referred to as, was non-existent as far as anyone outside the agency knew. Only a few very trusted people, were even aware of its existence. And fewer still knew Sarza was their agent. She had been trained as one since the ripe age of eight. Sarza began to relax, but her guns stayed pointed at the two Sparcus. Why were they here? What were they doing? Were they waiting for her? How and why would they be involved in the murders? Sarza swallowed hard.

"Why are you here?" Her question was still unanswered.

"Sarza. Lower. Your. Weapon," the male Sparcus ordered. Although she wanted to, her gut told her not to. Without obeying, Sarza repeated her question.

"Why are you here?"

"We have orders for you."

"Why did you wait for me *here* of all places, with a preming Bar'aat who tried to *kill* me? And neither one of you did anything to stop him?"

"Sarza," the female Sparcus took over the conversation. "That wasn't part of the plan, but we knew nobody would follow you here. You would make sure of that." She was right.

"What do you want?" Sarza wanted answers.

"Your cover may be blown."

That was the worst thing Sarza could have heard. After over a decade working for and with worthless humans, in addition to a variety of other bureaucracy peddling individuals, a blown cover would mean the complete failure of her mission. Sarza's blood froze, rushing to her temples.

"What do you mean *may*?"

"We've heard IPP chatter that some people suspect you are a double agent. But nothing is confirmed. Nobody has confirmed, for sure, that you are one of ours."

Sarza finally dropped her guns, placing them back in the holsters. Now she understood the urgency of receiving this message. If her cover was, in fact, blown, she suspected the Sparcus would execute her on the spot. Sparcus didn't kill Sparcus, unless . . . preservation of the SparIntel secret was at stake. In which case the Sparcus had, and expected, no mercy. Strangely, Sarza's mind went to Wes.

"Does my handler know?"

"Yes. He was briefed."

"By who?"

"His boss."

"How do we know?"

"Another Sparcus agent. She was able to initiate a relationship with Venta's direct superior." Sarza wasn't making the connection. The male Sparcus filled in the gap. "Venta's boss does a lot of pillow talking. Our agent does her business and listens." Sarza nodded. One of humanity's great shortcomings was their hypocrisy as to their own desires and sexuality. It was surprisingly easy to seduce a human into doing something they considered depraved — like linking with a Sparcus. The dirtier, more forbidden it was, the more certain humans were wired to do it. "How do they know?" That was the part Sarza was dreading. Had she been careless? Had she done something?

"We may have an internal leak. A mole in SparIntel." The thought of a Sparcus betraying the Sparcus people enraged Sarza. Her hair started to glow red, flying over her head like a halo of fire.

"You shouldn't let your emotions get the better of you," the Sparcus woman noted, looking straight at Sarza.

"I don't." After a brief pause, Sarza added, "How long do I have? Can we fix this?" Her hair was reverting back to black, although a few red streaks still highlighted her face. "And what does Maerah say?" Maerah was the SparIntel leader and she had been pivotal in growing and protecting the agency.

Some had described her as heartless. But Sarza knew to follow orders, especially Maerah's. Whatever Maerah's orders were, Sarza would heed them.

"We are running counterintelligence and trying to muddy the waters. So it may be salvageable. But you need to be careful." Sarza noted the awkward pause and then, "No orders from Maerah. Yet."

"Understood." Sarza looked back at the Bar'aat's body in front of her, remembering why she was there in the first place.

"I still need to know whether he sold any Sparcus Gloves." She nudged the broad white blood-spattered shoulders with her gun. "It's part of an investigation. And I have to get through it." Preserving the integrity of her cover was more important than ever, and looking as though she was still aggressively pursuing leads was crucial.

"I think that information disappeared when he got shot in the head." There was certain sarcasm in the Sparcus man's voice.

"Prem." Sarza was losing patience. Every lead was, literally, a *dead* end. She looked at the desk and saw the Bar'aat's deskrock. She grabbed it.

The Sparcus man looked at her quizzically. "I doubt he keeps records." That sarcasm again. Sarza was getting irritated at this pompous man. She shot him a glance, didn't bother to answer, and jumped over both of them to the door, deskrock in hand. She had nothing more to say to them. A few moments later she was gone. The two Sparcus agents stayed in the room alone. The sound of the GS-4322 reverberated through the street. Sarza was gone.

"Did she buy it?" The Sparcus man was still looking at the Bar'aat.

"Yes."

"Good. She needs to dislike the guy. They cannot become allies, no matter how hard we push them. They can't trust each other."

"How could they trust each other? He's human. She hates humans. She hates humans more than any other Sparcus I know. Now he knows she's a double agent, and she knows he's onto her. They will never trust each other."

"Fine. But she really has to dislike him. We can't have her solving this thing and saving him."

"I know."

"We could just kill her." The male Sparcus let the words slip out. The female Sparcus's voice twisted in disgust.

"That's *not* the plan. We have orders to let her investigate."

"If she's compromised, protocol dictates she should be killed immediately."

"We don't *know* that she's compromised," the Sparcus female answered. "She's been with them thirteen years. That's an investment SparIntel can't waste on a hunch."

Outside, Sarza hopped on the GS-4322 and flew away from the merchant's home. As she took a left turn, following little yellow lights on the floor through the Maka jungle, two other GS-4322s dropped out of the foliage and started following her. She wasn't sure how long they had been onto her, and she couldn't know for a fact they were the two Sparcus from the Bar'aat merchant's home. They sure weren't there for a courtesy visit. Sarza started driving faster and making evasive maneuvers. She ducked between two trees, leaving the path of yellow lights behind her and moving into darkness. Only the moon lit her way now, shining bright and white. The GS-4322s closed on her, following her through the trees. She pushed the machine to go faster, moving up and down as branches and leaves slapped her thighs, face, and arms. She didn't care. Pain was a minor inconvenience. And in fact, the harder the slaps, the harder the Velcra turned. They were still close behind. As she emerged from the forest, she found herself smack-dab in traffic. She tried to go faster, but the thickening congestion of the Maka capital, Bakchar, made it difficult.

Bakchar consisted of interminable skyscrapers interspersed with warehouses and factories. Unable to see who was after her while trying to steer clear of other drivers, Sarza took a quick left between two buildings. Her pursuers weren't behind her anymore. She dove between more buildings. She was less than arm's length from either wall, the corrugated metal flashing by her at tremendous speeds. Any deviation to the left or to the right would have cost her at least a limb. She stayed focused on a point in front of her, maintaining the GS-4322 as straight as it could go, ignoring everything around her. As she emerged on the other side of the buildings, the two GS-4322 slammed into her from the right, sending her machine in a tailspin. Sarza tightened her legs, holding the GS-4322 in place, and crouched down, her body flat against it. She managed to regain control of the machine. But just as she straightened herself, the two GS-4322 circled around and crashed into her again. She could see the blue hover lights flickering, signaling imminent failure. She wouldn't be in midair for much longer.

Thinking quickly, Sarza slowed the machine down and let it get close to the ground. She jumped off and, unable to properly amortize the fall, twisted her leg at the knee. Pain shot through her, exploding at the joint and reaching the back of her head. She rolled on the ground and kept rolling until she hid behind a parked hovercraft. She stood up and ran limping between two buildings. She was panting frantically, sweating from the exertion and pain, feeling the night air crushing her lungs. Without turning around, she heard her GS-4322 slam into the building across from her and explode. She felt the heat from the fire reach her as she kept running. The explosion was reflected in the hundreds of skyscraper windows, lighting up the night. She slowed down, took a right turn into an alley, and stopped. Her breathing was slowing down. She waited. Nobody was coming after her. She peeked round the corner of her alley. She could see the two GS-4322s circling the accident scene, no doubt trying to find her body. Sarza crouched against the wall, trying to make herself as small as possible. She had a good view of the riders—two bipeds wearing red suits. Their faces were covered with helmets and visors. She couldn't tell who they were. Human? Corsini? It was hard to tell. She ignored the voice in the back of her head suggesting the obvious answer. These were Sparcus. These were her people, and they were trying to kill her.

As Sarza stayed hidden, she could hear sirens blaring down the street. The two GS-4322s lifted away from the debris and flew away. Sarza began to run—as best she could—toward Car-ahic's house. It was a good thing he'd lived in the same place for decades. Feeling a bit panicked and more than a little exhausted, she stood in front of his door. Her presence set off chimes inside. *Door chimes – and genocide – were Earth's most widespread contributions*, she briefly, sarcastically, commented to herself. The door lifted, and Car-ahic's wife, Bansheeah, greeted her. She too was tall and covered in white fur, wearing two long-barreled weapons across her back and ammunition across her chest. The look on her face was concerned. She looked around behind Sarza, making sure nobody else was coming, and ushered her in.

The home was the standard rectangular Bar'aat home. A black square hover table sat in the middle of the living area. Four little Bar'aats were running around, chasing each other. The sight of cubs tightened Sarza's chest.

Sarza looked as Car-ahic emerged from another room in the house, chasing his children around, laughing with them. As he saw Sarza's face, he stopped. A frown wrinkled his wide brown forehead. Sarza wasn't smiling. She tried to move toward him, but her knee made her groan. It wouldn't take long to heal, but for right now, she was out of commission. Car-ahic's expression became even more serious. He gestured for the children to leave the room. Bansheeah came to stand next to them both, bringing a hover armchair for Sarza. Sarza sat in it, grateful to get off her legs. She leaned forward, knees open, elbows on her thighs, looking up at her two friends.

"I need help Car-ahic." She hated doing this to him. But she had nowhere else to turn.

"Yes. Of course." He crouched in front of her, waiting to hear what she needed.

"I need to leave. I need to leave tonight, and I have to do it discretely."

Bansheaah stood behind her husband. "I can get you to Astarte tonight. There is a transport—"

"Not Astarte. I can't do that." Both Bar'aats looked at Sarza quizzically.

"We can get you a Nego-Pod." Car-ahic suggested.

Sarza clenched her jaw. "No. No Nego-Pods. The two people who were after me think I'm dead. But I often use Nego-Pods. So if they know anything about me and they are checking . . . they'll find me." She took a breath, and looking at the floor told them, "I need you to help me get to Earth." Sarza forced the words out of herself. It pained her, but there was a distinct possibility the two people chasing after her were Sparcus. They flew like her, they could keep up with her, and they were the right size. She couldn't totally ignore the evidence. Both Bar'aats were obviously shocked at her request. Sparcus didn't run to Earth for safety. But if Sarza said she needed this, they would make it happen.

"Okay." Car-ahic sighed. "I'm sending a large cargo to Earth in the next three hours. I can get you on there."

Sarza didn't want to talk about this any further. "Sounds fine." She stood up. The pain shot through her, but she didn't flinch. She started walking toward the door, limping silently. Car-ahic followed her.

The last thing Sarza heard was Bansheeah's voice, saying "Be safe." *Fat chance of that*, Sarza thought.

Barely an hour later, Sarza was in the cargo hold of a large merchant ship headed to Earth. The ship was far larger than it had looked from the sky. Boxes were neatly arranged next to each other, filling endless rooms with tools of destruction. Sarza knew humans liked to stockpile, but seeing it like this put a whole other sense of reality on it. They obviously were trying to compensate for their well-documented weakness. She shifted on the floor, trying to alleviate some of the pain in her knee. She pulled off the boot and lifted her pants. She was black and blue, but the articulation itself looked fine. She sighed in relief. She couldn't afford down time right now, especially given the fact that she felt so vulnerable. As she sat in the dark, she was grateful for the break. But she knew she wasn't altogether safe. Although every fiber in her body screamed for sleep, she pushed off rest until she was somewhere more secure. Getting caught in a cargo hold would spell disaster. She would have to stay awake one more day. And then, she would find Wes.

#

Wes was sitting in his living room wearing a loose, synthetic blue t-shirt and grey running pants. He was drinking a glass of water, standing near a window, looking out. He had arrived from Sulpuro that day, increasingly frustrated that the rest of his investigation was proving fruitless. He hoped Sarza had found whatever she was looking for.

He glanced toward the door, inhaling sharply. He could smell her. There was a knock at the door. He opened it to find her with a Bar'aat deskrock in hand. Handing it to Wes, she said, "I need you to process the information on this." Wes noticed her limp as she pushed past him and into his home.

"Okay . . ." Wes didn't understand why she hadn't done it herself, or why she looked like such a wreck.

"It's locked to Sparcus hands. To anyone's hands. Only Bar'aat DNA can access it."

"You stole this from a Bar'aat?" Wes was surprised, and a little impressed. The Bar'aat were the most heavily armed creatures in the system.

"No. He wasn't alive when I took it." Sarza walked further into the apartment and moved toward the bedroom. Wes didn't answer. "I need to figure out who bought Sparcus Gloves."

"What? Why?"

"Don't ask questions. Just figure it out."

Wes became irritated. "I need to know why I'm doing this! I don't even know what I'm looking for."

Sarza relented. Wes had a point. "Find out if he sold an SG-33. To anyone."

Sarza reached the bedroom door. Wes wanted to ask more questions, but she was in no mood to talk. And he was not going to anger an exhausted and apparently injured Sparcus. Instead, he asked her, "What are you doing?" He didn't quite understand why she was going to his bedroom, of all places.

"Going to sleep." The idea of sleeping in Wes's home was not ideal, but they could be running out of time, and she wanted to get to the bottom of this. She had spent a whole day thinking this over during her trip. She had decided that this was really the only thing that made sense. Despite what Wes may or may not know about her, he had made sure to maintain her cover on Sulpuro. So for the moment, he was still playing along.

Wes looked at her across the room. This was completely surreal, but having a conversation about it wouldn't make it any less so. "I'll wake you when I get something. . . . On second thought, I'll talk to you in the morning." He saw Sarza's shoulders relax. She needed this. She hesitated for a moment.

Wes's nonchalance about her presence was dumbfounding. He seemed to be so comfortable when she was around. It created, even if only slightly, a shred of respect for the man, even if she still despised the humans, including this one.

"Fine." With that, she walked in his bedroom and dropped onto the bed, face down, still dressed and fully armed.

Wes had followed her and stood at the entrance of the bedroom. "How long has it been since you slept?" He seemed genuinely concerned and somewhat curious.

"Four days." Her voice still came through, self-assured and level.

"You want to talk about your knee?"

"No." The muffled voice came out of his pillow.

Wes paused for a moment longer and started closing the door. He watched her on his bed, her curves perfectly contoured by the Sparcus IPP uniform, her hair spread out across the sheets. A thought crossed his mind, bringing a little smile to his face. He walked back into the living room. She was no doubt one of the most impressive beings that he had ever met in his life. And she was fearless. Wes grabbed a few things from the dining room table, along with the deskrock, and headed to IPP.

At IPP HQ, one of his friends, a Bar'aat agent on night shift, lent a hand — literally — to trick the deskrock reader into unlocking. With the help of de-encryption software, the system turned on. Wes and the Bar'aat agent stood in his office. Scrolling through the files, Wes realized he was looking at a black market weapons dealer's database. Sarza certainly knew where to get information.

The Bar'aat whistled under his breath. "Your covert is good. Nobody gives this information up easily."

"She's good. Really good." Wes agreed. He knew Sarza was good, one of the best even. Both from her work with him so far and from reviewing her file. But he couldn't find anything even remotely related to the Sulpuro murders or the sale of Sparcus Gloves. He shut down the deskrock. "Want to keep it? Process the information on it. Maybe it'll be useful." The Bar'aat happily accepted the offer. "Absolutely! I'll tell you if we find something."

"Thanks." Wes handed him the deskrock. Before releasing his grip on it, though, he added, "Be careful. It wasn't easy to come by."

"I can imagine." His colleague answered.

With that, Wes relinquished the deskrock and walked out of the room. He walked down the immaculate white IPP halls until he reached his workstation, a small, cramped desk attached to the wall. No hover desks for agency employees. He sat on the hover seat. It dropped too far down. The energy ring on it was running out, and obviously nobody would bother to replace it until he was literally sitting on the floor. He hoped he would be able to get access to the crime scene records from Velin. Maybe he would be able to see the information collected at the scene and make heads or tails out of the situation. So much of it didn't make sense. He pressed the tips of his middle three fingers on the black surface of his deskrock. It read his fingertips and turned on. The screen flashed against the wall. He flipped through the familiar files, drilling down to his active cases. As his index finger touched the projection of the Braxian murder casefile, a black and red warning window flashed before his eyes: "Access Denied." The two words were utterly incomprehensible. He could not access his own file? He couldn't access his own ongoing investigation? What good was he if he couldn't review the collected evidence? He gritted his teeth and dropped his hands onto the desk. Nothing more could be done today. He would have to go home, with his tail between his legs.

He stood up from the hover seat and walked out of the office. Once back onto the street, he realized it was only one in the morning. He still had plenty of time to sleep. Then he remembered Sarza was in his bed. The idea of joining her crossed his mind, a very brief and fleeting instant. He dismissed the idea as a pleasant fantasy and resigned himself to sleeping on the couch. As he walked through his front door, he got a call. It was the Captain. She was angry. "There are six dead bodies on Maka, an exploded GS-4322, and half an office building up in flames. Are you involved in this? Is your Sparcus agent in this? And where is she, by the way?"

At this point, Wes was standing in his living room. Before he could answer, Sarza appeared leaning against the doorframe, awakened by his return. Although he was sure she wasn't doing it on purpose, her messy hair and sleepy eyes made her look anything but professional, and everything inviting. He was totally distracted, trying to focus both on the Captain and on Sarza, and failing at both. "I'm sorry, what?"

The Captain wasn't paying attention to Wes. "Tell your covert to get a grip. It's not a battlefield. Tell her to get that through her thick Sparcus skull."

"Yes Captain." The call disconnected.

Wes looked at Sarza, longingly, hoping she wouldn't notice. "Six bodies Sarza? Six Bar'aats? What were you doing out there, going on a hunting expedition?" She shrugged and stepped forward, lifting herself off the doorframe. "They tried to kill me. I killed them first. I did what I had to do. And I brought you back something for it." Wes went from angry to intrigued in a moment. And—to his surprise—he was concerned someone had located his covert agent so easily.

"How did they find you?"

"I don't know. They must have followed me." She had to find a way to keep him from sharing her location with his Captain, but she couldn't tell him outright what she knew. Sarza continued, "I think there is a leak coming from inside IPP." Wes could hear the palpable hesitation in her voice. She was choosing her words very carefully.

"Who?"

She couldn't answer that question without explaining how she knew. "I don't know. It's better to be safe than sorry. That's all."

"That's one hell of an accusation."

Sarza lied, trying to regain some footing. "I understand. But you and I know it happens. I would just prefer to keep a low profile until we work through this case."

Wes didn't answer. He sensed the deception, but he wasn't going to push the issue. They were both tired, and the room was filled with tension. It would do nobody any good to work through this now. Sarza turned around and went back into the bedroom. Sleep was the only thing on her mind at that point. Wes watched her walk away, a longing look on his face. He looked at the floor and then at his couch. He walked over to it, took his shirt off, pulled off his pants, and lay down. He waved his hand midair making the requisite finger gesture that turned off the lights, and fell asleep.

BOOK I
CHAPTER 4

S arza woke up in Wes's bed. Hunger gnawed at her insides, reminding her that she hadn't eaten in as long as she hadn't slept. She was still fully dressed. And her boots were still on. She swung her legs over the side of the bed and took a closer look at Wes's bedroom. It was bizarre to be in the intimacy of a human home. It was bland, clean, with barely any furniture. She was on a large bed with no headboard. The floor was made up of a black synthetic material. The walls were the usual standard, modular style, which was very common in human apartments. The concept was to allow people to change the number of rooms in any given apartment and even rent several apartments as one by altering the living space. If a tenant wanted a three-bedroom apartment, the walls could be moved to accommodate that. If a tenant wanted a large living room or party room, the walls could be moved to do that too. It allowed landlords to multiply their options, and gave tenants the option of enlarging or reducing their living areas depending on their family situation and income. On the walls was imitation wood paneling, a nostalgic throwback to a time when Earth still had enough trees to use as furniture. She looked at the floor, reminded by how petty and reckless humans had been with their planet. Their ability to needlessly destroy their planet was boundless.

Sarza looked back up and saw a single wardrobe against the wall. It was probably there when Wes had moved in. It wasn't something someone would buy — not willingly at least. The room had large windows across the entire southern wall, floor to ceiling. Black rolling curtains were pulled down, leaving the room still fairly dark. It felt as though Wes didn't live here — not really. The door to the room was closed.

She finally stood up and opened the door. Wes was sitting at the metal kitchen counter eating. The counter was floating in midair. The sight of a human doing something so domestic should have repulsed Sarza. In fact, being so close to such a lowly and disgusting creature should have made her uncomfortable at the very least. But it didn't.

Wes glanced at her, said, "Good morning," and went back to his breakfast. She was too busy looking at him to answer his greeting. He wore black baggy pants with multiple sets of pockets. The thick cloth was breathable, lightweight, and very resistant. It wasn't IPP uniform per se, but many IPP agents wore them. She had to admit to herself they looked great on him. Even sitting down, his ass was ridiculously inviting. His shirt was just as bad: light grey, short sleeved, and tight enough to let her see his muscular shoulders, his perfect strong biceps, and his broad chest. Although he was hunched over his bowl, he still looked as broad as the wardrobe in his bedroom. The tendons in his forearms flexed with power at the mere act of raising a spoon. She felt the urge of running her fingers down his spine. Her teeth clenched at such an outrageous instinct. And her the hair at her nape began its usual dance. He wore a double chest holster and a gun on each side of his body. She appreciated his readiness for action.

Wes continued, "You hungry?"

"Yes."

"Good." he slid a square plastic plate over toward the end of the counter. It was a strange mixture of eggs and potatoes. She sat down on the floating disc that served as a stool and started eating with her hands. He stared at her, blinked a couple of times, and slid over a fork that was also on the counter. She grabbed it and started using it. She caught a smile curling up his lips. It made her uncomfortable. They ate in silence.

Finally, she spoke. "Did you find anything?"

"No. There was nothing useable."

"Prem."

"I know." He played with his food. Then he looked up at her and looked into her eyes. "What do we do now?"

"I don't know. I'm all out of ideas." It was the first time she had loosened up to him. Or maybe he was imagining it.

"We could go to Hatuu-oh." He was thinking aloud.

"For what?" She was still eating—and doing so rather quickly, obviously happy to be in front of food.

"That's where the first victim was from. We could go back to the beginning."

"Okay." She was nearly finished with her plate.

"Okay?" He was surprised there had been no sort of argument from her.

"Okay." She had nothing to lose, and she wanted to find out who was committing these murders—and trying to kill her in the process.

"Hold on. I have a call." Wes applied pressure to his ear, turning on the cochlear implant and retinal display.

"Wes?" The Captain appeared in his view.

"Captain."

"The Bar'aat IPP is ringing my communicator like they've forgotten it's *in my ear*!" Wes looked at Sarza and remembered their unfinished business from the night before. The Captain continued, "And to make my life even more complicated, there's another murder."

"Where?" He straightened up, tensing.

"Nash'Amir." Wes tensed even more.

"Who? Who on Nash'Amir?"

"A male and his cubs."

Wes relaxed. Sarza had not been able to hear the other side of the conversation, so all she could do was read Wes's reactions. The tensing at the mention of Nash'amir wasn't him being responsive to his boss. It was a personal reaction. Something stirred him. Sarza watched him carefully. There was more to this conversation than Wes was letting on.

"We will be right there."

"We?" Asked the Captain.

Wes thought back to Sarza's suspicions about a leak. And he remembered that protocol did not require an overt agent to disclose his covert's location. He looked carefully at Sarza. "I meant I'll be right there." Sarza was looking at him in the eyes. There was a momentary connection. A common understanding of the stakes.

The Captain had noticed the change in pronouns. "Have you seen Sarza?" There was no reason for the Captain to ask that. Not quite understanding why, his instincts told him to lie. "No." He paused. "I haven't seen Sarza." If there was a leak in IPP, it would be better to let his covert stay covert. Disclosing her location right and left would do nobody any good. And the whole purpose of assigning handlers was to track the overt agent—him—and leave the covert out of the picture. Wes was rationalizing. He knew not all of it made sense right then and there.

Sarza saw the words cost him. He looked back at the counter. Sarza felt something stir inside her. She understood what he was doing for her. And it didn't leave her altogether cold.

"Let me know when she reappears. I want her debriefed on the Maka debacle."

"Yes Captain." Something occurred to him. "How do we know she was involved?"

"We know. That's all. I'll send the location of the Ishtar body to your transporter."

"Very well."

He went quiet. And a few moments later, he closed the connection. Sarza stood up. "Nash'Amir next."

"Yes." He also stood up and cleared the counter of the empty plates and dirty silverware. He then moved the floating counter and stools over to the side of the room, where they turned off and tucked themselves against the wall. This was all part of the modular home concept.

Wes's IPP transporter was parked on the roof of his building along with the other tenants' vehicles. The only difference was that his transporter was an off-world vehicle—and four times larger than any other transporter there. The arrow-shaped, light brown transporter had enough space for five people: two in front and three behind. Sarza sat next to him in the front row as they took off vertically. She looked at Earth disappear under them. She was always happy to leave.

By the time they arrived on Nash'amir, its two perfect purple moons were dancing in an orange sky. Nash'amir was truly a beautiful planet. The colors were more vivid than anywhere else. The planet was covered in endless mountain ranges. The tips were jagged and uninviting, reminding onlookers of the power of natural forces. These mountains were rich in metals and minerals, mined by thousands of Carlans, a population of small green creatures who were good at one thing only: manual labor. Nash'amir's main export was the metal used both by the Bar'aats to build weapons and by every other planet to construct buildings. Inside the mountains were caves where the Ishtars used to live long before their technological advances. The earth was yellow and chalky. Forests bathed the valleys, giving refuge to wide varieties of plants and animals. They created a dark, rich, deep green carpet of lush, inviting foliage.

But the most striking sight, whether on approach or while on the planet, was the seemingly improbable harmony between the males and the females of the Ishtar species. The male Ishtars were massive, dragon-like creatures, with human torsos and snake-like heads. They even hissed a little when they talked. From the waist down, their bodies were round, with short but tremendously powerful hind legs, and long scaly tails. They also had wings that spent most of their time folded up neatly on their backs. Their wingspan filled most rooms. Although they were perfectly capable of flying, they did so rarely.

The women, on the other hand, were humanoid, although their backs and the backs of their arms were covered in scales. They had fine, attenuated facial features, and their eyes were usually yellow with reptilian vertical slits as pupils. They also had three eyelids, which took some getting used to. Some of them had light scaling around their foreheads and jawlines. They walked around with no — or very little — clothing. They hardly needed them, given the total absence of external genitalia. They wore their hair long, to their knees, and they battled alongside their dragon husbands, usually leading the charge. Ishtar couples were among the most dedicated and proud once they were paired. Their affection for each other showed in every gesture and glance. Ishtar men tended to the young, using their bodies to keep them warm and transport them around. It was amazing to watch a massive lizard bend over and use its human-like arms to brush a child's hair or gently move eggs in a nest to make sure they were uniformly warmed. It had also caused the humans much surprise when they discovered that both the dragon males and the humanoid females were born from Ishtar eggs.

Sarza noticed that Wes had become pensive as they got closer to the planet, but she kept quiet.

Following the Captain's directions, they landed in a clearing and walked to a neighborhood. Ishtar males and their children were running all around the place. The homes were massive metal and stone caverns. The Ishtar's dragon population, by virtue of its sheer size, dictated that every building and structure had to be large enough to accommodate them. The roads were sandy and undefined, with a few women walking around on them. Most women were either totally naked or slightly covered by their long hair. They were tall, like Sarza, and carried weapons of all kinds in simple slings and straps against their bare skin.

As Wes and Sarza walked toward the address the Captain had relayed, they saw a larger crowd. Heavily armed women stood around their destination. There were lights on the floor all around the building, like crime scene tape. They were still quite far away from it all. Wes whispered to Sarza, "Stay discrete. Stay out of trouble." Sarza pulled her cloak over her head and quietly slipped away from Wes. He walked toward the scene alone.

As soon as he stepped into the Nash'amir home, Wes felt his stomach revolt. On the floor was a massive Ishtar male with six cubs, three males, and three females. The male's wings were outstretched, as though he had tried to protect his family or scare the intruder by extending them their full length. Its tough skin was iridescent and purple. Under them lay six small bodies. The three males were like their father, their dragon bodies still soft because they had not yet grown the hard scales of adulthood. Their bellies were white and smooth. Their little humanoid hands were outstretched toward their father. Wes swallowed past the lump in his throat. The three little girls lay under the Ishtar's other wing. Two of them had blond hair, while the third child's hair was red. All three lay peacefully, as though sleeping. Wes saw the flowers in their hair. He turned for a moment, afraid that he was about to throw up. He regained his composure and looked at the scene. Their throats had been slit: all seven of them. The Ishtar women couldn't bring themselves to look into the home. They all cried as they stood just outside. He looked around for signs of a leftover weapon, but couldn't find any. Three Nash'amir IPP agents—all women—walked in. Wes had his back to them and didn't notice.

"Do you need anything from us?" One of them inquired.

He turned around, a little startled. "Yes. Did you process the scene?" He was trying to look collected.

"Yes." Only one of them was speaking. The other two stood behind silently. "We took prints and scanned for biological materials."

"Anything interesting?"

"We don't know. We had to send all lab results to your IPP office on Earth."

Wes frowned. "Can I see the rapid results?"

The Ishtar was unhappy about turning him down. "I'm sorry, but I was told that protocol for this case is to send all raw data to IPP HQ Earth. Nobody else sees or touches the results before then." Wes wasn't pleased, but from the look on the woman's face, there was nothing she could do about it.

"Okay. Thanks." They walked out and he was left alone among the slaughtered innocents. The Ishtar women outside were dispersing. He waited a few moments more as Sarza slipped in behind him. "Who would do this?" He heard real emotion in her voice. He turned around. She had taken her hood off and he saw the tips of her hair turn red. He didn't know how to answer her. Who would do this? Who would slaughter cubs?

"To kill young. To kill the cubs. It's so despicable it's human." Sarza spat the words at him. "*Shikesha Bukeru.*" Wes translated the Sparcus warrior motto to himself: *A soldier can die or kill, but never dishonor or disgrace himself.* For the Sparcus, killing the young was a disgrace—the worst of disgraces. Wes stayed silent. He knew that her statement came from a place of great pain, fueled by the agony of her people at what the humans—his people, in some ways—had done to them. He walked toward the scene and crouched next to the bodies.

Sarza paused and then, out of left field, said, "Why did we get called to this?"

"What?" Wes didn't understand the question.

"Why did we get called to this scene? It has nothing in common with the Sulpuro bodies. Why did we get called?"

"I don't know."

"Why are they assuming these murders are related?"

Wes paused. "I don't know." Those were good questions. He was so used to taking orders and chasing murders that it had not occurred to him. He assumed he was called because it was part of the same string of crimes, but nobody had actually said that to him.

"Actually, it has nothing in common with the bodies on Sulpuro. Nothing at all." Sarza looked around the room. She caught Wes's emotion as he looked at the scene.

"Is there something you have to say to me?" She wasn't challenging him, but it wasn't an emotional question either. She was trying to gather facts.

Wes looked at her purple eyes. He wanted to tell her about his past. He thought maybe she would look at him like less of an outsider. But maybe if he did, he would have to try to explain things he couldn't explain to himself. He kept quiet. "No."

They walked out into the open, leaving the bodies behind them.

"Where do we go from here Wes?" The sight of the cubs still angered Sarza, her hair a mixture of red and the rare white of sorrow. He looked at her, and compassion swept through his eyes. She caught his glance, and quickly put a hand over the wispy white strands. He was seeing a lot more of her than she wanted to show. *Prem this hair*, she thought to herself. *Prem!* She covered her head again with her hood.

"I have to see someone before we leave. She might be able to help." Wes said.

"An informant?"

"Not quite . . . a friend."

"You have friends on Nash'amir?" Sarza really wished Wes's file had been available for review rather than sealed. It would have helped her avoid all sorts of surprises.

"I do." He walked at a faster pace. They got into the transporter and hopped over to a small town a quarter of the way around the planet. It only took a few minutes. The planet was very rocky, interspersed with large warehouse-like buildings.

Wes landed, and as soon as the doors lifted on each side, an older Ishtar woman, still strikingly beautiful, walked toward him with a small toddler on her hip. The back of her hands and fingers were covered in grey and silver scales, while her palms were soft white skin. The scales extended up the back of her arms, her shoulders, draping onto her collar bones, and ending just above her bosom. Her breasts were those of a human or a Sparcus. Her white and grey knee-length hair was laced with black streaks. Black freckles extended from her nose to her temples, like a smattering across her cheekbones, starting in small dots and increasing in size, turning into black scales as they reached her hairline. Her eyes were the usual Ishtar yellow, with a thin horizontal pupil. Her three eyelids flitted across her eyes as she kept the sands of her planet out of them. She walked toward Wes with a tremendous smile on her face. When she reached him, she put her arm around his neck, kissed his cheeks, and hugged him hard. He put his arms around her and returned the embrace. Sarza looked at the scene, bewildered.

"Wes, my Wes, welcome home my boy."

"Yes Nana. Yes. How are you?"

"I am fine Wes. Just fine. Come inside to eat something, my boy." The woman stopped and looked at Sarza, "Is she with you?"

"Yes."

"Then come on over." The woman gestured to Sarza to come in. Ishtar women generally didn't fear Sparcus women. Sarza was again reminded about how much they had in common. They were the warriors of their species, the workers, the leaders, the protectors, and the mothers. They were also of similar stature and had the same build as the Sparcus women. And their lack of shame at their own nudity made Sparcus women feel comfortable. Although their sexuality was as mysterious as it was bewildering.

They walked into a cloth and metal tent, massive enough to hold five or even ten Ishtar males. The three of them sat on the floor, sipping a very spicy tea that made Sarza's eyes water. Wes and the woman said nothing. Sarza felt like she was intruding, so she got up and walked out. It seemed so strange to have relied on the hospitality of a human twice in two days, but Wes seemed to be as comfortable with her as he was with the Ishtar. Sarza thought back to Wes's apartment that looked like anyone could have lived in it. Ironically, she concluded, the only place where Wes the human seemed out of place was Earth.

As Sarza stood outside, she saw a woman and a child walking toward the house. Reflexively, Sarza slipped behind the tent and waited for them to walk in. She stood by the doorway and listened. There were no doors on the tents. Some of the tents had cloths that closed their entrances. Others were open, like the one Sarza currently found herself standing beside.

Nana's voice came through first. "My dear, to what do I owe the visit?"

Silence, then the woman said, "Nothing good Nana. I am sorry. But . . . this child has something to say to Wes."

Sarza noticed the familiarity with which the Ishtar said the name "Wes."

Wes replied, "What is it?" He was talking softly, probably at the child.

The child started to cry quietly. The unnamed Ishtar woman continued, whispering, "She saw who did it."

Wes said, "Did what?"

"The murders . . ." The Ishtar's voice was barely audible. It took all of Sarza's Sparcus hearing to pick up the sound waves that moved out of the Ishtar's mouth.

"What did she see?"

"I'm not sure." The Ishtar woman choked up. "She keeps crying about purple eyes and fire hair . . . but, I thought you should know."

Sarza could sense the awkward silence in the room. Although only two of them knew she was out there, and despite the fact that she wasn't even inside the building, she felt like everyone was staring at her. Her blood froze. That a Sparcus would kill young was untenable, unimaginable, an affront to their suffering—to what they had endured and would continue to endure until they disappeared. Her hair turned shock white, although nobody was there to see it. The voices inside receded as she crouched on the floor, trying to steady herself. Her knee reminded her it had not yet healed all the way. She shifted her weight to accommodate it. A Sparcus had committed these murders: both the Velin Necrological Reviewer and the Ishtar family, for sure, and she wouldn't be surprised if the Braxian's murder came back to her species as well.

She wasn't aware of how long had passed when Wes walked out alone. He found her still crouched, black hair interspersing itself into her mane—the rest of it still white and red. She looked up at him, but didn't speak. He puckered his lips and looked at her, the sadness etched all over his face. He started walking toward his transporter, and she followed. They had nothing to say. He knew she had heard the conversation.

In the transporter, Sarza finally asked, "Why do they know you?"

He paused, hesitating for a moment. "I was raised here."

"Why?" she raised her eyebrows "Why would a human grow up . . . *here*?" She gestured.

"That is none of your concern." The conversation was over — for now. He paused again. He was searching for the words to talk to her about something else.

Sarza put two and two together, but wanted to make sure she was connecting the dots correctly, "Is that why you sealed your file?" There must have been something afoot if a human was raised on Nash'amir. It could explain why there wasn't anything on Wes predating his eighteenth birthday.

Wes had known, the moment he took Sarza to Nana's house, that he was giving her more information than was otherwise available. But she had trusted him enough to sleep under his roof, and she had come to him when she needed help. Against all odds, he trusted *her*. "Yes." He wasn't going to give her more information than that. And, to his relief, she didn't ask. Instead, she said, "We need to track down a Sparcus." The words came out as a whisper.

"Yes," he exhaled.

"We still don't know who committed the first murder though. Right? Or the one on Sulpuro?"

"The Necrological Reviewer was killed with a Sparcus Glove." They had both known this from the moment they had stood in that bedroom watching the leftovers as they oozed off the bed.

"Not necessarily worn by a Sparcus." She was overreaching a little, but she had to be sure.

"Okay," he relented, "That's why you went to Maka?"

She nodded. Wes turned on the transporter's communicator, "This is IPP Agent Venta. I need a watch order at the

Nash'amir Wormhole and at all Spaceports. Alert in case of a Sparcus female's departure. Purple eyes."

"That could be *me*," Sarza remarked bitterly.

"But it isn't." He turned off the communicator and sat there. "It's a long shot. She may be long gone already. But for now, we just wait."

"We just wait," she echoed. Barely a few seconds later, the communicator turned on and a female voice came through, "Sparcus female, purples eyes, approaching wormhole *fast*." The transporter was off the ground and into the blue so fast Sarza barely realized they had lifted off before the sky turned black around them. Wes looked like a mad man flying the machine with the utmost concentration, blazing through the sky. They caught sight of a Sparcus transporter. It was black, sleek, like a thin arrow. Sparcus markings emblazoned the tail and the tips of the wings, almost like they were dipped in blood.

Sarza gripped the side of the ship. Her nails were clawing into the metal. This went against everything she believed in. To chase a Sparcus was unthinkable. Unacceptable. Unforgivable. And to do it while sitting at the side of a human would have turned her stomach just a few days earlier. But all the while, she knew this was the right thing. Images of slit throats flashed across her mind. Finally, Sarza exhaled, "*Shikesha Bukeru*," and relaxed. She was on the right side of this confrontation.

Wes fired multiple rounds at the Sparcus ship. He was trying to damage it and force it to land. Killing the person on board would do nobody any good. The ship flipped itself, flying over their heads, and ended up behind them. Wes dropped underneath, slowed down, and lifted himself so now he was the one behind, holding steady fire. Two ray guns, one on each wing, delivered constant energy beams, while a third turret, on the underside, operated in small bursts. But they weren't hitting their target. The Sparcus ship banked to the right and moved away from them. Wes went to the left and circled back around. The Sparcus ship did the same. Soon, they were flying directly at each other, firing ceaselessly in each other's direction. The space between them was disappearing at an alarming rate. Wes knew playing chicken was no way to win a firefight. Both of them would eventually get hit. The issue now just came down to which one would get hit first.

Sarza and Wes jolted to the side as a shot hit them, damaging the rear wing. The transporter went into a tailspin. Smoke and fire blazed out of the machine. Wes was no longer in control of his machine. Seizing the moment, Sarza took over the commands. She managed to stabilize them and flew back toward Nash'Amir. She was glad they had not gone very far, relatively speaking. As she approached a canopy of trees, she realized her only chance was to crash land as gently as possible. The damaged metal body slammed into the ground, tearing through the vegetation, and narrowly missing several tree trunks. The impact caused Wes to slam his head into the front of the transporter and lose consciousness. They finally came to a stop. Sarza looked over at Wes. He was slumped in his seat. She opened the cockpit, undid his restraints, and pulled him out. She lifted him on her shoulders and started walking toward a village. She had no idea where she was.

A male Ishtar had seen the transporter come down with a trail of smoke and followed it to the crash. He landed next to her.

"Put him on my back. And get on." Sarza hesitated. "I won't hurt Nana's boy. Or anyone traveling with him." Convinced, Sarza dropped Wes's body on the green scaly back, just behind the wings, and jumped up behind it. The Ishtar flapped massive orange and blue wings, lifting them effortlessly. Sarza was holding onto Wes, lying in front of her, his back to the sky. She was worried for him. And that worried *her*! The Ishtar lifted them through the sky. The trees, the dirt, their vehicle all became small and retreated from her surroundings. Sarza looked at Wes. She put a hand on his back. *Just to make sure he doesn't fall off,* Sarza told herself. She hadn't realized how close they were to Nana's home or how far they had fallen. She saw the home as they approached, and a few moments later they landed in front of Nana's tent. Nana walked in a rush with a worried look on her face. Other women ran out and carried Wes into the house. They laid him on a thick pad on the floor. There were no such things as elevated beds on Nash'amir.

Minutes later, a female Ishtar arrived. She was a doctor. Her black hair was piled onto her head, but could have easily fallen to the floor if left loose. She wore a belt with gadgets, but nothing else. Her breasts were round, inviting, and proud. Her legs were muscular, her shoulders strong. The Ishtar doctor pulled out a small scanner from her belt and aimed it at Wes's head. Images of his brain and skull flashed on a screen. She turned to Sarza. "I can't see permanent injuries. Although with the brain, it's hard to tell. But give him a couple of days to rest, and he should be—could be—fine."

"When do you think he'll wake up?" Sarza was still worried. The doctor's words were not exactly reassuring.

"I don't know." With that, she turned to Nana. They said a few words to each other and she walked out, leaving Nana and Sarza with Wes. Nana moved toward the bed and started removing Wes's clothes. Sarza stood there and watched. She wasn't sure if touching him, even while he was unconscious, could elicit the usual inappropriate reaction from her. And she didn't need the world—especially Nana—seeing her turn blue for a human. Nana was soon done and walked out, leaving Wes naked with only a blanket on his body. Sarza kneeled next to the bed and watched Wes lying there. She wanted to touch his face, but she didn't.

As she wrestled with the thought, Wes opened his eyes slowly, breathing heavily, pulling himself out of the daze. And then, just as she had feared, Sarza's hair turned blue. Not just a little and not just the tips. But entirely blue. She watched him stir, push down the blanket as he tried to sit up, uncovering his lower abdomen, letting Sarza get a peak at the top of the dark curls. She couldn't stop the reaction. It was like she was built to be like this around him. Wes fell onto his back and turned his head to look at her. Seeing her blue hair, he sat back up and put his hand behind her head. A smile creeped on his face. He pulled her in, holding his mouth barely an inch from hers. "After pain, pleasure. Right?" He smiled, then winced — his head was pounding — "The Sparcus way!" Sarza was not amused.

She put her hands on his chest and pushed him away. "You will recover from the crash landing. You will not recover from what I will do to you if you don't let go of my head." Wes heard no humor in her voice, so he released her immediately. Her hair was now purple — a mixture of red and blue, her confusion more apparent than ever.

At that moment, an explosion shook the home. Sarza sprung into action. She pulled out her guns and walked toward the door. "Stay here and be quiet."

She stood behind a drape, quickly looked in, and hid behind the drape again. Six Sparcus agents filled the room. They were SparIntel — not IPP. Sarza knew as much by their lack of uniforms, the fact they were armed, and the fact they knew how how to find her. But she didn't understand why they were there or what they were doing. SparIntel was not supposed to exist. It was supposed to be a rumor. And yet, here they were in the flesh, blowing up family homes. Sarza heard Nana scream. She looked into the room, and one of the Sparcus agents was aiming her Liquifier at Nana's young toddler. Sarza reacted, not even thinking about her actions, and threw herself in front of the child. She crouched in front of her, arms outstretched, and stared intently at the Sparcus female. They were five to one. And Sarza had just gotten in their way.

Sarza jumped, faster than the woman could react, and kicked her in the face. Gravity on Nash'amir was the same as on Astarte. It didn't help her. And they were just as used to it as she was. Nobody had any advantage this time. Both guns blazing, Sarza shot the two Sparcus agents, who fell dead immediately—their torsos torn apart. Sarza thought to herself, *And then there were three.*

As she turned around, she felt a burn on her side and knew she was hit. She breathed out and steadied herself, letting the pain flow through her. She had lost the element of surprise. All three Sparcus agents had trained their Liquefier guns at her. She wouldn't stand a chance. And the pain from her side was starting to tear through her.

"We don't want any trouble! We just want *her*." He pointed at Sarza. "Just let us have her and we will leave you. We have a warrant for her." One of the Sparcus agents was talking to someone. Sarza turned around. Wes stood there, naked, holding two Ishtar guns, aiming one at each Sparcus. Sarza and Wes both believed them. If Sarza turned herself over, this situation would be over.

"I don't care." Wes's answer didn't skip a beat. Two shots flew past Sarza, from behind, each hitting their mark. Two of the four Sparcus agents crumpled to the floor. The Ishtar weapon was energy-based, but didn't cause external damage. Instead, it worked internally to stop a target's heart and, in the moments before death, cause unbearable and paralyzing pain. The last Sparcus standing dropped his gun to his side, turned around, and ran out.

Sarza turned and chased after the fleeing Sparcus, only to find that his transporter was right outside. By the time she reached it, he was already in the air. Sarza stopped running as she watched it lift off. Panting, she fell to her knees, unable to understand what had just happened. Her life has just been turned upside down. SparIntel had come out in the open to kill her. She couldn't feign not knowing, this time. Not like on Maka . . . They were tyring to kill *her*. And, maybe worse, *she* had killed Sparcus agents. And Wes — the human — had saved her from certain death. None of this made sense.

Sarza went back toward the cave-tent on all fours. She noticed her blood dripping through the Velcra, leaving drops in the sand and drying as soon as they hit the yellow chalk. She swayed from side to side, pushing herself to put a hand and then a knee in front of each other. Wes and Nana came out to grab her, but Nana stopped herself, remembering that Sarza was covered in Velcra. Touching her would have caused searing pain. Sarza kept moving on all fours, slower and slower, but she was inside the home now. A few more lunges and she fell onto pillows arranged on the floor. Wes sat next to her, a worried look on his face. He stroked her cheek. Her breathing slowed down, becoming relaxed. "Why are they after me?" The pain was making her confused.

"I don't know why." There was tenderness in his voice. His fingers still stroked her cheek as she rested her black hair on his thigh. And, he though to himself, he didn't know who these Sparcus were. They weren't wearing uniforms.

"Wes . . . a Sparcus would never kill another Sparcus. Jie-zer-yu. We are a dying race Wes. We can't . . ."

"Sacrifice the future for short-term gain." He finished her sentence. "I know Sarza. Jie-zer-yu."

"We have to go back to the first murder, Wes."

Remembering their conversation from that morning, Wes agreed. "We have to go to Hatuu-oh."

Realizing her head was still on his lap, she turned her body — wincing — to lay on the floor. The Ishtar doctor walked into the tent.

"She needs to undress."

Wes reached for the Velcra suit, hesitated, and dropped his hand to his side. "Can you take it off Sarza?"

"Yes. Of course." There was a little indignation in her voice. She sat upright, wincing again, and undid the back of her suit. It was slow, arduous, but nobody else would be able to do it. Wes sat by her side, watching the laborious process. The back was finally undone, and she pulled it off her shoulders, pulling out in front of her chest, and down over her arms. Wes's eyes grazed her body, resting for a moment on her bare breasts. He felt himself stir and looked away. Having grown up with women's nudity, he was fairly used to seeing it. But she did something for him. He wondered how strong his roots must be to reach for something he buried so deep inside him. Sarza didn't pay attention to him, instead focusing on getting undressed. She sat on the floor, her chest and stomach bare — her abdomen a wall of visible muscles, her chest athletic, and her breasts harmoniously proportionate to the rest of her figure, round, inviting, and womanly. She leaned back into the pillows as the doctor began examining the wound.

Wes stood up and walked out, leaving the women to the business of healing.

BOOK I
CHAPTER 5

T he wind swept the Nash'amir sands and lifted a fine dust into the air. Wes stood at the entrance of Nana's cave-tent. Sarza walked toward him, flanked by Nana on one side and another Ishtar woman on the other. Wes couldn't help but think how beautiful she looked. One of the Ishtars had brought them a Sparcus sparring outfit. It was dark blue and grey, with no sleeves or shoulder straps. It looked like a mix between a corset and chest armor, starting just above her breasts. The material, however, was flexible enough that the single-piece outfit included shorts that hugged the top of Sarza's thighs and ended just under her buttocks. Sarza was also wearing her ubiquitous thigh-holsters, that grabbed her thighs under the shorts, the straps pressing into her thighs. She walked barefoot and had foregone her Sparcus Gloves. She had healed very fast. They had spent barely a week on Nash'Amir, and already Sarza's wound had closed.

During that time, Sarza had also warmed up to Nana and the multitude of children that came and went from the household.

Wes had asked about the unidentified assailants, but Sarza had shrugged, and denied knowing anything about who they were or what they wanted. Aside from that, they had spoken little about the investigation. They both knew where they were headed to, leaving no point in discussing it any further. They had, however, spent most of their days fixing the IPP transporter to prepare it for takeoff. He had also fielded a few calls from the Captain. He had insinuated they were on the move, failed to mention the injury, and stayed vague about the progress of the investigation. He was glad Sarza would soon be ready to go. He wouldn't be able to keep this up for long. And of course, they had laid low, letting Nana tell people they had left. If anyone was looking for them, they would hopefully look elsewhere.

Sarza reached where Wes stood. She never smiled at him, but the glare was gone. She looked at him and walked into the cave-tent. Nana put her hand on Wes's arm and whispered, "Does she know who your mother was?"

"No Nana. And it is better if we say nothing." Nana nodded and followed Sarza in. The other woman was walking toward a different home, returning to her own.

Wes turned to face the inside of the tent and watched Sarza. She was sitting on the floor, surrounded by pillows, cleaning guns. Wes had been able to request additional weapons, which had quickly been delivered, no questions asked. They were now fully armed. Nana was slowly sharpening her traditional Ishtar dagger, sitting across from Sarza. Neither woman spoke. Wes stood near them. Sarza paused and looked up at him. "Are you ready to leave?"

Wes was a little taken back by her abruptness. "To Hatuu-oh?"

"Yes. Of course."

Wes regained his footing. "Are you ready for the trip?"

"Yes."

"We can leave tomorrow."

"Today would be better." Sarza's purples eyes stayed level on Wes. "We 've wasted enough time already. We should leave now."

"It's nearly dark." One day of travel meant it would be evening when they landed. They could just spend the night and leave in the morning.

"Even more reason to leave now and not later." Wes stayed silent. Sarza stood up and started walking out. "I will wait for you at the transporter." Seconds later, she was gone.

Wes hugged Nana and said his goodbyes. She looked at him. "Your mother would be so proud of you."

"For what, Nana?"

"She would be. That's all."

"Have you spoken to my father?"

"No. Since your mother passed he has not spoken to anyone. I don't think he has even left Terra. You had not spoken about him this entire time."

"Nana . . . Sarza doesn't know . . ."

"I understand, Wes. But . . ." she paused. "Your father and your mother made it work. So maybe you and Sarza . . ."

Wes smiled, then chuckled. "Sarza's hair would be bright red right now listening to you say such things." Still smiling, he added, "I don't need a minder anymore Nana. I'm all grown up."

"I know." Nana looked at the floor. "But I raised you as though you were my own."

"I know you did Nana. . . . I have to go."

Nana hugged him again and he left. The transporter roared through the sky a few moments later, Sarza at the commands. It disappeared into the orange sky.

It was early evening when Sarza and Wes landed on Hatuu-oh a Standard day later. The sun was setting on the side of the planet they were approaching. During the flight, Sarza had changed from the sparring outfit back into her Velcra IPP outfit. Wes had done his best to look ahead, avoiding eye contact with her or any part of her anatomy. Although his groin had certainly been aware of what was going on beside him.

Sarza, who had taken back commands as soon as she was dressed, was navigating. "Do we need to be on this side or on the other?" Sarza was trying to locate a Spaceport on either side of the planet. She pulled up a map of the planet on the in-cabin display, which flashed across the front window.

Wes answered, "This side. The IPP Hatuu-oh Headquarters are here."

"Are you sure you want to go to IPP?" Sarza actually sounded concerned.

"Yes. It's where I should start. I'm still IPP. Regardless of what may or may not be happening on Earth." He was referring to the leak.

Sarza guided the transporter through the boundary between breathable air and space. The heat created a white glow all around them. For moments they couldn't see anything, and then the blue contours of Hatuu-oh appeared. The planet was a large, aqueous mass. The Braxians, in fact, had built platforms to hold their civilizations. Most of the time, however, they enjoyed staying in the water. They ate and slept underwater, coming up for occasional breaths for air and communication. They were not actually capable of speaking to each other unless they had air to operate their vocal chords.

The landing was a smooth one. Sarza opened the doors, and Wes jumped out. "Wait here."

"Is that an order?" She wasn't joking. Wes stopped in his tracks.

"No, Sarza. It is not an order."

"Then I will go."

Wes paused, exhaled, and let the comment roll of his shoulders. She was baiting him, but he had no inclination to give her the satisfaction of reacting. She was childishly trying to create space between them after their time on Nash'amir.

Unaffected, and with a measured voice he simply answered, "Very well. I will meet you at the Cashax Inn. Do you know — "

"I will be there," Sarza interrupted him. She jumped out of the transporter, holding her cloak in her left hand. She pulled it over her shoulders, fastened the front, and walked away. As soon as Sarza was out of hearing range, he pressed on his right ear. "Suzanne, are you there?" He was running out of contacts, friends, and allies. But he knew an overt Braxian IPP agent, Suzanne, he could speak to. They had started at IPP together and stayed in close contact ever since.

"Wes! To what do I owe the pleasure?"

"Not a pleasure Suzanne, unfortunately. I need to talk to you."

"Of course."

"In person."

"Very well. Can I meet you at the HQ?"

"No. Meet me at the usual spot."

"Ten minutes."

"Done."

The line went dead. Wes was still standing next to his transporter, parked in the Braxian Northern Spaceport. The Spaceport occupied a floating metal platform. Two massive wing-like roofs covered several hundreds vehicles similar to the GS-4322s. Some were smaller, some larger. They were locked into their hover platforms. Each stood next to a small column with a hand recognition plate. Wes placed his hand on the first one in the row. It read his identity: name, age, and known address. The circle of light under the vehicle lit up, flashed three times, and turned green, signaling the vehicle was ready for release. He took out his personal payment card and flashed it in front of the reader, beneath the hand recognition plate. The green light turned blue, releasing the vehicle.

He jumped on and started flying toward the IPP office. The sun was finally setting.

Wes flew past the brightly lit Braxian IPP headquarters. The building was three stories and square in shape. The first floor was underwater, allowing Braxian IPP agents to spend time submerged during their workdays. The sound of his vehicle was the only thing disturbing the peace. Braxian nightlife took place underwater, which left the platforms eerily quiet despite the bustle taking place "downstairs."

He slowed down, still on his transporter, as he passed the headquarters. He knew from previous visits that the lobby looked exactly like the IPP headquarters on Earth, with the exception that the tiles were blue instead of white. The cameras detected people walking in and out, but the guns stayed motionless.

For the first time, Wes had a moment of doubt—a hesitation—about whether he would be allowed to walk in if he had tried. The idea that the Captain could be compromised was gnawing at him. Sarza had not said as much, but the Captain seemed quite interested in Sarza's whereabouts. And it came on the heels of a particularly well-planned attack. The coincidences were piling up.

Wes kept traveling and reached his meeting point. Suzanne was waiting for him. She wore no clothing as she always did; she didn't need to. The IPP had even made an exception for Braxians, who complained that clothing only made them heavier underwater, giving them a blanket dispensation as to wearing any uniform. The body of the Braxian female was entirely smooth and lacked any external gender marks.

"Suzanne." Wes greeted her.

"Wes." She knew this was business.

"I'm investigating the murder of a Braxian on Sulpuro." Suzanne did not interrupt him. "Nobody is claiming him, but I need to know who he was and why his death was so damn important. I need to know—"

"He was a Braxian covert. Braxian intelligence." Uncovering other coverts was a perk—and drawback—of the job.

"Not IPP?"

"Yes. That too. He was actually a Braxian covert *and* an IPP covert agent. Nobody will ever claim him. But the higher-ups are furious and want to know whether there was a breach, whether the Braxian intelligence is at risk, and who did it."

Wes took a moment deep in thought. His heart lifted a little. It was the first time in weeks he got information about the case that didn't lead to an absolute dead end. He wanted to hug Suzanne.

"What else? Can you get me the case file? The analysis from the crime scene?"

"No. I've kept my finger on the pulse about this the moment I found out you were assigned to the case. But the crime scene file is sealed. Nobody can access it."

"Why?"

"I don't know."

Wes pressed on. "Why was he on Sulpuro?"

"I don't know."

"Who was his handler?"

"A human."

"Do you know where he is?"

"A step ahead of you Wes." Suzanne smiled. "He is at IPP HQ. Here."

"Does he know I'm coming?"

"No. He is just there." She paused. "Don't get into any trouble."

Thirty minutes later, Wes was walking into the human's office. Wes wanted information and was going to get it out of the handler. The human looked up surprised.

"Who are you?"

"Wes Venta. IPP Earth. I need information from you."

"About what?"

"The Braxian agent murdered on Sulpuro."

The IPP handler visibly tensed up. "There is nothing to say." He stood up. "And I need to know why *you* need to know?"

"I'm investigating his murder."

"Nobody released his identity. You have no business knowing his identity." The human handler reached for the security button. "And you have no business knowing I was his handler."

Wes, without thinking, pulled out his weapon and aimed it at him. "You don't want to do that."

"What on earth are you doing?"

"Don't test me. I want you to answer my questions. Sit down."

The handler stopped moving but didn't sit.

"*Sit down.*" Wes's voice boomed through the small office. The handler complied.

"Why was he on Sulpuro?"

"Vacation." the handler was barely audible.

"*What?*"

"He was on vacation with a mistress." Wes couldn't believe his ears.

Furious was an understatement. His voice was a growl. "I've been chased around half the fucking galaxy over a guy who was getting off with a mistress? Are you fucking kidding me?"

"He was still a covert agent. And he still got murdered." The handler seemed sincere.

Wes calmed down. "Was he working on something in particular? Was his assignment particularly dangerous? What was he working on?"

"That's the thing . . . he wasn't working on anything. He was between missions."

"So there was no reason for him to be murdered?"

"Not particularly." The handler seemed dejected, and resigned. Wes relaxed but kept his gun pointed at him.

"Why was I assigned?"

"I don't know. But the IPP Council specifically requested you to be assigned, and nobody else."

"You mean they requested that an Earth IPP be assigned." A million thoughts were racing through Wes's head.

The handler looked at Wes trying to gauge his reaction. "No. I mean *you*. You, Wes Venta."

Wes's heart was pounding in his chest as the blood rushed to his temples. His arm dropped, his gun now pointing at the floor instead of the handler. "Actually," the handler looked up as though he was sorting through his thoughts, "to be more precise, the IP Council requested you be assigned. And the IPP Council approved the recommendation of the IP Council and actually did the assignment."

"Why me?"

"Who do you think you're talking to? I'm a handler, Agent Venta. Just like you. Decisions regarding assignment are way over my pay grade. What I'm telling you is gleaned from the grapevine."

Wes knew the handler was telling the truth. His gun was at his side. He looked at the ground, then at the human again. This made no sense. None of this made sense. It dawned on him that he had just aimed a gun at another IPP agent. For no good reason. He mumbled, "I'm sorry." But the look on Wes's face was obviously betraying much of what was going on. The human wasn't even thinking about the weapon anymore. He continued, "I don't know what's going on, but I have nothing left to say. And you look like you've had enough."

Wes retreated from the room, running down the hall and out the front doors. He thought the handler had seemed peaceable, but he was under a tremendous sense of danger. Someone had specifically asked that he be assigned to this case, which led to Sarza being assigned to the case as well. Although people were chasing *her*, he was the reason she was involved in the first place. None of this was connecting. He had to talk to Sarza.

Sarza's footsteps were inaudible through the streets of the Braxian capital. She hoped her Sparcus counterpart on Hatuu-oh was at his usual hangout. It was a bit of a shot in the dark, but well worth it. She was running out of reliable sources and contacts. What she really needed to know was the Braxian's identity. Despite her flippant remarks during her initial meeting with Wes, the piece of information that had yet to surface was the Braxian's name and occupation. Sarza needed information from someone, and right now, another Sparcus agent with as shady a past as hers was her best bet. She turned the corner down an empty street, turned down another one, and reached her destination: Club AquaMaxime . . . *So original*. A massive crowd of Braxians surrounded the entrance, trying to get into the club.

There were very few other-worlders around. She made her way to the door of the club entrance. The Braxians waiting in line were visibly bothered that a "human" was pushing in. They had been waiting for a while, would probably wait a long while more, and some would not make it in before sunrise.

She was wearing her visor. Which, thanks to interesting fashion trends on the planet, didn't seem odd. Wearing sunglasses at night was actually considered stylish.

The bouncer, a Kerouac, was standing guard. He had the lower body of a lion, standing on four legs, with a long tan-colored tail whipping behind him. His upper body resembled a mixture of a wolf and a human. His large, muscular, hairy arms crossed across his mighty masculine chest. His nose was in the shape of a muzzle, and his massive teeth protruded from his upper jaw, which comfortably pressed against his lower lip. His ears were human though, as were his eyes.

Kerouacs were reputed for their aggression. They neither tolerated nor accepted women who dared to be warriors, workers, or leaders. This one, however, must have had to adapt somewhat. He didn't seem all too irritated at seeing an armed Sparcus female. She walked up to him, standing less than a person away from him.

"I'm on official police business. I need to get in."

"What agency?"

Sarza clenched her jaw and snorted, "NYPD Earth." *What a ridiculous cover. It's like they want nobody to believe it.* The Kerouac laughed.

"Yeah! And I'm a Braxian. Sure. Whatever." He shifted to stand more squarely in front of the door.

Sarza was irritated, but she couldn't fault him for the comment. It was exactly how she felt.

"Listen. I'm not here to start a fight. It's official police business. We're investigating a series of murders. I can either shut the place down, turn this place into a blood bath, or I can go in and not make a fuss. Up to you."

The Kerouac leaned closer to her, his fists moving to his sides, squaring his shoulders, "You shouldn't threaten me." She knew he was right. Sparcus could take on a lot of foes, but Kerouacs were actually worthy of some fear.

"I'm not threatening *you*. I'm threatening *them*. You and I would, undoubtedly, make quite a mess." Sarza nodded her head toward the Braxians standing outside the club. The Kerouac relented. "Fine. Get in." He stepped aside, gracefully on his four legs, clearing her path through the door.

The dance floor was made up of rectangular aquariums that stood from the floor nearly to the ceiling, each about twelve by eight meters. About ten or twelve of them stood in rows throughout the club, each with a staircase that went to the top, where Braxians could climb and then jump into the water. There were muffled sounds of music coming from the underwater speakers in each of the aquariums. Braxians filled the water, silently dancing, making out, or generally entertaining themselves.

A shelf stood along the top edge of each of the dance rooms. Waiters and waitresses served Braxians sitting there, as their legs dangled in the water. Sarza walked between the dance rooms. At the back of the club was a dry land bar. There were a few tables, a hovering bar, and a single bartender. It was quiet and utterly devoid of Braxians.

Two humans were having a heated discussion at one of the nearby tables. Next to him, a Bar'aat was quietly drinking a purple liquid. A Sparcus man sat in front of a yellow cube of jelly. Salted fish fat, a Braxian delicacy. *Not* Sarza's favorite. She swallowed with mild disgust. The Sparcus man was about ten years older than Sarza. He had black hair and light blue eyes. His skin was light brown.

The Sparcus looked up as she walked toward him. She sat down on a hover disk directly across from him at the small circular hovering table.

"Sarza."

"Malik." They sat in silence for a moment.

"Is this a social visit?" Malik seemed hopeful.

"I'm not here to link." Malik was visibly disappointed. Intercourse was on his mind. She had assessed him a while ago, and he was a prime specimen. She had also experienced him personally a few times, both on Astarte and on other worlds. He had been everything that could be expected from a Sparcus male. She felt a brief pang of disappointment as well. It would have been a good diversion. "I know it's hard—"

"Not here to talk about that, Sarza. That's fine." He paused for a moment, then he added with a grin, "I miss Bashbathars."

Sarza laughed a little, "Yes. So do I. Although I suspect you just miss linking at this point."

"Yes." He was smiling. "Hatuu-oh is not the same thing, you know . . ."

"Is anywhere else the same thing?" she asked rhetorically.

"No. Never." He shifted in his chair and moved forward, ready to talk business. "What *are* you here for then?"

"I need to talk about something that happened on Maka."

"Did it happen to *you*?" His eyes widened with concern.

Sarza played it safe. "No. I just want to know what's going on."

"There is a compromised Sparcus agent."

Sarza felt uneasy. "Who?"

"I don't know. No name. It's just chatter among the Sparcus."

"Which Sparcus?"

"What do you mean?" He was playing coy and she wasn't buying it.

"Intelligence or IPP?"

"I don't know what you mean . . ."

"Don't play stupid." They were both wholly aware of SparIntel's existence, and Sarza knew it. Sarza rephrased her question in a way that made it clear she wasn't joking around. "SparIntel or IPP?"

He looked at her alarmed, glanced around them making sure nobody was listening, and then, leaning in as close as he could, "Are you out of your preming mind? Do. Not. Use. That. Word. *Ever!*" Sarza knew he was right and felt reckless. But she continued, "So? Which one is it?"

"Not IPP." Malik answered.

Sarza leaned back. "Fair enough." She paused and thought back to what Malik had said. "How do they know the agent's compromised? Is it a woman? A man?"

"Well . . . that's the odd thing. It seems *she* was seduced by a human?"

"*What*?" Sarza raised her voice, incredulous, humiliated, and angry all at once.

"Whoa! Don't get mad." Her hair was probably red. "We're not talking about *you*. Don't take it so personally."

Sarza swallowed and tried to regain some composure. "What the hell does that mean she was seduced by a human?"

"She's always in his company and there is chatter — just chatter — that she fell for him."

"What?" What did "fell for him" even mean? "That she's in . . . ," choking on the word, "*prem*?"

"Well, something like that. Maybe not, you know, *prem*." Sparcus couldn't actually fall in love. "But she seems highly loyal to him."

"That's rubbish." Sarza was adamant.

"Okaaay." Malik was raising his eyebrows not sure what to make of her reaction. "I know you hate humans but maybe . . . you know . . . she was so deep undercover we lost her."

Sarza grunted. "So what are they going to do?"

"The order is to kill her on sight. She's a compromised asset."

Sarza swallowed hard. "Sparcus don't kill Sparcus, Malik." *Except I did, a week ago.* She stopped talking, afraid her voice would betray her.

"I know. *Jie-yer-zu*. Long-term gain and sacrifice. Yaddah yaddah. But if she's compromised, she can bring down the whole operation. We've invested too much, too many agents, too many of our children trained since just eight years of age to infiltrate IPP and local police . . . one of us gets caught or goes to the other side, we are done." He reached across the table and put his hand on hers. "You know that as much as any of us. And none of us are replaceable anymore."

She sighed. "What else do I need to know?"

"Why do you need to know?" He was genuinely curious, but Sarza didn't appreciate being questioned.

"You don't want to know that. It's better for you if you don't."

"Okay." Malik pulled his hand off Sarza's. "The Sparcus agent could be getting in the way of a bigger plan."

"What bigger plan?"

"I'm not sure. Something about a . . . an intelligence plan for a number of targeted murders. On key foreign operatives."

"Key foreign operatives?"

"Yes. Other covert agents and such." He was sitting in his chair. "That's all I know." She smelled no fear or discomfort. He was either telling the truth or masking his reactions very well.

Sarza stood up. "Thank you."

"Welcome." Malik was looking at the table. Sarza leaned toward him, slid her hand behind his head, and gently grabbing his hair pulling him in for a kiss. She made it the best kiss she could possibly make it. His hands were behind her head, caressing it, while pushing his mouth into hers. She felt his body relax and try to return the favor of pleasure. It was something a Sparcus man would always do: return the favor. She was grateful for the effort. Finally, she pulled back.

He looked up at her. "Thank you."

"You are welcome. It's not much but—"

"It's a nice gift. Thank you." He seemed pleased. And the roots of her hair were blue, which delighted him.

Sarza turned around and left the chaotic club. The Kerouac didn't even notice her leave. She headed for the Cashax Inn. Traveling around Hatuu-oh as a land-faring animal was inconvenient. The public transportation system was largely underwater. It required actually getting wet to use it. The city had a series of underwater tubes interconnecting every building on Hatuu-oh. Roofless pods moved along those tubes and were available to travel from one floating platform to another. But using them required the ability to breathe under water for extended periods of time and the willingness to get wet.

There were also roofless pods on the surface. But they were few and far between. Sarza spotted one down the street from where she stood, waiting at a stop point. She ran toward it and jumped in. The oval-shaped transport held two red plastic benches facing each other. Each bench was large enough to accommodate three people. She sat on one bench alone. Green lights along the floor told her how much longer the pod would wait for passengers. After what felt like an interminable wait, all of the green lights turned off, and the pod departed. As it started moving, an automated male voice asked her where she wanted to go. She gave the voice a destination and sat back.

The trip took fifteen Braxian minutes. Her hair would have been a mess were it not for her cloak and hood. She had pulled it over her head and held it tightly. That was another disadvantage of using the roofless pods: they were designed for hairless beings. The pod came to a halt in front of a stop point just around the corner from the Cashax Inn.

Sarza jumped off and walked into the inn. The innkeeper looked up as she approached him. He was a Corsini—elegant, well-spoken, and human-looking, but a little smaller in stature. The Corsini enjoyed and thrived on art, literature, and political philosophy. They were very good in the service industry because they were naturally elegant and poised. Most importantly, they were discrete.

"Good evening Milady."

"Good evening . . . Sir." Sarza had to find the antiquated word.

"Are you meeting someone?"

"Hum . . . yes . . . no . . ."

"Milady, there is a gentleman here who reserved two rooms. If you know his name I would venture to guess he is expecting you?" The Corsini was doing this very tactfully.

"Yes! Ah, yes." Sarza understood. "His last name is . . ." She paused. Was he using an alias? Was the room under another name? They hadn't discussed this. Finally, she leaned forward, "He's a *human*," she said, emphasizing the last word, insinuating an illicit Sparcus-human affair she didn't want to discuss further. She hoped this would indicate and explain her unwillingness to use names.

Understanding what Sarza was implying the attendant straightened up, "Yes, that's right Milady. Room 3002." he gestured to the recognition plate on the counter. "If you could please?"

"Yes. Of course." Sarza placed her hand on the plate. It was exactly like the one in the inn on Sulpuro. The plate read her palm print and beeped, signaling confirmation. Despite tremendous technological advances, the galaxy wasn't on a single unified system. A simple palm scan at a hotel wouldn't have-or at least shouldn't have-raised any immediate red flags.

"We are all set. Have a wonderful night."

Sarza left the lobby and walked toward the elevator. There were three elevator chutes. Two of them had signage indicating that they were for aquatic beings, which meant they would go thirty floors down, to water filled rooms. The third elevator accommodated land faring creatures. She waved her hand in front of a red light next to the elevator door. The system recognized her as a registered guest, and the elevator door opened. She stepped in, stood on a levitating disk, and rapidly ascended thirty floors. The doors opened at the top and she walked into a hallway filled with yellow walls, covered in light blue drapes. The floor had visible wet footprints left by Braxians who had used the water elevators.

She found her room, waved her hand in front of the door sensor, and watched as the door swung open. Inside, a two-person bed — a mattress — lay on the floor. There was no other furniture. The rooms were the same color as the hallway. She heard a single long chime. It wasn't coming from the circular door she had just used. She looked around. She saw another circular door, off to the side. She walked toward it and heard another chime.

"Sarza?" It was Wes. She found the door sensor and activated the door, which swung out like a hatch. Wes was standing there.

"Hi."

"Hi." He seemed glad to see her.

"Have you been here long?"

"No," he answered as he walked into her room and sat on her bed. "I just got back from IPP. I held a human handler at gunpoint." It probably wasn't the most important piece of information, but it was the one that made him the most uncomfortable.

"Well," a smile curled the edges of her mouth, "At least you did something useful."

"Don't. Don't even go there. This situation is a mess!"

"Well, tell me about it."

"I was assigned to the Braxian murder. Not Earth. Me. You understand, *me*. Someone wants me in this mess." That news surprised her.

"Why?"

"The hell if I know!" Wes was exasperated. He had his head in his hands.

"Did you find out anything about the Braxian?" Sarza wanted to know more.

"Yes. That's the kicker." Wes looked up. "He was a Braxian covert. But he had *no* mission value at the time he was killed. He was with his mistress having himself a good time."

"But he was a Braxian covert?"

"Yes. But Sarza . . . this wasn't a political hit. I mean . . . why him?"

"He was an important covert. I don't know why. But he was critical to the Braxians. That's what I found out tonight."

"He was IPP Sarza! He wasn't critical to the Braxians. He was IPP!" Wes was shouting.

"He was both." Sarza stayed calm. She was looking at the floor.

"What?"

Sarza felt uncomfortable discussing the existence of double agents. "He was both IPP covert and a Braxian covert. He probably got compromised and one of the two sides had to get rid of him." Now she felt really uncomfortable. She and the Braxian had a lot more in common than she liked.

"Is that what you found out tonight?"

"No."

"What *did* you find out?"

"Nothing." He smelled no fear. And he saw no tension. "I don't know anything else about that."

"But why me? Why pick me for this assignment? There is more to this. It's like both sides are playing a game. And we're stuck in the middle." Wes was talking to himself more than to her. She didn't have anything else to answer. Wes looked up at her. "Anything else?"

"No." She couldn't exactly tell him SparIntel – the agency that didn't exist – could possibly want her dead because they thought Wes had seduced her and that she now was a rogue. She couldn't tell him any of the rest. It would blow her cover entirely. Although, given what she had learned on Maka, he probably already knew she was a double agent. The Sparcus had been clear: the Captain knew she was a double. It was plausible the Captain had relayed that information to Wes, if only to warn him to watch his back.

"You didn't find out why someone wants *you* dead?"

"No." She wasn't happy lying to him. This conversation was driving the point home that whether she liked it or not, they were in this together. Her own people wanted her dead.

Wes and Sarza spent the next hour talking about Wes's conversation with the human handler. Finally, seeing they were getting nowhere, Wes – sitting on the edge of the bed – put his hands on his knees. "We need to get some rest," he said. Sarza, sitting on the floor across from him, stood up and started getting undressed. Wes turned his back to her and walked back to his room. He left the hatch open. And she didn't close it.

As Sarza finished taking her clothes off, she realized linking would have really helped her right about now. Seeing Malik and then spending the evening with Wes had mellowed her. She lay down on the bed, staring at the ceiling. Chasing after Malik after turning him down was uncalled for. And right now, she didn't want to be anywhere near a Sparcus. The sentiment saddened her. Sarza slipped her hand on her breast, sliding it on her stomach and between her legs.

Next door, Wes was lying awake in his bed, staring at the ceiling in the pitch black. He noticed a gentle green glow coming from Sarza's room.

"Oh, for the planets' sake . . . Seriously? Seriously?" Wes muttered to himself. The green glow, emanating from Sarza's hair, could only come from one thing: she was having an orgasm. He turned onto his side, his back to the faint green glow. "Fuck this." It took him another half hour to calm down and fall asleep.

By then Sarza had already sunk into deep, restful slumber.

BOOK I
CHAPTER 6

Wes and Sarza were leaving the Cashax Inn. It was early morning, but both of them were far more rested than the previous evening. Wes had told Sarza he needed to go back to talk to the human handler and ask him a few more questions. He had not been in any state to conduct a proper interview the previous day.

"I don't know whether he is going to kill me or call security."

Sarza didn't respond.

They were walking toward the stop point that Sarza had used the previous night. No pod was in sight. They would have to wait. The temperature was comfortably warm. The weather on Hatuu-oh went from temperate during the summer to below freezing in the winter months. The Braxians didn't mind so much. They could stay underwater and indoors all winter, taking advantage of the very stable temperatures deep within the aqueous mass of the planet.

A roofless pod finally showed up. They both climbed aboard. Two Braxians, a Corsini, and a human were already in the pod, commuting to work. The male voice from the pod asked Wes and Sarza where they wanted to go.

Wes was about to answer when Sarza interjected, "Bait and Tackle Hole." Wes nodded. Bait and Tackle Hole was directly across the street from the IPP headquarters. It was best not to advertise where they were going. The voice interrupted his thoughts, "Estimated travel time: fifteen Standard minutes." Sarza and Wes simultaneously did the calculation. A quarter of a Standard hour was 0.2 Hatuu-oh hours, 0.6 Sparcus hours, and 0.4 Earth hours.

Nobody spoke for the entire ride over, which lasted *exactly* fifteen Standard minutes. Wes and Sarza were the very first stop. As they stood in front of IPP HQ, they both paused. "I'll go in." Wes had thought about it during the ride over.

"No. I will." The people who were after her were SparIntel. Which meant that, theoretically, IPP was still safe for her. The same was not necessarily true for Wes.

"I didn't think you saved your human handlers." Wes was half joking, half serious. Sarza pursed her lips. She didn't welcome the reference to her previous handler, and Wes had not spoken about it during their entire time together. And a lot had changed since then. Wes had preserved her cover on Sulpuro and protected her on Nash'amir, despite his suspicions she was a double agent and the knowledge that the Sparcus were out to kill her. Bringing it up now indicated he didn't trust her, which made her feel like a fool for trusting *him*.

Sarza didn't respond to Wes's remark. "I should go in. After what happened last night, you're at risk."

"I don't think he turned me in."

"You're willing to risk your life or freedom on that?"

Wes paused, looked up at the IPP headquarters building, and then at Sarza. "I could call him . . ."

"Sure," she sneered, "And give away our position? Forget it." Sarza was wary of ever using communication devices. They were supposedly shielded, impossible to intercept, and did not give away location, but Sarza never thought it was worth the risk. She exhaled.

"Then we both go in." Wes wasn't joking. "If something happens, we will have each other's backs."

"You would trust a Sparcus?" Sarza was daring him to admit the unthinkable, and indirectly looking for some comfort that she wasn't as much of an idiot as she felt.

"I already have." Wes didn't flinch, didn't overemphasize the statement, or try to make a point. He asserted a truth. Sarza, uncontrollably, experienced gratefulness at the human. Wes started for the front doors. Sarza caught up with him. They walked in. Both of them held their breath as they walked through the lobby, getting scanned. The guns didn't move. Apparently whoever was looking for them had not sent, or could not send, the information to the Braxian offices.

As they reached the steps and moved past the targeting area, both of them exhaled, noticing for the first time they had both held their breaths.

"Why are *you* nervous?" Wes asked Sarza under his breath. "IPP isn't after you. The people on Nash'amir were all Sparcus. And *not* IPP Sparcus." *Or at least, not wearing IPP uniforms.*

"My own have tried to kill me, Wes. There is no safety anywhere anymore."

Sarza and Wes reached the human handler's office. He was putting on his coat, getting ready to go home after his night shift.

"*Hm-mm.*" Wes cleared his throat. The handler turned to look at them. He looked at Sarza and his face went pale. He was terrified.

"I told you everything I knew last night. There is nothing else I can say. I don't know why you came back with . . ." Fear shook his voice. Both Wes and Sarza could smell it, too.

"No. I'm sorry about last night. I apologize and . . ." Wes held up his hands.

"What do you want?" The handler was staring at Sarza, incapable of looking elsewhere. He remained frozen in place.

"She's not going to hurt you. She's with me."

"What do you want? Get it over with already."

Wes realized that the conversation wasn't going to lead anywhere. "I need to ask you a few more questions about the dead Braxian."

The human handler obviously wanted to leave the office. "I told you everything last night."

"Yes, but . . . I want to ask you a few more questions."

Sarza observed the motionless man.

"Your handler statement wasn't in the murder report. Why were you not debriefed?"

"I was." The handler could barely speak.

"Where is your report?"

"I sent it to a captain."

"Where?"

"*The* Captain at IPP Earth."

Wes hated himself for instilling so much unnecessary fear in this man. "What did your report say?"

"There were Velcra ligature burns on the Braxian's ankles and wrists."

Wes sensed Sarza's anger and heard her exhale sharply. This confirmed the Sparcus were involved in the Braxian murder.

"Were there images of those? Images of the ligature marks?" Wes thought back to the absence of pictures of the Braxian's extremities in the report.

"Yes. The Necrological Reviewer took images, but they never appeared in the final report."

"Do you know why?"

"He said there was some sort of malfunction and the images were lost."

"Was the agent's mistress a Sparcus?" As soon as Wes asked the question, Sarza snorted in laughter. Sparcus would never link with a non-Sparcus. Seduce, yes. Link, no.

"No. No."

"Who was his mistress?"

"I don't know." The handler looked at Sarza as she shifted her weight, and the tension quickly rushed back to his face. He was keeping it together, but there was a lot to be worried about. A Sparcus was scary enough, even for a trained operative. But a Sparcus backed by a human, displaying such bizarre behavior, *inside* an IPP building meant something was very, very wrong. And he was on the losing side of this confrontation, if things turned violent.

Wes tried to calm him. "I believe you. I believe you."

"Was there anything else at the scene?" The handler looked at the floor. He had something else to say but was hesitating. Sarza took a step forward. The handler's tongue quickly untied itself. "It looked like it was staged to make it as confusing as possible. Multiple wounds, multiuple injuries, all attributable to various species."

Wes and Sarza knew that already, but maybe the handler had another read on this, "Why is that significant?"

"Because . . . because as soon as the scene was processed tensions began to run high. Every person on the case was accusing someone of another species—as though we all had to stick up for own. It got so bad that the IP Council was convened. And that's when you were assigned. I told you the rest before."

"Why? Why me?"

"Someone—I don't know who—recommended you personally. It had to be you and nobody else."

"Anything else?"

"No." the handler looked nervously at Sarza and back down at the floor, letting his eyes rest for a fraction of a second on her gloves. "I swear. It's all I know!"

Wes didn't know what to say. There was a silence. He mumbled, "Thank you," and then both he and Sarza were gone.

The handler exhaled, started shaking violently, and tried to sit on his hovering disk just before his knees gave way. Wes and Sarza were too far away to see someone slip into the office as they turned the corner down the hall. And they were nearly out of the building by the time the handler tried to emit a gurgled scream through his slit throat. The Sparcus standing behind him wiped his blade clean on the sleeve of his shirt and walked out as quietly as he had walked in.

Sarza and Wes were back in the roofless pod. Sarza finally broke the silence, stating the obvious conclusion about the Braxian murder. "It was a Sparcus." Her voice dropped. "A Sparcus did it." It was as though she was confessing to the murder herself.

"Yes."

"A Braxian, a Velin, and seven Ishtars."

"Yes." Wes could add nothing else. Nor make it easier on her.

After those few spoken words, the two of them rode in silence, observing the busy mornings of the Braxian commute. Some whizzed past them in roofless pods. Under them, the underwater pods moved around busily. The two worlds were visible to each other only when they went from one platform to the other. Over the short stretches of water, it was as though two parallel worlds were combined into just one, moving past each other.

As they observed the Braxian world around them, Wes glanced toward Sarza. Her hair whipped around her shoulders from the strong wind. For a brief moment, feelings flooded in him. He really did care for her.

Eventually, they made their way back to the inn. Wes swiftly exited the pod, but turned to find Sarza not budging.

"What are you doing?"

"Wait for me here."

"Where are you going?"

"Astarte. I have to go to Astarte." She laid her purples eyes on him, and he saw her reticence and sadness. He also detected her tragic resolve to see her task to the end.

"Why are you doing this?"

"You mean following the leads? Following the leads to *my* people?" Wisps of hair around her temples began turning white with sadness.

"Yes." He was barely whispering, the heaviness of the moment dawning on him. "You can stop. You can stop doing this." He paused, knowing that wasn't true. So he tried again. "You don't have to do it alone."

"Why are you trying to save me?" Now she was angry. He made no sense to her. He was so impervious to the fact she was a Sparcus—and so willing to protect her at all costs. She found it maddening, like he was challenging her to respect him, trying to dupe her into forgetting that her race would die out and disappear, unable to reproduce itself, because of people like him, because of filthy humans. That men on her planet crumbled into depression once they realized they were useless to their partners. That there were school buildings and child-minding rooms left empty—but not destroyed— reminding everyone of the fact that none of them would ever bear a child again. Sarza's hair was a flaming halo whipping around in the Braxian wind.

Wes didn't retreat. He understood she wasn't angry *at* him, but at what he represented. "I like you. I like you and you've done nothing wrong. And your people are trying to kill you."

Sarza calmed down a little. It was a reminder of why of she *had* to be on his side. Her people were trying to kill her.

The white around her temples had spread to the tips of her hair, framing her face in white.

"I need to know what's going on." That was the truth, and Sarza took comfort in being able to tell Wes something truthful.

"I'll come with you then."

"You *cannot* come to Astarte. They will kill you."

"Would you protect me?"

Sarza didn't want to answer, nor did she have to. They both knew she would—despite her misgivings about it. "That's beside the point. A human on Astarte . . . they would kill you."

"Sarza—"

"This conversation is over. I will be back in four or five days. If I'm not back by the sixth day, move on. I'm dead."

The roofless pod started humming as it prepared to leave. Before Wes could answer, she was traveling down the hover path faster than he could follow.

Wes walked into the hotel lobby. He felt uncomfortable being apart from Sarza. There was some comfort in facing this—whatever it was—with her by his side. A Corsini woman dressed in a lavish dress stood at the counter. Her dress was typical of sixteenth century Italy. Her dark red sleeves were overflowing and large. The top of her dress crossed over straight across her bosom, showing close to nothing. Her hair was wrapped in a cloth. And her chest was adorned with a tan v-shaped decorative panel, embroidered in red. Wes caught her looking his way. She held his gaze, longer than necessary. He slowed down. She quickly glanced at the elevators and then back at him. She was telling him something. He stopped. She lifted two fingers.

Wes started walking backward toward the door. Just as he did, two fully armed IPP agents stepped off of the landfaring elevator. Wes slipped behind one of the columns in the lobby. The IPP agents were two females, a Kerouac and a Bar'aat. They were both massive, fully armed, wearing full IPP body armor. Those uniforms were only worn in hostage situations, or when arresting armed and dangerous fugitives. He had no idea if they were there for him or for Sarza, but he wasn't about to find out. The two agents went to the counter. Wes hoped the Corsini woman would continue to show him the same courtesy she had shown by warning him. He didn't wait to see the end of that conversation. Wes made it out of the front door while the agents' backs were turned to him.

He started running down the same street Sarza had disappeared down moments before, but he wasn't moving fast enough. He turned around long enough to see the Kerouac and the Bar'aat barreling toward him. The Corsini lady had decided not to go out on a limb for a stranger, regardless of how attractive he had seemed. The Kerouac's lioness body was in full swing, her muscles moving like liquid, propelling her forward on all four legs. Her hands reached for the belt tied around the lower torso, and pulled out a massive energy launcher with rapid-fire capabilities. She took aim and fired at him, the blue balls of light barely missing. Behind her, the Bar'aat was also running. She was heavier and didn't have the agility or grace of the Kerouac, but her massive feet fell to the ground in heavy, relentless, ground shaking hits.

Both of them were heading straight for him. Wes kept running. He took a left around a building but realized he had reached the end of the particular floating platform housing the hotel and streets around it. He looked around. He saw no roofless pods and could think of no way to get back to the Spaceport. If Sarza got off the planet without him, in the transporter, he would be stuck there with two IPP agents on his tail. Wes looked down. The underwater roofless pods were traveling silently. The Kerouac had just turned the corner. Wes jumped into the freezing water and stayed there as long as he could. He swam under the next platform. He turned around and used his hands and legs to crawl upside down along the platform. He cut a forty-five degree angle until he emerged on the left. As he came up, gasping for air, inhaling as much as he could possibly inhale, he saw the Kerouac and the Bar'aat running across the bridge that would have put them right above him. The water was so cold he couldn't feel his feet anymore. He pulled himself out, his clothes soaked, the water running down his pants, and started running again. His grey t-shirt was stuck to his body, clinging to his pecs, slowly freezing him in the process. He didn't slow down.

Around the platform stood several tall skyscrapers. He could lose himself in the maze and hopefully gain a little ground. He saw no sign of his pursuers, but he wasn't going to slow down. He pushed himself to go faster and faster. The gravity on Hatuu-oh was sixteen percent less than on Earth. He was lighter but not so much lighter that he couldn't run properly. As he zigzagged between the buildings, he saw the Kerouac and the Bar'aat turning a corner to his right. He wasn't sure if they had spotted him yet. He ran in the opposite direction, making sure he knew where the closest shore was. As he crossed a street, a canon blast barely missed his head. He looked in the direction of the shot and saw the Kerouac, still aiming at him. He dropped to the right, toward the water. Instead, he found a wall. One of the few dead ends on this wretched planet, and he was in it.

"*Stop!*" The Bar'aat voice bellowed. He turned around and put his hands over his head. The Bar'aat was aiming a Paralair gun—a massive tube that ended with a cone. She had pulled it off her back and was holding it over her shoulder. A single pulse would paralyze any being for somewhere between six and twelve Earth hours. They were not interested in talking to him. Wes was cold, wet, his breath was ragged, and his heart was racing. He slowly looked to both sides and noticed a small hole in the wall, high above him, just big enough for his foot. Relying on the reduced gravity of the planet, he jumped—landing his foot in the hole—and used it as a stepping stone to jump over the wall behind him. His body felt lighter. He would never have been capable of doing this on Earth. As he dropped on the other side, he felt the tremor of the Paralair blast hitting the wall on the other side. The great disadvantage of the Paralair is that its shots traveled slowly, making them somewhat easier to avoid. On the other side of the wall, Wes nearly fell into the water. To his left was a smooth continuation of glass skyscraper windows. To his right, a small door. He ran to it and found the entry point for an underwater pod station. Arrows pointed him in the right direction.

Wes followed the signage down a transparent glass staircase that sank into the water. He heard footsteps behind him, but was unsure if they were the agents'. The water was now at his waist, and he didn't have a breathing device. It water fell warmer than before, given that had been running around in soaked clothes. He looked behind him and saw the Bar'aat agent turning the corner, followed shortly behind by the Kerouac. The Bar'aat had put the Paralair on her back. The Kerouac was still brandishing her gun.

Wes jumped into the water and started swimming furiously toward one of the tube entrances. Braxians were standing on an underwater platform, moving effortlessly underwater on roofless platforms in an orderly fashion. He swam by them. A roofless pod was leaving the stop point. Wes's lungs felt like they were about to burst. He kicked and got closer to the pod as it moved away from him. A few more moments and he would have to inhale water. Wes reached out as far as he could and finally grabbed the pod with a hand. It started dragging him through the tubes. The four Braxians on the pod were staring at him like he was a mad man, his body flailing wildly like a flag fluttering in the wind. He had lost the Kerouac and the Bar'aat, but in a few moments his lungs were going to fill with water.

The last thing Wes remembered was one of the Braxians grabbing his hand and pulling him into the pod. Soon after, he lost consciousness.

* * *

When he came to, he was wrapped in the female Braxian's arms. Her mouth was on his. She was breathing air into him in small puffs. Not much, but enough to keep him from drowning. The Braxian was swimming his body to the steps of another stop point.

Wes closed his eyes until he felt the fresh air on his head. The Braxian let go of him as they reached the stairs. His torso was now out of the water and he was sitting on the steps. The Braxian moved her mouth off of his. Wes coughed, spitting up small quantities of water, and watched her slip back into the water. He wanted to thank her, but she was gone.

Wes lay back onto the steps, trying to catch his breath, panting heavily and staring at the ceiling. He wasn't dead! Then he remembered. Sarza was on her way off the planet. He stood up, slowly at first, walking bent over, pushing himself off the walls, slowly finding strength in the adrenaline rush, until he limped, jogged, and finally was running again. He was looking for another stop point—one above the water this time. He found the nearest one, and moments later he was hurtling on a pod from platform to platform racing for the Spaceport. As he got closer, he saw that his transporter was still parked. The pod reached the stop point, which was still quite a ways from the takeoff area. Wes jumped off and started running toward his vehicle. He could hear the engines firing up. He got to it just as it was lifting. He waved frantically, hoping to attract Sarza's attention. If she didn't look his way, he was done for. The energy left him, he fell on his knees, waving and yelling until . . .

The transporter, only two-and-a-half meters above the ground, started to come back down. Wes was still kneeling, desperately catching his breath. The transporter's side doors lifted. Wes stood back up, slowly, looking at Sarza. He reached his arms toward the transporter, finding the handles to lift himself in. He pulled with everything he had left and dropped like a dead fish on the floor of the transporter. The door came down behind him and they took off. Minutes later, they were a small dot in space.

As the transporter left the waterworld behind and approached the wormhole, the display in front of Sarza indicated that it had detected an IPP vehicle waiting toward the wormhole's edge. Sarza reached behind her and grabbed a small box on the back of her belt. She pulled it off. As she pressed her fingers on it, a small plug emerged. She ran her free hand down the front of the guiding console in front of her. Her second and third finger found a small slit. She inserted the plug into the slit. Wes looked at her quizzically. "What is that?"

"A Masker."

"A what?"

"It masks the vehicle's identity. It picks a name at random from the general civilian population and makes us look like regular people."

"Where did you get it?" Wes had never seen something like it. Sarza wasn't surprised.

"None of your preming business." The object was highly illegal — it certainly upset IPP not to be able to track everyone accurately — and it was also, not coincidentally, classified SparIntel technology.

The last thing she wanted was to be spotted, so she decided to wait it out. She wasn't going to engage the vehicle. But if it was scanning her, she had some protection. The wait went far beyond what she had expected. A half-day passed, and finally the IPP vehicle sped off. If it was waiting for them, it probably thought it had either missed them or they weren't heading its way.

Sarza maneuvered cautiously through the hub into the wormhole to Sparcus. Upon exiting, an arrow-shaped, black Sparcus vehicle, its wingtips covered in the distinctive red paint, was waiting at the checkpoint, recording the identities of visitors to Sparcus space. It wasn't armed—given the embargo on Sparcus weaponry—but it could alert others to her presence.

"Who are you?" One of the Sparcus asked through coms.

"Sizler Wayne."

Without any further questioning, the vehicle slid to the side. Sarza exhaled.

"Who is Sizler?" Wes asked.

"It's an identity that my mentor gave me just in case I ever needed to hide. He and I are the only ones who know about it. Well . . . and now you."

Arriving in Astarte space, the resemblance of the planet to Earth was striking. Large portions of the planet were covered with vegetation, while some areas were filled with sea and a handful of deserts. There were plains of grey sand—deserts—where the Sparcus trained and lived, learning to adapt to the harsh surroundings. The dark green jungles were purposefully left dangerous, unkempt, filled with animals, allegedly to create more training ground. Wes knew better. The Sparcus didn't believe in eliminating the creatures that surrounded them on their planet. It made little sense to them to destroy nature.

As he laid eyes on Astarte for the first time—the great home world of the Sparcus people he had heard so much about—he saw there was something raw and strong about the planet. It was like Sarza herself. Vast expanses of water created a stark contrast with the sand plains—nature at its most beautiful and powerful. The water seemed freer, wilder than on any other planet. The jungle stood thicker, deeper, more daunting. The deserts lay breathtakingly beautiful in their harshness. Even the mountains seemed to cut deeper and jut higher than any others he had ever seen. To survive this planet, to live on it, meant to be acquainted with forces that only barely allowed for animal survival, and to understand, deeply, the beauty of raw, natural, balanced strength. Wes then caught site of the cities, immediately realizing their triumph over the undeniable forces of the Sparcus planet.

Either in the midst of vegetation or in the middle of deserts, Sparcus cities stood impervious to the wilderness around them. Every city was visible from miles away. The walls of old times had been kept and fortified rather than replaced with technology. Tall, light grey, and made with Astarte mud and clay, they created squares and circular town fortresses, within which highly advanced people lived. Soft shimmering blue lights—energy fields that kept out animals and enemies—flowed from the top of the walls to the floor like waterfalls.

"Why were you able to keep those?" Wes pointed. Sparcus weren't supposed to be able to keep anything that protected them from weapons.

"We argued that they protected us from the animals on our planet." Sarza answered. Wes smiled at the Sparcus ingenuity. Living in a dangerous place had turned, even if only a little bit, to Sparcus advantage.

"Do you get to keep weapons too?"

"Only for hunting and killing wild animals."

"Who checks for that?"

Sarza smiled at Wes. He was obviously enjoying this little exercise in loopholes. "The very, very, very careful Astarte IPP." He had no doubt that there were at least three "verys" too many in that sentence. They both sat back and kept looking out the windows.

The Sparcus lived inside the light grey walls in disc-like, one-story constructions. These living spaces were stacked on top of each other, sometimes directly on top and sometimes overlapping to create stair like buildings. The outside of the buildings were immaculately white, and most of them had single, continuous windows wrapping around their circumference.

The buildings were distributed randomly, with none of the straight avenues of Sulpuro. In fact, the ground had no roads, paths, or streets. All transportation occurred in the air anyway, and apparently land transportation had either never existed or had disappeared too long ago to leave a trace.

But, as Wes knew only from books, what really made Astarte stand apart from any other planet was its twin, Qetesh. The Sparcus people actually inhabited two orbiting planets of similar sizes. Before the Great Conflict, the Sparcus people had been so numerous that they had actually needed two entire planets. Astarte had large blue expanses of water, while Qetesh was dryer, with more desert areas. But both supported life. As they got closer to the ground, the twin planet looked like it was dipping itself in the sea, delicately hovering in mid-air. The two planets gravitated around each other with such elegance and grace that approaching them took people's breath away. Sarza glanced toward Wes upon their approach and noticed that he seemed deeply moved, although she was not sure why. *I guess he finally sees the lion's den.* She wondered if he saw the beauty of the Astarte-Qetesh dance the way she did. She also wondered whether it was awe or pride she saw in his eyes. Maybe he was gloating? He finally got to see the vanquished monster's home? She resented him for a moment. Her thoughts moved on.

As they got closer to Astarte, Sarza relaxed. When close enough, she softly landed at the Spaceport. Despite everything, she enjoyed being home. The Spaceport was surrounded by water. Qetesh looked over them like a protective orange giant. As Wes diverted his attention from the sights, he noticed they were in a very public — and probably monitored — Spaceport.

"Is this not dangerous?" Wes asked, as he grew concerned.

"Landing anywhere else other than a Spaceport would attract a lot of unwanted attention. We made it past the checkpoint, and that was the hard part."

Wes looked around at the rundown Spaceport. The few ships that were docked nearby were all in need of repair. Massive carcasses of what used to be magnificent works of technology lay in heaps. The rust was eating away the fuselages. The wings were useless to provide any lift. And the engines had long ago become unable to turn on. It was a stark contrast to the proud and ferocious fleets the Sparcus had boasted during the Great Conflict. Off to the far left were hangars filled with space vehicles that also could no longer fly.

"Come on." Sarza caught Wes's attention as they exited the pod. He immediately felt the heaviness of Astarte's stronger gravity. It was only about 1.4 times that of Earth's, but it made a significant difference. The Sparcus were, in part, tremendous fighters because they naturally lived and trained in more difficult conditions. Fighting on any other planet was child's play when everything felt like it weighed less. On Astarte, their muscles — which were impressive as it was — were continuously working more than any other species' even to fulfill normal daily activities. Not only were they genetically superior, their surroundings had given them tremendous advantages over everyone else. From the moment they were born — when birth still took place — to the day they died, the Sparcus had to exert nearly one-and-a-half times more effort than other creatures on other planets to exercise activities of daily living. As a result, fighting on Earth, for example, allowed the Sparcus people to jump higher, move faster, and get less tired. On planets like Hatuu-oh, the effect was even more pronounced.

Wes followed closely behind Sarza as they made their way to one of the hangars, which was similar to those where they had each previously retrieved personal hovercrafts. Sarza walked toward a two-seater GS-3242. She jumped up and sat behind the commands. Wes slid next to her. His grey t-shirt clung to his body. He noticed Sarza's quick glance at his torso. Seconds later, they took off.

BOOK I
CHAPTER 7

The GS-3242 was an oversized flying motorcycle. Wes was sitting at Sarza's side, but slightly behind. This gave her — as the pilot — better visibility. Wes looked at Sarza's intent gaze as she piloted the vehicle into the air. The white hair around her face had still not disappeared. He wondered if sorrow was ever so profound that Sparcus hair would never return to its natural color. This was hard for her. She was hunting her own people. And every Sparcus was — quite literally — irreplaceable. Added to that was the fact she was hunting her people alongside a human. She probably felt like a monster. And Wes understood. He had come to terms years ago with the inherent conflict between humans and Sparcus. How could he not? It was a necessity for someone who grew up in a household consisting of a human father and a Sparcus mother.

Sarza and Wes flew through the Sparcus air. It was warm, balmy; the evening air made the trip comfortable. Sparcus had large bodies of water that were similar to Earth's, but the whole planet was like Earth's Mediterranean region two or three hundred years ago. The seasons weren't as extreme here, but they still followed recognizable patterns: fall, winter, spring, and summer. These days, weather on Earth was like extreme Russian roulette—usually unpredictable and often extreme. The ground had bright white lights that marked the airspace for vehicles to follow. They were visible day and night. Pilots of the hover vehicles knew to stay within a certain range of the beams coming up. There were, as a result, very few old-style roads anywhere on the planet although in some places traces of the old complex infrastructures still remained.

Sarza looked at Wes. He was moved, looking out the window with longing. She had expected discomfort, fear—disgust maybe? But not this. Wes shifted in his seat, and she saw his eyes well up. Then she remembered his sealed file and his childhood on Nash'amir. Maybe this had something to do with that? But why would a human raised on Nash'amir have anything to do with Sparcus? They were so far gone at this point he would probably tell her if she asked, or she could seduce him and get it out of him. Sarza shifted uneasily in her seat. She had been asked to seduce numerous targets over the past decade. And she had always done so success-fully, usually—although not always—killing them or getting what she wanted before ever having to link. But the thought of seducing other targets had always repulsed her to no end. Thinking about seducing Wes was—well—an attractive thought. And that would have made it a very difficult task.

"Where are we going?" Wes's voice interrupted her thoughts.

"Lilithian." The Sparcus capital.

"Anyone in particular we are going to see?"

Sarza paused. He probably deserved to know at least that. "My mentor."

"Who is he?" Wes was pushing the limits. But although he was fully aware that she was on the defensive answering his questions, this was completely unknown territory. If he got killed, nobody would ever even find his body. He wanted to have some information in case he needed to get out on his own.

Sarza paused again. Her mentor was on the Sparcus governing council. He was also a member of SparIntel. In fact, when Sarza was eight years old, he recruited her and trained her to be a double agent. The training had been brutal: hours of hand-to-hand combat, technology, weapons training, piloting, driving, languages, customs and cultures, political structures, military strategy, secret service, resistance to torture, ability to inflict torture, and—after puberty was over—introduction to the art of seduction. Every simulation used live ammunition. Surviving the training was a feat in itself.

Her training had lasted seven years, until she was conveniently placed in a home where IPP agents were expected. She was fifteen years old. She remembered their arrival: a Kerouac male and an Ishtar female. She was outside, play-sword fighting with a boy her age. They took one look at her, walked into the home, and negotiated with the woman acting as her "mother" to hire her as an IPP agent.

Wes repeated his question gently. "Can you tell me who he is?"

"He is a member of the Sparcus Council." She could tell him that much.

"How do you know him?"

Sarza internally conceded that that was a good question. An IPP covert and a Sparcus Council member? Usually those people didn't mix. Unless, of course, SparIntel was involved. Which she couldn't tell Wes about. Despite everything they had been through she couldn't blow her cover. She couldn't reveal to him the most closely guarded secret in Sparcus history, a secret so important they were willing to kill each other over it. So she didn't answer. Wes had the good sense to take the hint and drop the subject.

They were flying through a city on the outskirts of Lilithian. Sparcus women and men in civilian clothes were training. The men wore loose white cloth around their hips and buttocks. They were short to allow maximum mobility. The women wore a short white dress that did little to cover their bodies. It fell off their shoulders and reached just under their buttocks. They also wore white and gold waist cinchers that went halfway across their breasts, holding them in place during battle. The men were bare-chested. One woman was in a fistfight with another woman. A Sparcus man was sparring with a third Sparcus woman. The man threw a right hook into the woman's face. The punch landed on her nose, which erupted into a stream of blood. She threw her left into the man's stomach, followed by a quick right into his cheek. He was on his knees. She grabbed the back of his head and pulled it onto her knee at half speed, more to make a point then to actually harm him. She released the man's hair and stepped back, raising her hands. The fight was over.

Wes saw schools, playgrounds, and children's areas that were all painfully empty. He wanted to ask Sarza why the Sparcus had not just gotten rid of them, but at the thought of asking the question he realized it would have meant a complete abandonment of hope. Project Geno had consisted of spraying a sterilizing agent that only worked on Sparcus men into the water, the air, and the Sparcus food supply. Within months, the entire male Sparcus population had been exposed, and every Sparcus man had been irreversibly sterilized. Wes felt ashamed. It wasn't something he could express on Earth because the party line was that the Sparcus deserved it. They were getting the upper hand, and a life dominated by sex-crazed bloodthirsty heathens was worse than no life at all.

But the thought of this slow, inexorable, genocide wrenched his heart.

As they entered Lilithian, Wes saw a massive building to his right, easily one of the largest buildings he had ever seen. The white, rectangular edifice displayed large columns in the front. While it likely only held somewhere between six and ten floors, its footprint was easily half a mile by half a mile.

"What is that?"

"The capital's Bashbathar hall." Sarza answered in a-matter-of-fact tone. Wes was stunned. This was the hall of orgies. He had very likely been conceived *in that hall*. That was a very, very weird thought.

"Why is it . . . so big?"

"When . . . before . . ." Sarza was looking for words. "Before the Slaughter, the Sparcus had Bashbathars every night. And in order to keep siblings and family members separate from each other, there had to be a lot of rooms running at the same time. We also controlled for age . . ."

Wes looked at her quizzically, so Sarza continued, "Fifteen- to twenty-year-olds are kept in separate halls if they want to participate." Wes was still looking at her. He wasn't understanding. Sarza was a little irritated. "Their skill level isn't where it needs to be. The boys especially."

Wes smiled, chuckling to himself. After a brief pause, he asked, "How did you keep family members separate?"

"Everyone has a DNA analysis done at the door, and you get a room number based on your family affiliations. Some nights it's just impossible to keep bloodlines separate. So people can get private rooms upstairs or go home."

Wes smiled. She was making sex sound so organized.

"Do you . . .?" It was a stupid question. Of course she went to Bashbathars. And he couldn't even finish it.

She sighed, finishing his question for him. "Do I go to Bashbathars?" She didn't like the fact he had to beat around the issue. There was irritation in her voice. It reminded her of human sexual dysfunction. Which she found repulsive.

"Yes, do you go?" Wes was trying to sound nonchalant. Knowing full well that ship had sailed ten seconds ago.

"Yes. I love Bashbathars." Sarza just threw the words out like she was expressing a preference for an ice cream flavor. There was no shame, no self-consciousness, and she was obviously not saying it to seduce him or put thoughts of sex in his head.

The Sparcus had quite successfully achieved sexual equality between women and men. Most humans could never get their heads around it. But Wes—although it still made him uncomfortable and feel out of his element—appreciated the honesty of it. Although right now, despite his best intentions, he wasn't totally detached from the conversation. He shifted in his seat. The thought of Sarza having sex had caused all sorts of tension below the belt. And staying seated was most uncomfortable. He, again, tried to readjust discretely.

Sarza kept talking, oblivious to his genital gymnastics. "But we don't have them as often as we used to. So most of the building stays empty."

The Bashbathar hall was behind them now. They were working their way through busy Lilithian traffic. Vehicles were flying both above them and under them, all following the lights on the floor. Some were blue, some were red, some were green, some were orange, some were purple, and some were white. Each color was directing traffic at a different height. As a result, the floor had dotted lines of colored lights intersecting, winding around, and sometimes running parallel to each other. But because each of the colors was only being followed at one particular height, traffic stayed orderly in the skies.

Wes was thinking about what Sarza had just said. There weren't many Bashbathars? Why not? Curiosity was going to get him killed.

Giugi Carminati

"Why are there fewer Bashbathars?" He braced for Sarza's reaction, watching her hair. Sarza was surprised more than angry. She glanced at him like he was an idiot, then looked back at the street. She wasn't angry. But she definitely thought he was a few brain cells short.

She sighed as she slowed down the GS-3242. They had arrived. But she didn't park yet. She let the GS-3243 hover at a standstill for a moment. She looked over at Wes, then at her feet, and then at Wes again. He wasn't talking. He looked genuine. There had been no judgment in his voice. Sarza didn't have the heart to be angry with him.

"After the men were sterilized," it was the first time Wes saw her refer to that without directing anger at him, "they largely became depressed. It's hard to feel . . . like a man . . ."

Wes didn't need her to lay that out in front of him. "I get it. I get it."

But Sarza continued, "Well, it's not just that." Sarza was looking at the floor. "Sparcus women only ovulate when they orgasm. They work very similar to the men in other species in that respect."

Wes was looking at the ground too. "Wow," he muttered. He was *not* expecting that. And his mother had *not* talked to him about that particular aspect of Sparcus reproduction.

"So in order for children to be conceived, both the male and the female have to orgasm. The Sparcus men became depressed when they . . ." Sarza paused. "Anyway . . . and it became less pressing for Sparcus men to fulfill Sparcus women. For some, not all, it seemed pointless to put in the effort to make a woman orgasm if her resulting ovulation would be wasted. So as a result, it became less important for them to learn how to do so. And linking with a Sparcus man who won't make a Sparcus woman orgasm is pointless . . ." She paused again, then continued. "At least . . . among *Sparcus*, women linking with men unable to make them orgasm is pointless. So the attraction of Bashbathars was diminished."

133

Sarza sunk back in her seat, staring at the building in front of them. They sat in silence.

Sarza continued, "Before I was born . . . I am one of the last children of Sparcus . . . before I was born, Bashbathars were joyous occasions where people linked, and some people Matched, and children were conceived. It brought the Sparcus together and ensured our survival as a species . . ."

"Matched?" That was a word Wes had never heard of.

Sarza looked at him, raising her eyebrows. "You've never heard of Matching?"

"No. Never."

"Of course not . . ." Sarza sneered and sighed, which Wes didn't realize someone could do at the same time until he saw her do it. Sarza knew it was common for other species to ignore the kinder aspects of Sparcus culture. It didn't fit the image of the Sparcus as bloodthirsty monsters.

"What is it?" Wes wasn't letting this one drop.

Sarza looked at Wes as she spoke. "Sparcus men and Sparcus women are attracted to each other based on aesthetics, strength, intelligence, and sexual ability. Men can be attracted to men and women, and women can be attracted to women and men. But there are certain things that are biological. In most circumstances, we are most attracted to Sparcus specimens who will provide the best possible offspring."

"Okay." Wes reflected on that for a moment. What did it mean, then, that her hair turned blue any time they were close to each other? He wasn't going to ask about *that*. He probably wouldn't live to hear the answer.

Sarza continued, "Eventually, after many, many, many partners, Sparcus women will Match. They will find a male that will provide the absolute best offspring. It's not something we control. It's not like human prem, that overrides any considerations of compatibility, sexual fulfillment, and reproductive ability." There was contempt in that last sentence. "A Match is *the* perfect partner."

"What happens when people Match?"

"Usually, they stay together for the rest of their lives. They are a perfect Match. It would be pointless to attempt reproduction with any other being."

"Well . . . but sex is not just about reproduction."

"Right. And in fact, even after a Match some women will maintain relations with their Match and other women and men. And the same for some men, with other women and men. But because Sparcus women need orgasms to ovulate, a Match is usually—necessarily—the most fulfilling sexual partner a Sparcus female will ever find. Reproduction is linked to sexual prowess. They depend on each other. So it's not . . . I mean . . . it really *is* a Match." Sarza paused.

"Like falling in love?" Wes looked very surprised that such a thing existed.

"No!" Sarza answered quickly, decisively, and impatiently. "It has nothing to do with prem, love, whatever you want to call it. Your 'love' is nothing but some ridiculous infatuation that leads people to make terrible decisions. It creates obsessions about monogamy. And it brings together utterly genetically incompatible creatures. It also leads to women and men to stay with partners utterly incapable of bringing them adequate sexual satisfaction. Love makes humans miserable. It's idiotic. And it's harmful."

Wes had not expected the outburst. But it did clarify things about Sparcus views on human relations. He certainly wasn't going to have a debate about the meaning of love now—or ever. If he could help it.

Instead, he had another thought. "Are you Matched?"

Sarza laughed, but there was bitterness in her voice. "I will never, ever Match. No Sparcus will ever Match. Ever again." The laughter was gone, leaving only the bitterness. "There is absolutely no possibility of reproduction now. Since you humans condemned us, there have been no Matches." Sarza's voice trailed off. She went back to working the commands and lowered the GS-3242 to the ground. It landed softly, and the gentle hum of the blue lights turned off. Wes sat silently. He had heard about Project Geno and the sterilization of the Sparcus people. He had listened to his parents talk about it his whole life. But seeing this was like nothing he had experienced before.

The GS-3242's reinforced clear polymer hatch opened toward the sky. Sarza and Wes stepped out, each on their side. The hatch closed behind them. Wes saw what had probably been a school—there was a large open area with a fence all around it—across the street. The building was falling apart.

He looked at Sarza walking ahead of him. She was in her late twenties and she was one of the youngest people of her race. There would be nobody to replace her. That was a weight he had never felt. But he felt it now. He shared it.

They walked into a tall and narrow palace, which shared walls on either side with other buildings. It was ornate on the outside, with marble statues and carvings, standing four stories tall. Sarza waved her hand in front of the door sensor. The door was just a force field, which dissolved as it recognized Sarza's credentials. She walked in. An older Sparcus was rushing toward her. There were guards at the door, inside. He gestured at them to stand guard at the door. The man had a white beard, shoulder-length white hair, and wore a white robe fastened by a black belt that crossed over his chest and reached the ground. He ran to Sarza and hugged her, holding her in his arms, burying his face in her hair, the way a father would.

He pulled back from her, holding her shoulders. "Are you okay?"

"Yes. I'm fine Vigor."

"I was so worried about you." His voice was shaking. He was looking at her with so much love. Wes stood there watching the scene, unsure what was expected of him.

"He is *the* human, right?"

"Yes," Sarza answered quickly. She turned to glance at Wes and then looked back at Vigor.

"He is very tall for a human." Vigor was surprised.

"I know."

"And a very good specimen."

"I know." *It's exasperating!* But Sarza's voice betrayed no emotion. She sounded like she was assessing a piece of meat. "But he is human."

Wes swallowed hard. Sarza had just admitted finding him attractive? Blue hair notwithstanding, hearing it in her words was exhilarating. Then it hit him that Vigor had just made that same assessment. He knew men did this. Hell, he did it himself. But hearing Vigor express it so nonchalantly reminded him how different he was from them. He must have looked at Vigor with an expression that betrayed his thoughts, because Vigor shook his head. "Here comes the human male . . . tsk, tsk, tsk. So worried about the man-on-man attraction."

Sarza looked back at Wes again. "So disappointing Agent Venta. Pleasure is pleasure, no matter where it comes from." Wes knew this, but getting a lecture from Sarza made him feel foolish.

Sarza and Vigor went back to paying attention to each other. Wes was grateful to be ignored. The Sparcus pair walked away from him, leaving him in the middle of the entrance. Wes saw Vigor stop in front a wall with a black panel. Vigor put his hand on it and spoke into it. Wes couldn't hear most of Vigor's words, except for "Dress like a Sparcus." Apparently, someone was on the other end, because Vigor was engaged in a conversation. It lasted a few moments. When it was over, Sarza and Vigor kept walking and disappeared into a hallway.

Wes was facing a large staircase, covered in red cloth. The steps split in the middle, and each kept going on either side of the second floor. Doors lined both sides of the room, while a force field created a red haze, obscuring his view. He could look through it and make out the furniture and large objects, but nothing more. One of the force fields disappeared, and a Sparcus man walked into the room. He was only wearing a cloth around his waist. He was tall, muscular but lean, his shoulders as wide as the door he had just walked through, and covered in sweat. His black hair was cut short, and his eyes were purple like Sarza's. His skin was very dark brown. As dark as the inhabitants of the African continent on Earth. He was about five inches taller than Wes. No muscle was left unworked, unsculpted, or unused. He was all power. Wes wondered, for a moment, how Sarza could find *him* a decent specimen when she was surrounded by *that* her whole life. He was a good build, but he didn't look anything like that.

The Sparcus man took off his loincloth. Wes blinked a few times and looked at the Sparcus man's face. He had no idea what to expect. The Sparcus man then threw the scent- and sweat-filled cloth at Wes, who did not catch it as he let it hit his chest and fall to the ground.

"Vigor said you have to wear this."

"What?" Wes hoped it was a joke.

"You need to dress like a Sparcus." Wes could hear the hatred in the man's voice. He tensed. He had no weapons on him, and he wasn't sure he could take on a Sparcus like this one barehanded. "Vigor said you needed some clothes and mentioned I should find you something to wear."

"I'll talk to Vigor." Wes kept his calm. This wasn't a joke, and this man was looking for a fight.

"Suit yourself. Let me know if you need any more of my clothes." The Sparcus gave a sardonic smile, turned around, and went back the way he came, naked. Wes — unable to help himself — noted he was an excellent specimen.

Wes stood there while the two guards stared at him. If they were amused, they weren't letting him see it. He took a few steps forward and sat on the lowest step of the staircase. He would just have to wait until Sarza came back. He hoped that wouldn't take too long.

Sarza and Vigor were in Vigor's kitchen. He was throwing small balls of nutritional material into a bowl. Sarza stood watching him.

"I didn't know if you would make it here alive, Sarza."

"You knew I was coming?"

"I hoped you would. You still refuse to use communicators." He wasn't happy about that.

"They are too easy to trace."

Vigor continued, "You're at risk."

"From who?"

Vigor sighed as he covered the bowl with a white disc of cloth-like material. He pressed the edges of it onto the bowl for a few moments. The white disc glowed, and when he removed it, the balls had turned into meat, vegetables, and a starchy substance. Sarza's stomach growled at the sight of her favorite foods.

"The Sparcus."

Thoughts of food disappeared as Sarza's stomach sank. She had suspected all along some Sparcus wanted her head. But to hear Vigor say it broke her heart. A strand on the left side of her head turned white from root to tip. She looked at him, unable to formulate a word.

"I know, Sarza. I know. I'm sorry." He pushed the bowl of food across the hovering bar toward her.

"Why? What did I do?"

"Nothing Sarza. It's just . . . The Council is divided 25–42 over this issue."

"What issue? Killing me?" Sarza was incredulous. How had she become so important all of a sudden? And what had she done to deserve this?

"Forty-two Council members want to find a way to amass enough weapons and destroy Earth. Of course, none of these discussions are public." They couldn't be public. The regular Sparcus Council discussions were closely monitored by human—and other—observers, which meant most of Sparcus decision-making took place at Bashbathars or in people's homes.

"What about the other twenty-five?"

"They want to ally themselves with Earth, convince them to hand over the antidote for Project Geno, and then move on. They believe in the existence of Project Genesis."

"*If* the antidote or Project Genesis exists. I haven't found it yet." Sarza quickly pointed out. "We don't have proof that it exists. Only rumors."

"Some people are convinced Project Genesis exists." Vigor made it clear he wasn't one of those. "They are ready to stake their lives on the fact that the humans developed an antidote."

"Fine." This conversation would go nowhere right now. "So what does that have to do with me? Would it not be better for me to keep looking for Project Genesis, as I am supposed to be doing?"

"Sarza," Vigor had a pained expression, "I've already said too much. But . . ." He hesitated. "It has to do with the human you have out there."

"What? Why?" Sarza's stomach was in her throat.

"The forty-two think you are compromised."

"I'm *not!*" Sarza raised her voice.

"Good." He seemed relieved. Sarza could see that even Vigor, her closest ally, had had some doubts. "But your only mission for the past thirteen years has been to find out about Project Genesis. And . . . well . . . you haven't had much success."

Sarza dropped the piece of food she was about to put in her mouth. She had spent thirteen years chasing Project Genesis: the alleged human antidote to Project Geno. But in all that time of searching through databases at night, questioning people covertly, and breaking into IPP agents' homes, she had found nothing. It was like someone had destroyed every piece of evidence and research about such an antidote, and that even the mere existence of Project Genesis had been forgotten. Sarza felt Vigor's words crush her. She had failed her people.

"So what does that have to do with anything?" Her voice was soft now. She was staring at her plate in shame.

"Well . . . The Council asked whether you were more useful dead or alive, given that you have brought no information and the general belief is that you are compromised. And . . . SparIntel analyzed the situation and stated that, in their opinion—"

"I'm more dangerous alive than I am useful. If I get caught, I might crack and give away SparIntel and our covert ops in IPP. Alive, I've done nothing good. So I should be dead." She knew where he was going. She was going to spare him the pain of having to actually say the words. His silence confirmed she was right.

"But what about Wes? Why is he involved?"

"Sarza!" He was irritated, but more abiout the fact that he couldn't help her than at her. "That is SparIntel information that I don't have."

"Why not? You are one of the most trusted SparIntel agents on the Council."

"Precisely. SparIntel is doing this internally. There is no crossover of information. So I was cut off from any additional data."

"Who were the Sparcus on Maka?"

"SparIntel agents."

"Why didn't they kill me?"

"They tried, Sarza. You got away." Now there were tears in Vigor's eyes.

"Why didn't they kill me in the Bar'aat's home?"

"Those were different agents, Sarza."

"What? Two Sparcus tried to warn me in the Bar'aat's home about my cover being blown and two tried to kill me outside?"

"Yes." Vigor was letting Sarza do the talking, just confirming the facts and suspicions she already had. But he couldn't quite keep his composure, "I don't know why they tried to warn you, and then kill you. I don't know . . ."

"The Bar'aats outside the arm's dealers home tried to kill me too . . ."

"They were probably paid off by the two Sparcus agents who wanted you dead. Or their boss didn't like you poking your nose in his business. Who knows . . ."

"Why would the Sparcus agents want me dead?"

"Sarza . . ."

"*Why?*" Sarza slammed her fist on the table, sending her bowl flying.

"I don't know the details. But—"

"Does this have to do with killing key agents on planets around the system?"

"Yes."

"Why are they doing that?"

"Sarza . . . I can't . . ."

"This is a stupid game Vigor. Just tell me what you know—"

"I don't know, Sarza." Vigor was exasperated. He wanted to give her answers, but he didn't have them to give.

Sarza looked at the spilled food on the floor. Her mind was racing. She had to see her SparIntel file. Any information about agents, targets, and missions was contained in their files. Something about her current IPP assignment with Wes was bending people out of shape.

"Who can log me into SparIntel?"

"You mean who can lend you their credentials to access your file?"

"Yes."

"Sax is here."

"Oh." Sarza wasn't thrilled about seeing him, but he would do anything for her.

"Where is he?"

"Talking to your human friend."

"What for?"

"I told him to give him some of his clothes so the human would look like a Sparcus. He can pass for one, if he covers that brown hair of his." Sparcus men's hair, just like the women's, was either blond or black. Wes's hair would have been a dead giveaway. But based on build, however, Vigor was right—Wes could definitely pass for a Sparcus.

"Does Sax know I wasn't supposed to seduce Wes?"

"No."

"Prem." Now she would have to deal with a jealous Sparcus man, of all things. Sarza stood up and walked back to the entrance where she had left Wes. Maybe Wes would still be alive. Sax was uncharacteristically possessive about his linking partners. Most Sparcus were happy with the Bashbathar lifestyle, but others insisted on monogamy—even without a Match. Sarza exhaled in relief. Wes was sitting on the bottom step with his head in his hands. He looked up as she walked in. Vigor was close behind.

"Thank the planets you are back." Sarza looked at him briefly, and then at the loincloth on the floor.

"Whose is that?"

"Some man said he was supposed to give me some clothes, and he chose to throw that at me." Wes sneered.

"So you've met Sax." Sarza was sure this was Sax's doing. It was totally his style.

"Who?"

"That was Sax."

Vigor was stifling a laugh.

"He thinks I'm just going to wear his clothes?"

Sarza wasn't going to discuss the details of her life with Wes. She didn't answer. Instead, she looked at Vigor. He gestured to someone, who disappeared upstairs.

"Did you find out why someone is trying to kill you?" Vigor was surprised at Wes's ease. He hadn't noticed it until then, but the Earthling was mighty comfortable in a roomful of Sparcus.

"Yes. It's the Sparcus. They want me dead."

Wes knew this was tearing her apart. He wanted to hug her. But if he did, he would have to explain why her black Velcra suit didn't hurt him. Now was not the time for that.

"Why?"

Sarza looked down at Wes sitting on the staircase. She bit her lower lip and looked at Vigor. She looked back at Wes. If she told him, she would confirm everybody's suspicion that she was a liability. She would be telling a non-Sparcus about the existence of SparIntel and her covert life. Even Vigor would have good reason to kill her where she stood.

Wes saw her face and Vigor's, and understood something was going on, something that couldn't be said. "That's fine Sarza. I don't need to know." He stood up. "We just have to keep you safe."

Vigor was staring at Wes dumbfounded. A human who wants to protect a Sparcus was unheard of.

Sarza forgot Vigor was there for a moment. Wes's dedication moved her, even though it shouldn't have, even though it went against all battle-hardened notions of herself. He moved her. "We still don't know who those people in your hotel on Hatuu-oh were. We need to figure that out too."

"True." Wes thought back to running away from the Kerouac and the Bar'aat on Hatuu-oh. "I don't know how they are connected. Or even if they are. It could be about my recent . . . unorthodox activities." He paused. "Or it could be something else."

Vigor interjected, "They are connected. I don't know how. But they are."

Sarza sat next to Wes on the staircase. "Why would someone want to kill people all around the system? What good does it do anyone?"

"Well . . ." Wes stared pensively at the loincloth still on the floor. "I can tell you it's creating a lot of tension between the various planets. The Interplanetary Council is a mess.

Everybody is blaming everybody else for the murders. And then blaming each other for not caring and not solving them quickly enough."

"Who would benefit from that?"

Wes was still deep in his thoughts. "If everyone hates everyone, and things get bad, we could end up with a Second Great Conflict—"

"And Earth would get blamed for not solving the murders fast enough." Sarza looked at Wes. "You would get blamed for not solving the murders fast enough—"

"Because humans don't care about any other species but humans." They were finishing each other's sentences.

"So the Sparcus," Sarza swallowed hard—what she was about to say was heresy—"the Sparcus kill other worlders and make it impossible for you to solve the murders. Then, when you can't solve them—"

"They blame Earth. And Earth *has* to turn to the only planet that doesn't blame them for the murders—"

"Sparcus." Sarza hated that this made perfect sense.

"But why Sparcus? Why would the Sparcus want Earth to need them?"

"To humiliate them?" Sarza suggested. This was likely at least part of the truth.

"Start a war to humiliate a planet? Maybe, or the Sparcus want something from us." Wes looked at Sarza. Her expression betrayed the fact he had hit the nail on the head. "What do they want from us, Sarza?"

Project Genesis, she wanted to say, but she couldn't tell him. That was *her* mission. Her real mission. Sarza was painfully aware of Vigor's presence. Maybe she would have answered Wes's question if Vigor had been elsewhere, but even she wasn't sure what she would have done in that situation. So she lied. "I don't know. I don't know that the humans *do* want something from us. They took everything we have already."

Wes stood up. "There is only one thing we can do, Sarza. We have to solve the murders faster. We have to do it before an all-out conflict erupts. This means we have to find the Sparcus who committed them."

"Okay." Sarza agreed. "I have to do something before that though. I need to look at . . . something." She caught herself. She was about to say "a SparIntel file." A Sparcus man walked in with a cloak. He handed it to Wes, who put it on. It smelled of Sparcus male. It had probably been used during a training session.

Sarza looked at him. "You need to cover that hair." Wes reached into his pocket and pulled out a comb. He flipped the switch on the back of it and ran it through his hair. It immediately turned black. "That's better," Sarza mused.

"It's actually my real hair color." Wes watched for a reaction.

"Why do you change it?"

"Aesthetics." Wes lied. Sarza looked at him with an expression somewhere between derision and incredulity.

She turned to Vigor. "Where is Sax?"

"Training." Sarza walked toward the door from where the Sparcus man had come. Wes followed her.

"Who is Sax?" Wes asked again.

"A Sparcus soldier. He can help me get what I need." Sarza waved her hand in front of the door sensor, and the force field disappeared. They stepped through and found a large room with black synthetic walls. The floor and ceiling were black too. The man who had thrown his dirty underwear at Wes was now wearing a full battle outfit—a flexible, thick, heat- and puncture-resistant material that covered his torso, hips, and groin. The material came down like a skirt just under his buttocks, and a pair of sturdy shoulder pads completed the ensemble. Under it, he was wearing a thinner version of the material that laced with Velcra, which turtlenecked at the top and ended as leggings on the bottom. Sax also wore heavy boots that rose to his knees. Another man was there, shooting at him using the same guns Sarza had at her sides. The two men were using adhesive boots to be able to run up the walls and across the ceilings. Sax fired a shot and hit the other Sparcus in the chest. The other Sparcus was thrown back against the wall, groaned, and slid to the floor. Wes was stunned. The man looked dead.

"Sax!" Sarza said his name, and he quickly turned his head to look at her. He was delighted — an understatement — at seeing her. He walked toward her and took her in his arms.

"Sarza. So good to see you." He was growling her name into her hair in a soft bedroom voice as he held her. Wes was *not* happy.

"This is — " She turned, gesturing toward Wes.

"Yeah, we met." Sax cut her off. He wasn't interested in knowing Wes's name.

"Good." Sarza continued, "I need to get into my . . . file." She pulled away from him.

"Okay? Why do you need *me*?"

"I can't use my credentials. It's complicated. I need you to pull it for me."

"Fine. Meet me at . . . meet me tonight." Wes saw the look on Sax's face. If he could have devoured Sarza he would have, and he wasn't at all shy about it. "I'm available if you want to use me before then." Wes was a little taken aback at how direct that was.

"Sax, I thank you. But I need to focus on other things today." Sarza was also very matter-of-fact.

"Very well. But if you would like some company tonight, I would be delighted."

Wes felt ridiculously uncomfortable. He wanted to leave. He turned around to look at the other man in the room. He was waking up, only stunned by the weapon. Wes heaved a sigh of relief. Noticing his reaction, Sarza explained, "The weapons are on blanks. They'll stun, even burn a little, but they don't actually injure." *We can't afford to kill each other in training. Not anymore.*

Sarza walked out of the room and up the stairs. Wes followed. "We will sleep a few hours here until I can go meet Sax."

"Okay." Wes walked up the stairs. Sarza's buttocks were swaying in front of him. He stared, glad for the sight. Then he thought of Sax and felt like a fool. The man downstairs probably didn't have to just think about Sarza that way. He could actually have her.

"Who is he?" Wes was trying to ask the question in a way that didn't sound like he was prying. But Sarza was no fool and this was the third time he tried to ask.

"He's a Sparcus man."

"He likes you." Wes knew he sounded like a jealous partner. Which he was not. He was not a partner.

"Yes. But we are not compatible."

"Oh!" Wes didn't know what that meant.

Sarza walked in front of him. "We linked. We linked numerous times. And although I am very good for him, he is not good for me."

"Oh!" Wes's answers were repetitive. But this wasn't a conversation he was used to having. Or had trained for—either at IPP or through his mother. That would have been the epitome of awkward. They walked into a bedroom with two mattresses on the floor.

"I orgasm once. Maybe twice. At *most*. It's insufficient. The chemistry isn't really there." Wes stopped walking. Being behind Sarza for the whole walk up the stairs had been difficult. Hearing her talk about sex was excruciating. But listening to her talk about her orgasms was torture. Before he realized what he was doing, he grabbed Sarza's hand and pulled her between him and the wall. The Sparcus Gloves were not made of Velcra. He didn't have to fake this. His lips were on hers, his tongue pushing into her. It took a few seconds before he realized she wasn't pushing him away. Her hands, actually, were in his hair. He adjusted to push his pelvis harder against hers. He pulled back to look at her. Her hair was waving around her head madly, the brightest blue he had ever seen it. Total Sparcus arousal. Her eyes were closed; she pulled him in hard. He kissed her again. Harder than the first time. The frustration at not being able to touch her clothes was pissing him off. But she was taking care of that. Her corset was on the floor and she was pulling her turtleneck over her head. They were still kissing as she pulled off her boots and her leggings. She was finally naked in front of him. His hands reached around and grabbed her ass, pulling her legs around his hips, holding her against the wall. She wasn't slowing down the kiss. She used her legs to pull him in tighter. Her hands were under his shirt, feeling his back, grabbing onto his shoulders. He turned around and took her to the bed.

Standing at the foot of the bed, he undressed as fast she had. Moments later they were both naked on the mattress. She whispered, "No linking . . ." He heard her choking tears in the back of her throat. What she was doing was exactly what she wanted — her hair didn't lie — but it was tearing her apart. And she was doing it in Vigor's home, which only made things more complicated and risky. If they got caught, they would assume she was "compromised." But she obviously wasn't thinking about that. And he wasn't about to bring it up.

"No fucking. Okay." His ego was a little bruised at that. But some sex was better than none. "I want to feel you. I just . . ." She nodded, pulling him against her again. His chest was crushing hers. And although it went against everything she believed, it was the best she had felt in years — maybe ever. The force field for the bedroom was black, making them invisible to the rest of the home. Wes traced kisses down her breasts, over her stomach, until he found her with his mouth. She moaned, bucked into him, and held his head in place with her hands. He worked her with his fingers and his tongue. He took his time, got her there slowly, pulling back and then coming down onto her with full force. He repeated the cycle over and over again, enjoying her scent, relishing her moans and mewling.

Her fingers ran through his hair and brushed against the top of his shoulders. Finally, when he was ready to let her go, she lifted pelvis off the bed, holding herself up on her tiptoes, pushing the back of her head into the mattress, letting out a tremendous groan as she came. Wes looked up. Her head looked like it was bathed in a sea of green lights. Her hair floated in midair, like a halo of static green luminescent filaments. As she let herself drop back onto the bed, her chest heaved with heavy panting. Her eyes were still closed as she put the back of her hand across her forehead. Leaving his fingers in place, he lifted himself onto her and put his mouth on hers. She responded in kind. They weren't done. They wouldn't be done for hours. They both knew that. The investigation would just have to wait.

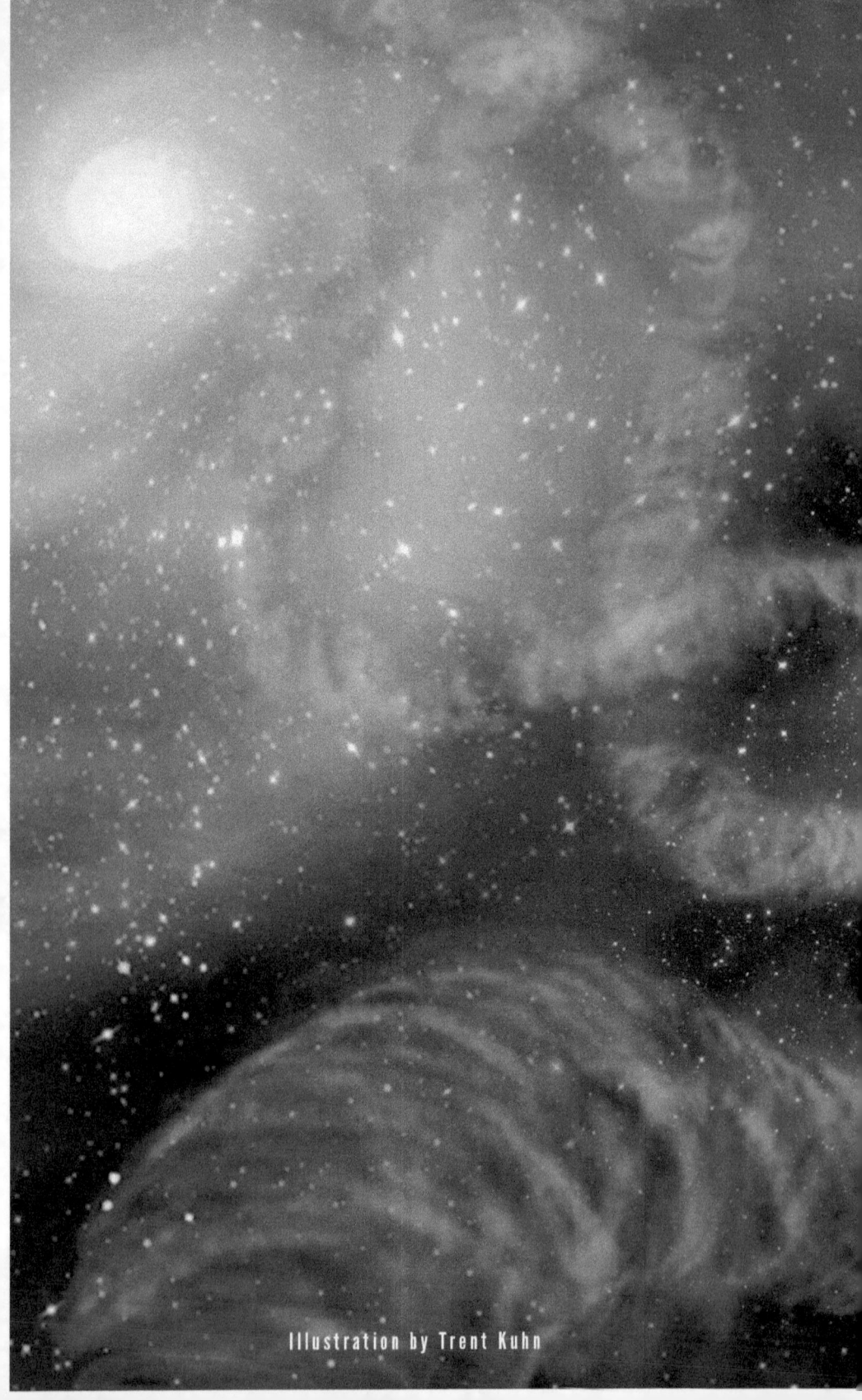

Illustration by Trent Kuhn

THE HUB

BOOK I
CHAPTER 8

When Wes woke up, the early afternoon had changed to evening. There was no light outside their window. Sarza lay motionless in his arms, sleeping soundly. He felt inexplicable joy at seeing her there. He stroked her face. She stirred. He wasn't sure how she would react to what they had done. Or to the fact he was in her bed. He rolled onto his back and stared at the ceiling. This was the best non-sex he'd ever had. She had more than returned the favors, and enjoyed every moment of it. The total abandonment between them had taken him — and probably her — by surprise. She was shameless in her enjoyment of her body, and it made the experience liberating for him. Sarza sat up and slid her legs onto the floor. She crossed them in front of her.

"Hey."

Sarza didn't turn around. "We have to go."

"Okay." Wes turned to sit with his back to her. They were sitting back to back, each looking at opposite sides of the room.

Sarza stood up and got dressed. Wes did the same. Their clothes were strewn all over the floor. She wasn't talking to him.

"Where are we going?" he asked.

"I'm going to see something with Sax. I think it's better if you stay here." Her tone was sharp, acidic, one could even call it threatening.

"I don't particularly like you going around alone." The Sparcus—the people on *this* planet—had tried killing her, multiple times. Wes saw no reason for her to go around the planet on her own. She wasn't safe here. In fact, neither of them were safe anywhere.

She snorted. "I don't need *human* protection, Wes. We aren't going there to talk about *feelings*."

"You are dead wrong if you think, for a moment, that I believe I can do anything to protect a Sparcus covert agent. There's a reason we use you as our mercenaries." Wes was treading sensitive ground. But her attitude was ridiculous. Two people were better than one. No matter where they came from. "But I need you alive to get to the bottom of this. And having backup won't hurt you. I haven't been a liability to you so far."

They were both dressed now, standing in the room, the bed where they had lain was between them. She was picking a fight. He would give it to her if she came looking for it.

"It's better if you stay here." She mellowed. "Sax will be more cooperative if you aren't there." Sarza looked at Wes, gauging his reaction.

"Okay. If you think it's better for us if I stay here, I will. Can I do anything while I'm here?"

"No."

She started walking out of the room. When she reached the door, she stopped without turning around. She hesitated, waited for a beat, then opened the force field door and stepped out. It closed behind her, and Wes was alone in the room.

Sarza had planned to meet Sax at SparIntel. She would let Sax do all the talking and logging in. It would be as though she wasn't even there. But as she walked down the staircase in Vigor's house, Sax was walking in.

"Sarza! You have to leave." He was tense.

"How soon?" She stopped on the staircase and was getting ready to go back up to get Wes.

"Now. Now, now, now. You have to go. You can't stay." He was running up the stairs.

"Why now?"

Sax grabbed Sarza's shoulders and held her. "There is a SparIntel warrant for your execution. The instructions are to kill you on sight. No questions asked."

"Okay." She didn't flinch. She wouldn't give anyone else the satisfaction of knowing how much they were hurting her by betraying her. By treating her like she was an outsider. And this was old news. Sparcus agents had been trying to kill her for a while now. Sax, noting her lack of reaction added, "It's an official warrant. No confusion. No inconsistent instructions. You've been officially condemned." Then he added, glancing at the white streak across her temple, "Sarza . . . I'm sorry."

"It's not your fault, Sax. It's the way it is." She turned and went up the stairs, two steps at a time.

"Where are you going?"

"I have to get Wes." She didn't turn around to see Sax's disgusted expression.

An hour and a half later, Wes and Sarza were on their way to the Sparcus wormhole. They had traveled on their own, declining Sax's and Vigor's offers for help. The fewer people they involved, the better. And the less attention they would attract. Vigor had let them use his Vex. The Vex looked like a giant elongated mushroom on its side that lifted vertically. This particular Vex was large enough for six people. It had a seating area in the front and a living area in the back. Three tiers of beds lined each side of the capsule, which also had a shower bubble and a toilet. The transport was an ugly brown color on the outside, but it was fast and sturdy, and the food on board meant they could spend a long time in it if necessary.

"Where are we going?" Sarza was flying and trying to fix coordinates.

"Vedic. The poison for the Braxian murder was Arapesh. It's worth a shot."

"We have nothing else." Sarza was busy going through the navigation protocols. Wes heard two beeps. It was the IPP cochlear implant. He pressed on his ear. The Captain's image appeared in his eyes.

"Agent Venta, where are you?" She was irritated.

"Investigating murders, Captain."

"Don't be impertinent. *Where* are you?" She'd had enough of the vague responses he'd fed her for weeks.

"I'd rather not disclose that, Captain."

Sarza was frowning. Any longer on the communicator and all of IPP would know exactly where they were. She was sure of it.

"Agent Venta — !"

Wes interrupted her, "Captain, we are about to lose comms. Do you have something to say to me?"

"Yes. You need to hurry up and get to the bottom of this. There were three more murders, two Kerouacs on Styx, and a Carlan on Sebera. There was also an attempted murder on Terra."

Sarza noticed Wes tensing. "Very well. Can you send us the crime scene files?"

"We would rather not transmit those," the Captain answered. "You should come see them here at HQ."

Wes swallowed. If he had doubts about the Captain's integrity, they were confirmed. This was a trap. "We are losing comms Captain. I will see what I can do." He disconnected the call.

"News?"

"Three more bodies."

"Prem," Sarza muttered under hear breath. "Where?"

"Styx and Sebera."

"We need to hurry up."

"Right." Wes sat back.

"Which one do you care about?"

"What?"

"When you found out there were bodies on Nash'amir, you tensed up. Just like you did right now. And then I come to find out you grew up on Nash'amir. So which one do you care about this time? Have a Kerouac girlfriend I don't know about?" She smirked.

"None of those." He paused. "There was an attempted murder on Terra."

"Ah! So Terra. What do you have with the Corsini?"

"My father lives on Terra."

Sarza took her eyes off the horizon and looked at him. "Why is your father on Terra? Who the prem are you?"

"Nobody. He moved there when my mother passed."

"Is your father Corsini? Was your mother an Ishtar?" This man made no sense.

"No. And no! You know Ishtars can't reproduce with humans. They don't have a uterus for heaven's sakes."

"Well, I don't know. You're an awfully weird human. And I have no idea how Ishtars reproduce. Nobody does." She was telling the truth.

"Sure." The Ishtar were notoriously coy about their sexual habits, Wes mused. They didn't want the galaxy to know that all it took to impregnate an Ishtar *male* was the kiss of an Ishtar female. It caused the Ishtar male to release male and female reproductive material inside their egg sacs, which triggered the growth of eggs, which when laid by the Ishtar male, would eventually lead to young. Growing up on Nash'amir, he had obviously learnt this much. But this wasn't the time to give Sarza a course in Ishtar sex ed.

Sarza was looking out the front window again. They were about to fall into the Sparcus wormhole. As they did, a light blue tunnel surrounded them. Mere seconds later they reappeared at the Hub. The eight wormholes, each headed for one of the civilizations, floated in a perfect circle, each equidistant from its neighbor. The space inside was cluttered with checkpoints and vehicles from every civilization in charge of monitoring the transport of people, goods, and information. It was — by agreement — demilitarized. This meant they were safe from weapons, although not safe from detection. They could see hundreds of IPP vehicles flying around the Hub. Which meant nobody actively checked the vehicles or tried to determine who was controlling them. It was somewhat of a free zone. Sarza pulled out the Masker and programmed it to look like a nondescript, run of the mill, patrolling IPP vehicle. It worked. Nobody bothered them.

Wes looked at her. "I want one of those." He was attempting humor. Sarza appreciated the effort.

"Not a chance."

The wormholes appeared on Sarza's display. Each of them showed the corresponding civilization in the native language. Wes pointed at the Vedic wormhole. Sarza had not bothered to turn on the translator, which meant Wes could read the Arapesh word for Vedic. "You can read that?"

"Yes. I can read Arapesh."

"Can you speak it too?" *Highly unlikely,* she thought.

Wes uttered a series of gurgles, to the best of a human throat's ability, which sounded remarkably close to the real thing. Sarza heard the Arapesh words over the gadget translating in her ear: "Shut the fuck up and drive." She laughed. She sounded sincere.

She turned back to the screen and tapped the image of the Vedic wormhole on the map. The transporter locked on its destination and began moving toward the appropriate worm-hole, automatically dropping into it, and a few moments later, reappearing at the mouth of the wormhole near Vedic. The trip would take another half day from there to the surface of the planet. Sarza turned to Wes. "You should sleep. We had a few hours at Vigor's, but it's been a while. I can't have you crashing when I most need you."

This was the closest Sarza had come to talking about what had happened. He looked at her, expecting her to continue. She was looking ahead. She must have felt his stare because she turned to look at him again. Still nothing. She went back to handling the controls, although what she was doing was unclear, given that the ship's autopilot would handle most of the trip from this point on. Wes leaned back in the seat and closed his eyes. He was asleep moments later.

Sarza stayed at the control for what seemed like an eternity. Finally, she spotted the blue dot that was Vedic. The planet was cold. Very, very cold. The Arapesh people were exactly like the Velin, except they were blue and could not stand sulfur. The two had originated from the same species, but millennia on different planets had led to very different adaptations. The Arapesh did not like the warm temperatures of Velin. They moved slowly, and their ooze tended to be a little more solid. Which, Sarza mused, made it easier on other-worlders' shoes. The Arapesh were medicine people. If something chemical was needed, they could provide it. In fact, they had been instrumental in developing the sterilizing agent for the humans. They also used particular poisons for particular killings. War called for certain substances, suicide for others, and crimes of passion yet for others. The issue with the poison used on the Braxian was that it should only be used by the Arapesh—it was a highly ceremonial poison. The blood analysis identifying the particular toxin had actually made it into the file. It was certainly not something that got sold to non-Arapesh. Or, if it had been sold to a non-Arapesh, that would have been a singular event.

Sarza turned to look at Wes. He was still wearing the grey t-shirt they had left Earth with. Changing anywhere else had not been an option. She would have to get him clothes. Of course, he had the Sparcus cloak on him. It was ironic that at this point, passing for a Sparcus was safer for Wes than being human. Sax's smell came strong from the cloak. He had probably taken great satisfaction in saturating the piece of cloth in sweat, knowing Wes would have to wear it. But then she noticed another smell. Sarza recognized it as a Sparcus smell, but she had never smelt it before. She wondered if Sax had loaned his cloak to some army friend of his, just to mess with the human.

Sarza sighed. Vedic was finally looming larger in front of them. Half of it was dark and half of it was light. She landed on the dark side of the planet. She would take advantage of a few hours of darkness. It would attract less attention, and they would be able to sleep undisturbed.

As she landed in the Vedic Spaceport, Wes woke up. He didn't say anything. They reached into the stockpile of re-loaded weapons Vigor and Sex had handed to them on their way off Astarte. Fully armed, they got out of the transporter and started walking. Vedic didn't have a vehicle hangar like most other planets. Travelers were expected to either have their own transportation or use public systems—the way they had on Sulpuro and Hatuu-oh. The hovering bus stop was a ways down a narrow footpath. There were a few lights, just enough to see where to go, but not enough to forget it was nighttime. Sarza and Wes walked in silence. Their footsteps were soft on the biosynthetic material meant to provide a path without harming the environment. Wes had pulled his hood over his head. In the dim lights, he could look like a Sparcus. He stared at the floor as he walked along. Sarza pulled her hood over her head as well. They were two shadows walking along to the hover stop. A public transporter was already there.

Sarza and Wes jumped in the hovercraft, which was shaped like an oversized pill. There were no benches or other similar objects for sitting, which meant travelers either stood or sat on the floor. Sitting on the floor was an option of last resort because it entailed getting covered in Arapesh goop. The walls of the transporter had circular windows that didn't open, and the entire thing was very light grey. The door to get in was just a rectangular opening that didn't actually close, which for the Arapesh was of little consequence. They usually adhered very well to any surface, making accidental falls out of the moving transporter unlikely.

Although the transporter could hold thirty or forty people, it was currently empty. Wes and Sarza stood and waited. They remained silent. The electronic voice asked for destinations. Sarza gave an address unfamiliar to Wes.

"Why did we come here?" He had just let her do the navigating. Vedic was not his cup of tea.

"To this city?"

"Yes."

"This is Aceso, the third largest city on Vedic. We have as much chance of finding what we want were as we do at the capital, Asklepios. If we are being expected, they will expect us to go to the capital."

"True." Wes looked out the window at the Arapesh landscape. The buildings were similar to Sulpuro's. It was remarkable how the two species had developed so similarly, largely based on their identical bodies, and yet had done so in such different climates. The buildings had ramps that were textured with small winding corrugations, allowing the Arapesh to go up and down with their jelly bodies. The structures were made with see-through mixtures of glass and plastic, as well as metal from Nash'amir. As they traveled around, both notes how empty the streets were. It was a stark contrast to the bustle of Sulpuro.

Wes's stomach growled. Sarza heard it. Then she remembered that although she had eaten on Astarte, Wes had not. He didn't say anything, but kept looking out the window. She was a little impressed at the man's resilience. She expected a human to spend his time whining.

The hover vehicle stopped. Sarza got up and Wes followed. The neighborhood they were in was a little livelier than the rest of town. A mixture of Arapesh and other-worlders walked up and down the footpaths.

"Where are we?"

"Where those who don't ask questions go." Sarza wasn't about to explain the life of a double agent. The nature of her job required becoming familiar with the shadier parts of the system.

Wes was about to ask another question, but thought better of it. He followed Sarza down narrow paths, where they barely fit. She took a left, then waved her hand, and a section of wall dissolved that only moments earlier been a featureless surface. She walked in and took her hood off. Wes did the same. They had entered an inn. Three small tables stood to their left, with a nondescript counter to the right. The Corsini attendant was short—like all Corsini—with red hair and green eyes. She was playing with images emitted from a deskrock, but neither Sarza nor Wes could see what she was looking at.

Corsini and humans were among the few species that could reproduce together. And some had done so, although the children of those unions had difficulty fitting in among either humans or the Corsini. Thinking about inter-species relations, Wes's thoughts went back to what had happened with Sarza. He thought back to the rumors of Sparcus women sleeping with human men in the hope of having children, but he had never heard of children being born from those unions. He had never actually met a Sparcus woman, or a human

man, who admitted to having such relations—except for his parents of course. He had, for the most part, ignored those rumors over the years. But after what had happened with Sarza, he wondered if there was any truth to it. She thought he was a human, but had accepted linking with him, even if in a slightly limited way.

Wes walked toward the counter and checked in. He didn't give his name. The Corsini attendant didn't ask for one. He pulled out IPP money—the preferred currency—in paper certificates of value. It wasn't totally untraceable, but it was better than using his card. He asked for one room. There was no reason to separate.

Wes turned around and Sarza was sitting at the table behind him. An Arapesh waitress brought her two plates of big, green and red, gelatinous slices of Vedic caterpillar. Vedic caterpillars were the size of Earth raccoons. Wes felt his hungry stomach revolt, but he *was* hungry. Anything else would probably be more revolting. He walked to the hovering table and sat across from Sarza. The waitress had also brought two small glasses of a semi-transparent white liquid.

He grabbed a slice of the caterpillar and started eating. The caterpillar tasted worse than it looked. At first impact, the meat was covered in cold green gelatin that attached itself to the top of his mouth. The inside was meaty, and tasted like human beef. But after a few moments, the whole thing turned into an acrid paste that left an awful aftertaste at the back of his throat. He reached for the Arapesh drink in front of him. He didn't know what it was and wasn't going to ask. It was extremely sweet and kind of thick in consistency. He drank a mouthful and thankfully realized the sweetness very successfully wiped out the acrid taste of the meat, making it much easier to ingest. He looked up at the other tables and then at Sarza. She was putting a piece of the caterpillar, covered in the white liquid, in her mouth. Wes self-consciously realized the white stuff was actually a sauce. Sarza smiled, highly amused at the scene, and then looked back at her plate. She reached for another piece, dunked it into the container of white liquid in front of her, and slipped it past her lips.

Wes finished swallowing. He reached onto his plate, picked up the half-bitten slice of caterpillar, and drowned it in the sauce. This time, the experience was a lot better. Chewing on the second bite, and feeling unexpected relief as the hunger pangs subsided, he became very grateful for the meal. Realizing he had drank half of his sauce, he caught the Arapesh waitress's attention and gestured for another container.

Sarza, trying to keep a straight face, changed the subject. "You need new clothes."

"My fashion sense offends you?" Wes was both sarcastic and rhetorical.

"You stink."

"Great."

"You stink of Sax. And then some. He passed the cloak around, I think, to the other guys. You need new clothes."

"Do you have contacts?" Wes changed the subject.

"On Vedic? No. No contacts. The ones I had were Sparcus. But I can't go there now."

"I would go to IPP. But that would compromise us."

"Do you have any informants? Non-IPP?"

"No. Everything on Vedic was above board." Wes chewed off another piece of caterpillar meat, obviously enjoying his meal at this point. Suddenly, Sarza stood up, aiming her guns at the door. Wes stood up instinctively. He pulled out his guns — the same as Sarza's — from his chest holsters. He had one on each side.

"What am I aiming at?" He still couldn't see what had alarmed her. A Sparcus then shifted out of the shadows next to the door.

Sarza said, in a very low voice only he could hear, "She's been following us. At least since the hover stop." The Sparcus raised her hands and placed them on her head. Sarza relaxed.

Wes didn't. "My name is Ceram. I'm here to protect you. Vigor sent me."

Sarza lowered her weapons. Wes did so too. But slowly. Ceram walked toward them. She was blond, sporting a clean crew cut, and a little shorter than Sarza—but only by an inch. She had a slighter figure, although she maintained the broad Sparcus shoulders and solid hips. She was wearing the same outfit as Sarza: black Velcra turtleneck, black corset, and black Velcra leggings with knee-high boots. Her eyes were black. Both Sarza and Wes, instinctively, assessed her as a very good specimen. She could probably kill anyone in the room with her bare hands. And she was athletic, healthy, strong, with intelligent eyes. She was standing by them by the time they were done looking her over.

"I am sorry I alarmed you. I didn't mean to. I was supposed to stay at a distance." She was embarrassed that Sarza had seen her.

"How old are you?" Sarza was asking the questions, although Wes wondered why age had any relevance.

"Thirty-two."

"Who do you work for?" Sarza asked.

"Sparcus." Ceram answered without batting an eyelid. But the answer wasn't an answer at all. It didn't tell Sarza if Ceram worked for SparIntel, the Sparcus Council, or for Vigor personally. And Ceram knew that.

"Do you know who you are protecting me from?"

"Other Sparcus." Sarza had to give credit where credit was due. Ceram stayed calm while admitting that her mission was defending a Sparcus from other Sparcus, which would eventually mean aiming her weapons at her own. Sarza sat down. Wes remained standing. The people in the Inn ducked silently under their tables. Violence was common around the galaxy, and this wasn't exactly an elegant locale. But everyone knew to stay out of the way. And they weren't quite sure the interaction was over.

"Are you hungry?" Sarza was acting like this woman had just walked into their dining room for a leisurely meal.

"No. Thank you. May I sit here?"

"Yes." Ceram maneuvered her way to the other side of the table, positioning herself between Wes and Sarza, facing the door.

Wes sat back down with his back to the door, and resumed eating, in silence, observing Ceram very closely. There was nothing he could discuss in the presence of a third-person. Sarza looked at Ceram, then looked at Wes, then looked at Ceram again. Finally, she stood up. Ceram stood up as well. "I'm going upstairs."

"Very well," Ceram answered.

Wes wasn't comfortable being left alone in the middle of a shady dining room on Vedic. But he wasn't about to chase down two Sparcus for protection. "I'll be up in a while." The two women disappeared. Wes sat there and ate his sliced caterpillar. Although he had briefly enjoyed eating, at this point the aftertaste was cathing up with him. But he was determined not to go upstairs. He picked at slice after slice, pushing it into his mouth. Wes looked down: there were two pieces left. He'd given enough. He stood up and walked toward the back of the lobby, where he found two elevator doors. He waved his hand in front of the sensor. Nothing happened. He waved his hand in front of the other sensor. Nothing happened. This was irritating. He looked behind him and saw a standard Arapesh ramp. Wes was thankful his IPP boots had gripping soles. Not quite like the ones Sax had worn on Astarte, but good enough to go up the ramp.

Wes reached his room and waved the door open. Sarza was naked, walking towards a bed, reaching for her clothes. He surmised, from the droplets along her shoulders, she had just finished showering. Ceram was standing by the door and evidently guarding it. The moment he saw Sarza, Wes had an urge to kick Ceram out of the room. Instead, he walked toward the shower stall that stood in the corner of the room. As he started getting undressed, it occurred to him he would have to get naked in front Ceram. He hesitated, then remembered Bashbathars, and kept going. By then Sarza had finished getting dressed and was sitting on a bed, cleaning the Sparcus guns obtained on Astarte.

Wes was naked when he walked by Sarza. She glanced at him, for less than a moment, and went back to reassembling her weapons. But, even though imperceptible to anyone but the two of them, he saw the hair at her nape raise itself. He would have bet money it was turning blue. He smiled to himself, and stepped into the shower stall.

"Water on." The jet hit him. It was freezing. He turned to face the wall. This was putting a damper on his self-confidence. "Warmer." The temperature rose a few degrees. "Warmer!" A few more degrees. *"Warmer!"* Finally it had reached bearable temperatures. But he didn't bother turning back around. This was embarrassing enough. He quickly finished taking his shower. "Water off." The water turned off. "Dryer on." Warm air started blasting from the bottom of the shower stall. It actually felt nice. It was always so pleasant to be clean after weeks chasing leads.

He stepped out and walked past Sarza's bed. She had not looked up or stopped cleaning her guns the entire time he showered. He was about to pick up his dirty clothes when Sarza stopped him. "Don't. I will get you clean clothes tomorrow morning."

"Okay. Thanks." Wes looked at Ceram. She was looking at him, but betrayed no emotion. He didn't want to say anything—but the truth was that he was exhausted. He had slept four or five hours on the transporter, not the entire trip-which was unfortunate-and it had been a long time since he had gotten a real night's rest. He laid down on his bed, turned his back to Sarza, and fell asleep.

While Sarza finished her task, Ceram silently indicated that she would wait and stand guard outside. As she left, she turned off the lights in the room. Sarza lay down, in the dark, and waited until Wes's breath was regular. She had hoped that allowing things to progress on Astarte would have dampened the arousal, scratched the itch. But it had done nothing of the sort. If anything, it had grown worse—now she knew what he could do. It enraged her that a human could turn out to be such a fantastic specimen. Even without going all the way, the way a man and a woman could, he had known how to please her. He had also proven himself able in combat—when he protected her on Nash'amir—and intelligent as he worked through this murderous mess with her. She just couldn't understand why her body would betray her like this and have such a violent reaction any time he was near her. Wes stirred. She listened carefully, but he was definitely asleep.

She walked out the door, making no noise. She walked down the hall and Ceram, following Sarza's lead, left her poast and began walking half a meter behind her. It was nearly morning as they stepped out of the inn. Ceram and Sarza had decided what to do, but Wes could not be involved. First, he probably wouldn't want to be involved. Second, Sarza didn't want to make him more vulnerable than he already was. Ceram and Sarza walked in silence into the chily Vedic air. The sun was rising. The two cloaked women walked down the streets, their black figures moving rhythmically to the beat of their boots hitting the floor. The few people who crossed their paths changed course, took abrupt lefts or rights, or aboutfaced and walked the other way. Sarza had forgotten how good it felt to be a Sparcus—to be so feared that nobody would stand in her way. It was exhilarating. She breathed in, then out again slowly. This felt better. She wasn't hiding behind Wes's identity, nor did she have to use a ridiculous cover. She was just her, in the imagined monstrosity of her people. A hunter rather than a hunted.

Sarza replayed her conversation with Ceram. There was a single planet-wide database on the purchase of poisons, but only certain people had access to it: healers and apothecaries. The latter would be armed, on the lookout, and ready to "greet" people intent on stealing product. Although Sarza and Ceram had no intention of stealing anything, apothecaries would be well guarded nonetheless. But healers were rarely bothered, and they were revered. They would not expect two Sparcus to show up demanding answers. Ceram had identified a healer very close to the inn. Its close proximity meant they could avoid having to run through the city and that they could get away, get Wes, and leave quickly. Ceram had a transporter ready at the Inn.

They reached the healer's office. Everything was still quiet. They let themselves in, breaking into the back window on the first floor, and found the healer's office. The metallic furniture included a cube the Arapesh used as chairs. They would prop themselves on top and let the ooze drip to the floor, engulfing the object, so that the middle of their bodies were held up on the cube while the rest of their mass hung like a skirt around it. Sarza and Ceram each sat in the back corners, in shadows, keeping in mind the spots where the sun would light up the room when the healer arrived. They sat in silence for a while, stone-faced, ready for action. As the minutes turned into a Standard hour, Ceram broke the stillness. "Was your mission to seduce him?"

Sarza had no idea where the question came from. They had not even discussed Wes while they were in the room.

"No." Then she thought about the question. "Why?"

"I just was wondering." Ceram was lying, and Sarza knew it.

"Why? Is the assumption that I seduced him?"

"Yes. No. Well, the assumption is that he seduced you, although some people—"

Sarza stayed silent. She'd heard this before. But she was losing patience. They had to return to silence, but this woman had opened a can of worms. Sarza wanted to see the conversation through to the end.

Seeing Sarza's hair start to veer color, Ceram was trying to back peddle. "Some people say *he* seduced *you*." Her voice trembled just a little. She'd been possessed to ask the question, but now would have preferred to return to the dead silence of the past Standard hour.

Sarza kept her composure. "Neither one seduced the other." Her tone was stern. She didn't like being questioned like this. Ceram didn't say anything. They sat in the room as the sun filtered through the large open windowpanes. They were sitting on the second floor, and the sights were beautiful. The sun was glinting on the cold, geometrical, metal-and-glass structures.

Finally, the wet-paper smell of an Arapesh sliming its way in reached them. Both women tensed, crouching, waiting for the moment entered. And he did. The healer was a typical Arapesh. They showed no sign of age and were always the same color with the same consistency until they died. He positioned himself in front of the door and let the sensor in the floor detect his Arapesh body mass. The door slid open, and he entered. He moved slowly, still a little congealed by the morning cold, and made his way to the back of the desk. At that moment, Ceram stood up, rushed to the Arapesh, and placed her gloved hands on either side of his head, "One word and you will be nothing but a pool of ooze on my boots."

Sarza stood up and stayed where she was. "I need to know if any non-Arapesh bought ceremonial killing poison in the past two months."

The terrified Arapesh healer was unable to utter a word. Sarza reached Ceram and tapped her shoulder, indicating her to let go of the Arapesh's head. Ceram looked surprised, annoyed even, but she did as she was ordered. Sarza walked around the table to face the healer. "I need to know who bought the poison, because whoever they are, they used it to kill a Braxian and pin the murder on the Arapesh."

The Arapesh healer was slowly regaining his composure. She could tell from the decrease in shaking of his gelatinous body. He did exactly as he was told, oozing his hand on the deskrock in front of him. It read his signature, and a display appeared in front of them. A single long member, like a finger, emerged from the Arapesh body and began working its way through the displayed field, moving the icons in midair. He finally found what he was looking for and gave Sarza the information she requested. Sarza wondered about Ceram's methods: the threat had seemed somewhat premature. The healer had not even attempted to resist the request. She was perfectly comfortable with brutality. But needless violence on innocents was uncalled for. It occurred to her that maybe she should have brought Wes. Although the scene with the human handler on Hatuu-oh reminded her that maybe he would have not been much better.

On the way back to the inn, Ceram stopped by her transporter to retrieve a packet. She handed it to Sarza, who took it to her room moments later. Sarza walked in while Ceram stood outside guarding the door. Wes was still asleep, but he woke up as she walked in.

"Where have you been?"

"Solving murders." She was nonchalant and not at all defensive.

"Is it solved yet?" Wes's tone was surprisingly warm.

"Probably. Only one non-Arapesh purchased the poison over the past two months. And it was a human!" Sarza was very pleased with herself. He could see that from her lit-up face.

"Who?"

"Carl Vogan."

Wes turned white, his features freezing, then falling apart. He sat up in bed, pulled his legs up, propped his elbows on his knees, and dropped his head in his hands. He began sweating, and Sarza could smell the distinct odor of fear.

"What? I thought you would be happy. We have a lead! If we find out where Carl—"

"That's me, Sarza."

"What?" Sarza had been pacing back and forth in the room, but she froze. "What?"

"That's my IPP alias. It is what I use if I have to go undercover. That's me, Sarza . . ."

"What do you mean that's *you*? It's someone pretending to be you."

"It doesn't make a whole lot of difference in the IPP, Sarza. My undercover alias was used to purchase poison illegally, and then that same poison shows up in the system of a murder victim? I can never explain that away." Wes felt sick. Years of working for IPP, of appearing normal, of doing his job for his father's planet, and here he was. *I'm getting royally fucked by someone with access to inside information*, he thought. He wanted to throw up. And he was furious. He stood up and looked around for his clothes. Sarza remembered the package Ceram had given her. It was on the bed. She pointed to it. "Clothes." Wes went to it and tore off the wrapping material. In it were a black turtleneck, a chest plate, black pants, and boots: it was the non-Velcra version of a Sparcus uniform. To let him wear Sparcus clothes was a tremendous step. He looked at her, then at the clothes, then at her again.

"Think you're up to disguising yourself as a Sparcus?"

"Yes." She had no idea how close to the truth she was. "Totally ready." As he got dressed, he saw her staring at him. He looked at her casually, reached for his guns, slipped them in the holsters in the leather-like chest plate, and walked past Sarza to the door. He was still reeling from the revelation that someone had used his alias to buy a murder weapon—for a murder that he was later specifically chosen to investigate. Sarza followed him out the door, saying, "Where do you think you're going?"

"I'm fed up with this shit, Sarza. I am not some fucking rat that gets chased from planet to planet." He stopped, turned toward her, stopping his face inches from hers. "And I will be damned if they are going to chase us around the fucking planets any longer. We're taking them on."

"Who? Who are we taking on Wes?"

"The people who assigned me to this fucking investigation. The order to assign a human was approved at the IP Council. The conflict about who would be neutral enough to investigate started at the IP Council. The arguments about how badly the investigation is being led take place at the IP Council. So I am going there in person and figuring out what the fuck they want from me. I am fed up with their political nonsense. We are getting answers." Wes was storming down the hall toward the stairs. Sarza was pleasantly surprised by the fire in Wes's belly. She appreciated his rage at being betrayed. And she felt like they were in the same boat—albeit for different reasons. Ceram followed close behind. Wes started walking toward the hover spot when Ceram got in front of him and gestured for them to follow her. Their transporter was at the Spaceport, and the only way to get there was the hovercraft. But they followed Ceram. Behind the building, in an abandoned lot, Ceram's transporter was parked and cloaked. Changing transporters was a good idea. If they had been tracked, at any point, this would make it harder for anyone to stay on their scent. The three of them got on and took off seconds later.

BOOK I
CHAPTER 9

Terra was a tremendous sight at approach. It was surrounded by three gaseous giants—blue, yellow, and green respectively. A fourth planet, Inferno, somewhat more in the distance but visible from the surface, was also yellow and utterly uninhabitable due to the ring of asteroids circling it. Terra was a relatively small planet in comparison. It was a little bigger than Earth, but looked quite similar given its giant neighbors. The seasons were largely the same as Earth's, as was the passage of time. And the gravitational pull on Terra was the same as on Earth.

Ceram, Sarza, and Wes approached the planet. The three of them had tried unsuccessfully to hash out Wes's plan. Wes knew the IP Council was at the heart of his assignment to this case. He also knew that the IP Council had directed IPP to assign him. The case itself now seemed like a tremendous, cruel, and pointless farce that had cost the lives of beings all over the galaxy. He also knew that the supposed tensions his Captain kept relaying had transpired at the IP Council. If he wanted to get to the bottom of this, he had to get to the heart of the matter, which meant finding someone close enough to an IP Councilmember to talk. Finding someone who would speak to him would be difficult, but he was up against a wall with nowhere else to turn.

Wes was at the commands, focused, angry, and done with this nonsense. Sarza was sitting beside him. Wes had noticed her shift in attitude. There was less resentment, even in public, and maybe a twinge of respect, but he may have been imagining that latter part. What they did have was a significant degree of comfort with each other's presence, even in public. This latter development had not gone unnoticed to Ceram. She sat behind them, in the center, utterly disgusted. She had made it clear on multiple occasions—both on Vedic and during the flight—that she found Wes despicable and pathetic, and that the only reason she tolerated his presence was because she had been assigned to protect Sarza. Sarza had failed to react, which for Ceram was a certain sign something was afoot.

Wes overshot the Spaceport on the northern side of Terra. As the neatly parked space vehicles on the ground zipped under them. Their Sparcus Vex was highly recognizable in Corsini airspace, and it was designed for interplanetary travel, not for on-planet transportation. This would attract a lot of attention. Ceram looked at Sarza, expecting a reaction. Sarza betrayed none.

Seeing the Sarza and Wes were apparently in tacit agreement on this crazed trajectory, Ceram broke the silence by clearing her throat. Sarza glanced at her, over her shoulder. Ceram raised her eyebrows quizzically, silently asking Sarza for an explanation. Sarza indulged her, "If someone is waiting for us, they will be waiting at the Spaceport."

Wes added, "And I don't have time to fuck around with spaceports and transportation," which was a better expression of his feelings, tactical considerations notwithstanding.

Despite her approval of their trajectory, Sarza wasn't thrilled at the speed with which they were approaching the surface. They were now hurtling through Corsini airspace, and Wes wasn't even trying to blend in the air traffic. He stayed well above it all, at near orbital velocities. Exhaling, Sarza reached out to the console and slowed them down. Wes opened his mouth to object but was met with Sarza's two raised fingers, midair, "We are going to generate sonic booms all over the preming place if you don't slow down. And by the way, the heat signature of entering atmosphere—at these speeds—probably alarmed half the galaxy." Wes closed his mouth, suppressing whatever was about to come out. She was right. A little less speed would make for a lot more discretion.

Cities and towns passed them below, eventually becoming more sparse, and finally giving way to a plain of desert sands which would have taken a few days to cross on foot. In the midst of the sea of dust the IP Council Chamber stood solitary and small. The IP Council had 100 representatives, consisting of ten from each of the civilizations. The building was circular, on a single floor, with large columns all around the outside. It had been built out of marble. The Corsini had a passion for it and used the metamorphosed limestone on every possible surface. This particular building was multi-colored—painted blue, yellow, white, pink, purple, orange, green, and had a million shades in between. The colors looked like a child had grabbed a paintbrush and randomly streaked the walls. The inside was painted the exact same way. The center—which took up three quarters of the building—was made up of a single large chamber. The rest of the building consisted of smaller meeting rooms and comfortable offices used by the IP Council members when they came for meetings.

Shortly after the end of the Great Conflict, the planets had begun the laborious process of creating an official body to air out their differences, in hopes that such a body would avoid any future conflict of the same proportions. The Corsini, who had been useless during the war, were eminently suited for this task. Their culture thrived on political and philosophical discourse, as well as a profound appreciation of the arts. Given their ineptitude at conflict, they had managed to leave every other planet relatively unscathed. The IP Council, as it later came to be called, was therefore seated on Terra. However, the Corsini people believed that the IP Council itself could not merely be *on Terra* to ensure neutrality. It had to meet far from the pressures of daily living and political payback because this would allow more reasoned and levelheaded discourse. Hence, the desolate location of this central building.

The Vex kept flying. After hours of negotiation, one of the few things the three of them had agreed on was that Wes's first stop would have to be the Corsini home of one of the Earth IP Council representatives. Wes said he knew her and he could speak to her. He also knew for a fact she was on Terra at this time of year to avoid the winter in her part of the world on Earth. Further, traffic around cities was utterly unregulated. Thousands of hovercrafts jostled around along demarcated air corridors, making it very easy to blend in the crowd.

Leaving the IP Council Chamber behind them, more desert plains lay underneath, until finally they started approaching a medium-sized town. The overlay on the cockpit window labeled it as Vatra. The buildings stood three stories high at most. The streets were small, with just enough space between them for shoulder-width walking. It was a pedestrian town, so space vehicles — or any vehicles — were left on the outskirts. The resulting distribution made the entire thing look like an island of tightly packed buildings, holding each other for safety, surrounded by a moat of interplanetary vessels.

They began slowing down as the buildings grew larger through the cockpit. Wes was always struck by how quaint Corsini looked. It felt to him as though, when visiting, he was going back in time and seeing a planet where someone had pressed the pause button and arrested its cultural and architectural development at Earth's Italian Renaissance. Even the clothes had not changed. Women and men adorned themselves with clothes of sixteenth and seventeenth century Italy. Some posited that the Corsini were, in fact, Earth humans who had traveled to another planetary system during the Renaissance. But there was little evidence of that, and it seemed quite implausible.

Wes wondered for a moment if his father would be in danger, but he pushed the idea aside. His file had been sealed and purged when he turned eighteen and joined IPP. He had officially made the request for the purpose of protecting his father's identity, but in reality, it had been a way to avoid any inquiry into his mother's heritage. Either way, it was a good decision.

They landed. Sarza and Ceram were on the ground in minutes, looking around for danger. Everything was quiet. Sarza sniffed the air. "There are Sparcus here."

Ceram nodded. "There are Sparcus everywhere though. It doesn't mean they are here for us."

Wes was barely listening. He was walking toward town. Vatra had forty thousand inhabitants, and most of them were not out and about that day. In fact, the streets were completely empty. The wind whistled through the small alleys and avenues, winding its way unimpeded. Sarza walked behind him, Ceram by her side. Wes was wearing the Sparcus cloak and, underneath it, Sparcus clothing. Puffs of sand flew up from the ground upon contact with his steps. His boots crushed the ground underneath him, while the heat caused him to sweat despite his clothes' thermoregulating properties. As she rested her gaze on him, from underneath her hood, it struck

Sarza how broad his shoulders looked, how assured his walk, and how his arms stretched the sleeves of his shirt the way she liked it. Sarza tugged the edges of her hood tigher around her face to hide her hair from Ceram. It was maddening how much she wanted the man. Sarza knew that her setting of "boundaries" on Astarte by refusing penetration was ludicrous. She had linked with women often enough to know that linking did not require that, but at the time, she wanted him so bad she had to find a way to forgive herself. It had worked, but not because of the limits she set. It had worked because he had left her with nothing to regret. In fact, he had left her nothing to regret five times. Had he been a Sparcus, he would have been prime Bashbathar material. Looking at him from behind she could nearly fool herself that he was Sparcus.

An instant before it happened, Sarza knew something was wrong. A shot was fired, missing her, and barreling between her and Wes. The wall beside them exploded, throwing shards of stone all around. She pushed her cloak from her face giving her better peripheral vision and pulled out her gun, trying to determine where the shot came from. She scanned the tops of the buildings, all around them, but couldn't see anything. The shooter clearly knew to make them face the sun when looking up. Wes had thrown himself into a nearby alley. After a moment, Sarza followed suit. She turned around to check on Ceram, but she had already disappeared.

Sarza and Wes stood against the alley wall, side by side, flattened against the surface behind them—waiting. Both were breathing slowly and deeply, preparing for a battle that was sure to come. Then, a Sparcus wearing a SparIntel uniform jumped down from the roofs and landed half a meter behind them, in the alley, guns locked and quick-charged. He stood between them and the cul-de-sac of the alley. Sarza ran toward him faster than he could react. She fluidly slipped into his arms, put her two hands around his head, as though she were about to kiss him, and applied pressure. Wes saw the man clumsily pull the guns up closer to himself, trying to take aim at Sarza, whose body was pressed against his. But in vain. The Sparcus Gloves had done their job. The man's arms fell back to his side, and he slumped against Sarza. She stepped back, letting him fall to the ground. They looked up and saw they would have more company soon. Without other options, Wes and Sarza ran back into the street they had come from, painfully aware that this made them perfect targets. Sarza was ahead, Wes less than two meters behind. A paralyzing blast exploded from a door and took Sarza with it, thrusting her against a wall with such incredible force that Wes didn't think she would survive it.

She collapsed on the floor, utterly immobile. Her opened eyes stared at the sky. Wes's heart exploded, the rage ran through his body, he heard himself scream in agony at the sight of Sarza on the ground. He wanted to throw himself on top of her and protect her. Instead, he pulled out his guns and aimed them in the direction of the blast. He fired blindly, hoping that whoever was there would duck or die. He took a few steps forward and saw a human IPP agent standing there, a canon in hand. Her complexion was pale, her skin nearly transparent, and she looked straight at Wes. He shot her in the head, her brain exploding all over the wall behind her. One thing his mother had taught him, by her mere identity, was that men and women were equal: in life, love, family, and battle. The IPP had always tacitly approved and appreciated Wes's ability to engage enemies, whether male or female, with equal force. The humans had never gotten over their queasiness with women in battle. And now, more than ever, he didn't care. This woman had harmed Sarza. *His* Sarza.

Having neutralized the immediate threat, Wes put one of the guns back in the holster and reached down for Sarza. He found the standard issue IPP handle on her back, between her shoulder blades, gripped it firmly, and started dragging her paralyzed body into another side alley. He knelt and held her head on his knees. She still wasn't moving, but Wes was able to detect a faint pulse. She was still alive. He closed his eyes and exhaled gratefully. He put her head back down as he heard footsteps running down the street. He wished everything wasn't so cramped, but they were trapped, like rodents in a wall. He pulled out his other gun from his chest holster and prepared for the next assault.

As he stepped into the narrow street, he saw a wall of Sparcus, wearing no uniforms just like on Nash'amir, running his way. There were maybe fifteen of them, fully armed, charging directly at him. He started shooting. He was clearly outnumbered, so he threw himself back into the alley where Sarza lay. He stood over her and noticed that her hands were moving. The paralyzing blast was losing its effect. He knelt and kissed her mouth, hoping she still resented him enough for this to trigger an adrenaline rush that would jump-start her. "Come on Sarza. Kick my ass. Come on!" he muttered under his breath. She wasn't coming back yet. He stood back up, gently laying her head on the ground, reached for the handle on her back and dragged her further into the alley. The Sparcus footsteps were approaching fast. He didn't know where he was dragging her—he was just trying to get away from the Sparcus. All of a sudden, he heard a voice booming from somewhere around him. It was the Captain's. He straightened up and turned around. He inched toward the end of the alley, to look at the main road. On one side, the Sparcus were still approaching. On the other side stood the Captain. He would soon be trapped between the two, and Sarza still lay motionless at his feet.

"Agent Venta, you are under arrest for the murder of a Braxian, a Velin, a Human, an adult Ishtar, six Ishtar young, a Bar'aat, a Kerouac, a Carlan, and the attempted murder of a Corsini." The wall of guns surrounding the Captain which all pointed directly down the street, ready to shoot him at a moment's notice, told him not to ask questions or resist. He raised his hands over his head and felt something against his leg. He looked down. Sarza was finally sitting up on her own and leaning against him. She looked at him. "They're insane," she whispered to him. He could have laughed at her off-beat comment, had she uttered it at any other time.

By then, the Sparcus had also reached their destination on the other side. Wes and Sarza were caught in between armed Sparcus and armed humans. Wes knew which ones would be more ruthless: the ones who wanted *him*. A tall man from the Sparcus side of the standoff stepped forward, unarmed, "Sarza Beshemet, you are under arrest for treason against the Sparcus people, the murder of Sparcus agents, and collusion with a human hostile." Sarza felt her heart in her throat. She had spent the entirety of her adult life trying to heal her people, trying to find the solution to their slow demise, and now they were accusing her of treason. She didn't know who she despised more right now. The humans arresting Wes or the Sparcus destroying her.

The Captain shouted across the narrow path to the Sparcus man, "You take the Sparcus. I'll take Agent Venta."

"Agreed." The Sparcus had what he wanted. "Sarza Beshemet, if you don't come out we will kill you."

Still in the alley, Sarza and Wes looked at each other. Sarza reached up for Wes's hand. He gave it to her and she pulled herself up. Standing in front of each other, face to face, they both raised their hands above their heads and slowly walked into the street, leaving the alley behind. Just as they had expected, fifteen to twenty armed Sparcus stood to their left, and the Captain, with her armed agents, stood on their right. Sarza turned her back to the Sparcus, and faced Wes. Wes turned his back to the Captain and faced Sarza. If they were going to be executed, he figured, she would be a better sight to look at. Moments later, each of them was dragged from the other by their respective species. Sarza saw how Wes didn't flinch and just looked at her with deep concern. They were being walked backward, facing each other, the distance between them increasing.

Suddenly, Sarza, who was looking at the Captain over Wes's shoulder, saw a spot appear on the her head. Seconds later, the Captain's lifeless body crumpled to the floor. Wes saw the same spot appear on the Sparcus man's head, also seconds before he fell to the ground. Three more people on each side collapsed. Wes and Sarza were free. They instinctively ran back toward each other to the middle of the street and turned to stand back to back. Three Ishtar and three Sparcus women ran out of small alleys that fed into the main street and came to stand around them—three in front and three behind—fully armed, some with shield-swords across their backs, some with energy bows and arrows, some with knives, but all of them holding guns.

Sarza was stunned. The women wore Sparcus Special Forces uniforms, which consisted of black and grey waist cinchers made of reinforced mixtures of cloth and metal— virtually impenetrable. Underneath it, they had a grey hard shells that covered their chests and wrapped around their shoulders and backs. Underneath that, they wore black turtlenecks like Sarza's. On their shoulders, they had massive epaulettes with metal spikes. Their black leggings tucked into tight fitting thigh-high boots, made from the same material as the waist cinchers. They also wore sheer, free-floating skirts that reminded every one of their opponents that they were being killed by a woman. The skirt was developed during the Great Conflict, when fighting the humans. The Sparcus—and most other civilizations—had realized that human morale plummeted when they were being decimated by women. And, aside from the strategic advantage this gave them, the Sparcus had also reveled in being able to add insult to injury.

Sarza had never actually seen one of the elite Special Forces units. She had only heard tales and seen them in images from the First Great Conflict. The women must have been fifteen to twenty-five years older than Sarza and Wes, but they were battle machines finely tuned to kill and destroy. The woman closest to Sarza was a Sparcus, about an inch taller than her, muscular, but of average build, her skin the blackest of blacks. She had green eyes. Her long, blond, tightly curled hair created a halo around her head. She was aiming a bow with energy arrows, getting ready for another headshot. The weapon was deceptively simple. A dark, blunt, black quiver placed in a bow. But as soon as the bow was drawn back, and using the kinetic energy accumulated and mixed with the properties of the quiver's material, the "arrow" turned into a stick of energy capable of tremendous speed, distance, and penetration. The woman on Sarza's other side was an Ishtar. Her brown skin blended perfectly with her black hair, softly curled against her shoulders. Her yellow serpentine eyes framed by the copper-hued scales freckling her hairline and extending down her neck. She had perfect features except for a scar that ran from her forehead and down her cheek to her jaw. Both her guns were ready for battle. For the first time in her life, Sarza knew — for sure — she was in the presence of superior force.

Another one of the Sparcus women — a tall, black haired, olive-toned woman — pulled her shield-sword out from her back holster and threw it in the air. It was massive — easily two-and-a-half meters long. To Sarza's surprise, Wes's hand reached effortlessly to grab it, like he had done this a million times before. He pulled it down to his side and took the Sparcus battle stance. One knee hit the ground, the other leg lending support. Both his hands gripped the handle and held it off to the side at waist level, his upper body twisting to counter balance the weight. All of this had taken mere seconds. The shield-sword activated, creating a faint vanishing glow around Wes as it established the shielding force field, locking itself on his person, and allowing him to move freely with his weapon within it. Wes stood back up, the flittering sheen protecting him now by both significantly slowing down projectiles that hit it straight on and deflecting those that hit it at the slightest of angles. This was a classic Sparcus weapon. Someone must have modified it to activate to non-Sparcus hands. Sarza noticed a smile creeping across Wes's face as he wielded the formidable weapon. He was obviously in his element and enjoying it.

Three Special Forces started running down one side-alley, grabbing Sarza by the wrist and pulling her behind them. The other three pulled Wes in the opposite direction. They ran faster than Sarza was used to, but to them it looked like it was nothing. She may have been a highly trained operative, but these women were the stuff of legends. They quickly disappeared into another alley, then another, then yet another. Sarza tried to keep track of their direction. Finally, one of the women, an Ishtar with brilliant red hair tied in a braid that reached her buttocks and freckled skin, pushed Sarza into a cul-de-sac. She fell backward. The three other Special Forces showed up with Wes and threw him in the cul-de-sac as well. He slammed into Sarza, pressing her up against the wall, his hands coming to rest on the wall behind her, on either side of her head.

Five of the Special Forces then disappeared to the left, drawing off the IPP and the Sparcus, who had no idea they were running directly past Wes and Sarza. The two of them crouched in the darkness of their small, recessed space. Sarza looked up and saw the sixth of the group still standing with them. Her sinewy body made her look deceptively fragile. But Sarza had no doubt this woman, like her counterparts, was all physical power. Her head was shaved, exposing the Ishtar scales that started just above the warriors' nape and disappeared into her turtleneck. The scales were grey, black, and silver. She turned around, her three eyelids closing and opening rapidly as she blinked. The vertical pupils in her yellow eyes began examining Sarza. As she looked at them, she shrugged her shoulders, readjusting the laser canon hanging diagonally across her back. Her very defined facial features, including a prominent nose and marked jawline tensed as she focused on Sarza and Wes, looking for something.

"Wounds?" She asked.

"None." Wes answered immediately.

Sarza knew instantly the two of them weren't strangers.

The woman nodded, looked back towards the street, making sure it was still clear, "Let's go."

Wes stood up, Sarza followed suit. The three of them ran in the same direction as the Sparcus, the IPP, and the other Special Forces, tailing the hostile crowd. The Special Forces had led everybody to an open space, a plaza, with a fountain in the middle. By the time Sarza and Wes arrived, the fight was raging. The women wielded laser-powered knives, swords, guns, and bows, jumping over Sparcus and IPP alike, slitting their throats, and covering themselves in blood in the process. They were unstoppable, unbelievable. Sarza was in awe at their efficiency. An IPP agent lunged at her. She grabbed his wrist, pulled him in front of her, and broke his arm behind his back. He fell to his knees. She pulled out her gun and fired a shot into his head. Wes had left her side. She looked up and saw him battling a few yards to her right. He was semi-crouched, holding the massive sword in front of him. He slashed an approaching woman across the stomach, turned around to stab a Sparcus man, and jumped up to impale a male human. Sarza didn't understand, couldn't comprehend, where he had learned to fight exactly like a Sparcus, down to the way he held the sword over his head as he waited for the next attacker.

Soon, the water in the fountain was pink with the blood of the fallen, but the Special Forces weren't done. They now outnumbered what was left of Wes's and Sarza's assailants — four IPP agents left and three Sparcus. They started running away from the public square as fast as they could. Sarza saw

Ceram running with them. She looked over her shoulder at Sarza and kept running. She had not been sent by Vigor at all. She had probably given away their position on the planet. And spied on them all along.

Sarza and Wes ran with the Special Forces in the opposite direction. All of a sudden, a booming female voice reached them from behind. "Stop, you Sparcus scum!" Wes slowed down. Sarza didn't understand why. The comment was obviously not directed at him. "I have your father," the voice continued.

Wes stopped dead in his tracks, but his heart raced hard, pounding inside of his chest. The Special Forces women surrounding them stopped with him. Sarza watched Wes turn around, raise his hands over his head, and slowly walk back toward his inevitable arrest and likely execution. The women did nothing to stop him. Sarza looked toward the booming voice. A woman with brown hair and a tall, eerily skinny figure, stood behind an elderly man on his knees. She held a knife under his throat. The man was clearly was terrified. Wes looked at Sarza as he walked past her and paused for a moment. Sarza could see the resolve in his eyes. She didn't know what to say to him. How could she tell him not to save his father? How could he do anything other than what he was doing?

The dark-skinned, blond-halo-haired Sparcus turned to the redhead. "Can you kill her from here?"

"No. She's too far."

"Can we go to the other side?"

"Not fast enough."

They all stood in silence. Then one of them resumed her retreat. A second one followed. Then a third. Sarza felt like she was tied by a string to both the women and Wes. She couldn't move in either direction. She wanted to protect the human. If anything, she knew he wasn't guilty of murder. She watched his inexorable walk to the center of the plaza. He kneeled, put his hands on his head, and waited. The sun beat down on his body. His cloak draped all around him. An IPP agent approached him and removed Wes's guns from their holsters. Another one, a woman, approached and took Wes's sword. The man then pistol-whipped him so violently Wes's body fell across the floor. Sarza caught sight of the blood spattering either from his mouth or his nose — she wasn't sure which. Wes fell to the ground and didn't move for a moment. He then picked himself up, slowly, pushing up against the ground until he got his balance and got back on his knees.

Sarza's hair raised itself, red, flaming, fury running through her. She overheard something but she wasn't sure what it was. She seared both the man and the woman's face in her memory, vowing to kill either one if they were ever unlucky enough to cross her path. She tightened her fists, clenching her hands at her side. She swallowed hard and gritted her teeth. She was powerless to do anything. It was the worst feeling ever. Moments that felt like eternity passed her by. Eventually, she pulled herself from the spot where she had stood, and ran after the women. After running for a few minutes, they stopped. All was quiet. Sarza was panting, trying to catch her breath. The others were exerted but still in control, looking at each other knowingly. It was clear they had known each other a very long time.

One of them, a Sparcus, punched the wall in front of her. "Prem! Prem, prem, prem, prem!"

"We will get him back, Mika," said the redhead Ishtar. "We will get him back before they kill him."

Sarza was bent over, still standing, her hands pressing into her knees, catching her breath. She looked up at these creatures of myth. Finally, in between ragged breaths, Sarza asked, "Who are you? Why are you saving us?"

The redhead answered, without smiling, "We aren't saving *you*."

The blond who had punched the wall continued, "We are here for Wes."

"Wes?" Sarza asked "Why Wes?"

"We promised his mother."

"Who is his mother?" Sarza didn't understand.

The Ishtar with the scar running down her face walked up to Sarza, stood inches from her, and as though she was delivering the words directly into Sarza's mouth, hissed, "One of the fiercest Sparcus warriors that ever lived."

BOOK I
CHAPTER 10

A day before Wes's arrest on Terra, the Captain had sat at the briefing table in the same exact room where Wes and Sarza had first met. At her side stood her boss, the Earth IPP Chief. He wore the dark burgundy uniform of the IPP. They faced a large, glowing screen, which took up most of the space in front of them. It flickered, then stabilized, then flickered again, throwing shadows on their faces. The rest of the room was pitch black. The Captain and the Chief were the only two people in the room. The Captain looked glum, a nervous wreck, her eyes still red. The Chief had not even noticed. He was focused on what was about to happen. An emergency IPP meeting had been called over the failing investigation into the murders taking place all over the system. The other nine IPP Chiefs appeared on the screen, one from each planetary system, including the Sparcus system. The Chief took the lead. "Thank you for agreeing to this meeting. I appreciate everyone showing up on such short notice."

Silence.

"I first want to assure you that we are doing our best to get to the bottom of these murders. And we have finally identified a suspect." He swallowed. This was going to be a hard thing to sell.

The Sparcus IPP Chief immediately jumped in, "Who is it?"

Silence. The Chief paused. "Agent Wes Venta."

Through the static of the communicators on each planet, he could hear chatter, murmurs, and gasps coming from the various rooms.

The Braxian Chief's voice was the first to reach him. "How did you all miss this?"

Then the other voices came through. He couldn't tell who was saying what: "That's outrageous!" "You had him under your nose the whole time?" "Why was he assigned to this case?" "Why was he chosen for this?" "You are telling us you didn't know this?" "How long have you been covering for him?" "How long have you known?" The questions continued to pour out, the venom, resentment, and indignation mounting.

The Chief held up his hands. "Please, please, please. I understand it's a shock. We are floored, and appalled, but . . . we will find him. He will be brought in for questioning. He will be arrested—" The rumbling at each end of the system wouldn't die down so easily. The Captain, speaking out of turn, leaned forward. "We didn't know! Okay! We did not know." Her voice was trembling. She looked like she was on the edge of tears. "We had no idea he was among us."

"How did he get assigned to this case?"

The Chief looked at the Captain sternly. She had overstepped and now he wanted her to clean up her own mess. She should have sat back and shut her mouth. He whispered, "The stage is all yours Captain. Try not to fuck it up—again!" He moved aside, allowing the Captain to become the center of the screen for everybody else watching. "I recommended he be assigned. . . . He is — was — one of our best agents. And he was. . . . It was my recommendation." The Captain thought back to the events that had led her to this moment, and she felt her stomach turn to ice. Blood rushed to her temples, the anxiety and stress of the past month overwhelmed her. She had spent days crying at night and trying to act impervious during the day.

The Corsini's voice came through. "You understand that nobody was left unscathed? Except for you and the Sparcus."

"We lost a human handler." The Captain said tentatively, knowing full well that would hold up all of fifteen seconds.

"Because he was our guy's handler!" The Braxian voice was so angry it was shrill. "He was probably in on it and became an inconvenience. We trusted you to do this right." He was choking on his words, nearly apoplectic. "If you had cared that a 'fish' — right, because that's what you all call us, *fish*! No, I'm sorry, 'frogs' is it? — had been murdered, you would have dealt with this faster. Instead, you just sat on your hands — "

The Bar'aat interrupted, "We had an outright execution. A maraking execution! Right on our planet, and your guy's prints were all over the office!"

The Captain tried to defend herself. "He was an arm's dealer. We couldn't necessarily link it — "

"*We are all arms dealers!*" The Bar'aat roared through the galaxy. "That's what we do. We gave you guns, weapons, and armaments when you needed them. We saved your sorry little hairless bodies from . . ." he caught himself. "We saved you and then you have the gall to answer, 'He was an arm's dealer.' How does that make any difference? It's who we are!"

The Captain was trying to explain herself, trying to take back the words, when the Kerouac jumped in. "Do you have any other rationalization for why the killing of one of ours was no big deal? Why you couldn't pin it *on your own guy*?"

The Ishtar's voice came through next. "You paired him with a Sparcus! Of all things. And then they came here and slaughtered our children! Children! Do you hear me? Children." The pain in her voice was stronger than the anger. "We let him walk around our planet because we thought he was investigating. How could you let that happen?"

"We didn't know—" The Captain tried to answer.

"To hell with you!" The Ishtar woman was having none of it. "You should have known! We are all just animals to you. You've always made that clear. It's been forty years, and you still think you are so superior. What have you done to make yourselves so superior, huh? You didn't even have space travel you backward, antiquated, limited little creatures." The Captain stayed quiet. This wasn't new. This resentment, this tension, this inability to truly see each other as equals had always been an undercurrent of the fragile peace. It was coming to a head over a few murders. A few insignificant murders. The appearance of partiality and injustice was far stronger than any actual malice on anybody's part. The guilt that had slowly grown over the past few weeks was now crushing her chest. She was having trouble breathing.

The Sparcus representative, a woman with light brown skin and very fine features, spoke for the first time. "What we have here is not just a botched investigation." Nobody interrupted her. "What we have here is Earth's evident attempt to protect one of its own at the cost of everybody else's safety." Her voice was calm, non-judgmental; she was keeping perfect composure.

"Now listen—" The Chief had had enough.

"I think we've done enough listening. You have given us weekly updates that were all but useless, while 'creatures' were being slaughtered left and right. We're done listening to you. I don't care about what you want to *say* about this." The Sparcus was taking tremendous satisfaction in this. "I think we all want to know what you are going to *do* about it."

The Chief didn't miss a beat. "The Captain here and I will go immediately and arrest Agent Venta."

"Where is he?" The Corsini woman had immediately noticed the omission. She was an older woman, with grey hair gently embracing her face that was held at the back of her head in a lose bun. Her blue eyes were piercing. She showed the signs of many years of wisdom on her face.

"We—

"You don't trust us with the information." It was a rhetorical statement, sourly delivered. Rumbling and muttering spread through the room, transmitted from across the galaxy, making it abundantly clear that all Earth's credibility was gone. Finally, the Kerouac representative's voice broke through, "You understand that when I go back to my superiors with this, they will want the human to be tried on Styx?"

"Same for Hatuu-oh."

"Same for Nash'Amir."

"Same for Sulpuro."

"Same for Maka."

"Same for Terra."

"Same for Vedic."

"Same for Sebera."

It was like a roll call of discord. Each species announcing its interests as being at odds with Earth's.

"It is better for him to be tried here on Earth." The Chief knew it would make them irate, but even though Agent Venta was probably a murderer, humans would not agree to him being tried anywhere other than on Earth. One of theirs was one of theirs no matter what. It would set a poor precedent that humans could be arrested and tried anywhere in the galaxy. He added, "We agreed it is usual protocol. The IP Rules dictate that every species is responsible for . . ." His voice trailed off. He felt the futility of his statement. They were too far gone to care about rules that had been set up decades ago.

The Braxian's voice came through the communicator. "I have just received a command from my superiors. If the human is not handed over, we will come get him by force if needed." The Chief's stomach sank. The Captain was about to throw up.

"Now, let's be reasonable . . ." The Chief tried to calm things, feeling the situation slip through his fingers.

"Even if the Braxians decide to be reasonable, we won't be," the Kerouac's predictable response was laden with threat.

"You have operated with impunity long enough. We can no longer trust you. Nor can we trust your airspace." The Bar'aat lay his cards on the table. The screens of every other planet turned off until the Captain and the Chief were looking at their own images; the only remaining ones on the screen.

It was as though everyone had just been waiting, for years, on an excuse to re-open the conflict. This wasn't about a single murder, or a single agent. This was about years of trying to find agreement between planets that never saw eye to eye, never saw each other as equals, and had accepted Earth out of necessity rather than respect. When the Sparcus were on the verge of taking over, Earth had brought them to their knees by making it far too dangerous for the Sparcus to continue with conflict. Each dead Sparcus would never be replaced by a next generation. But winning such acceptance—and peace—by being the most ruthless had done nothing to bring the planets truly closer. All the cracks were coming to a head. The Chief was watching the Second Great Conflict begin before a shot had even been fired. The room was quiet, dark; the Chief and the Captain sat in silence. At least, the Chief thought it was silence until he realized that the Captain was crying at his side, shaking uncontrollably, sitting in her chair, only her shoulders moving. She could barely breathe through her sobs. He stood up. There was nothing he could say. Finally, she crumpled onto the table, shaking her head from side to side.

"What?" He didn't know what else to ask.

"I can't . . . I can't . . ." She was trying to talk through the sobbing.

"You can't what?" The Chief was a little intrigued. This wasn't going in the direction he thought it would go.

"I can't do it anymore. I can't."

"You can't do what anymore?"

"I can't. I . . . I pushed for Wes to be assigned to this case because . . ." She looked up at him, "I've been," she breathed in, trying to regain her composure, "I had a . . . with a Sparcus . . ."

The Chief's face betrayed his profound shock and realization, mixed with fear, the emotions crisscrossing his face. "You had a relation with a Sparcus?" His voice, however, remained businesslike. He was still the Chief, and there was information to be had here.

"Yes."

"And?"

"The Sparcus, the one I was . . . she threatened to . . . tell . . . if I didn't do what she said." The Captain had stopped crying. She was looking at her hands on the table, her arms stretched out in front of her, her fingers clasped around each other. Her hands were shaking from her holding them so hard.

"What did she tell you to do?" The Chief sounded like he was disarming a bomb, trying not to push too hard, but trying to get to his goal.

"Assign Venta to the case."

"Why?"

"I don't know. I don't know. Nothing was ever explained to me."

"But how . . . coverts are assigned to cases, not handlers. How did you know to assign the covert? Normally, coverts were assigned and handlers came as part of the package. For this investigation, the IP Council had asked the IPP Council to approve an exception.

"He requested assignment to a Sparcus agent. He always does. So I paired them as handler and covert while, simultaneously, assigning Beshemet to the Braxian murder."

"Did they ask you to do anything else?"

The Captain nodded, the tears starting to well up again. "To not allow access to the crime scene reports until they were here."

"What do you mean no access?"

"The information was collected and sent here. Nobody on the ground saw it."

Hundreds of questions were flying through the Chief's head, but he could only ask one at a time, "Who looked at them here?"

"She did."

"Who?"

"Mesheah . . . I . . . the Sparcus that I . . ." The Captain looked at the Chief. She was desperate, sad, and heartbroken. The genuine heartbreak the Chief had not uncovered until now. He wasn't just looking at a compromised agent. He was looking at a jilted lover.

"How could you . . ." His voice softened, "How could you fall in love with a Sparcus . . . Jane . . ." He used her first name, probably for the first time since they worked together. He was disappointed. "The one thing they despise the most about us . . . love . . . and you fell for it . . ." He trailed off, shaking his head as he looked at the floor.

"What else did they ask you to do?"

"To leak that she was a covert Sparcus Intelligence agent."

"There is no such thing!" The Chief exclaimed "We've kept our eyes and ears open, we've had people in the Sparcus government for years. There is no such thing as Sparcus Intelligence! You know that. I know that. Most agents across the system know that—"

"I know," the Captain was nodding, "but I had to say it."

"To who?"

"To Venta."

"That's it?"

"Yes."

The Chief was still standing there looking at what was left of the confident, capable Captain he had worked with for years. "You understand you will be tried for this."

"Yes."

"Is Venta even guilty?"

The Captain shook her head. "I don't know. I don't know. I don't know." The Chief knew, however, that her answer was irrelevant. They couldn't go back now. They couldn't tell the others that he wasn't guilty after all. It would look like a cover-up. They had to go through with the arrest and hope the legal system could hold up its end of the deal. He turned around and headed toward the door. "Captain. You aren't relieved of your duties yet. And you had better get your ass ready to go to Terra. I promised you would be there, and we are going to see this through." He didn't wait to hear her answer. He waved his hand in front of the door sensor and walked out.

* * *

Three days later Maerah, the head of SparIntel — the "non-existent" Sparcus covert intelligence agency — stood in her large Sparcus quarters on Qetesh. She looked out the window at Astarte, peacefully orbiting, dipping itself into the dunes on the horizon. Maerah's blond hair nearly touched the ground. She had sworn to only cut it the day she could return to combat. She smiled to herself: that day was very near. She wore a floor-length white tunic made of see-through material that left nothing to the imagination. A white and gold cincher wrapped around her waist and stopped under her breasts, lifting them just a little. She was curvy, like a typical Sparcus woman, and very athletic. Her arms were toned and her back sculpted. The top of the tunic fell around her shoulders, leaving them bare. She had been described as "breathtaking" by many other Sparcus in the not-so-distant path. Although now, she was more commonly known as callous, ruthless, single-minded, and tenacious.

Behind her, the room was large and empty. She had never seen the need for furniture, preferring to sit on the floor. She had a few pillows for that purpose. Four floor-to-ceiling windows surrounded her. She stood in front of one of them. The building sat on an island in the middle of a lake so large that it was basically a sea. Astarte—the planet—dipped its massive body just under the horizon of Qetesh. It looked like it was bathing in the waters of its twin planet. Carad walked in. Her hair was brown, a sign that at some point in her life she had Matched with a fertile male. Women with brown hair were few and far between. But, as had become common, the Match had fallen apart after Earth unleashed Project Geno on them. She also had permanent white streaks, marking the sorrow that life and experience had brought with it, including the loss of two daughters and a son to the First Great Conflict. She had mentored Maerah through the years, facilitating her rise to power. Carad wore the black Sparcus outfit, including turtleneck, leggings, and boots. She had never liked the tunics, finding them impractical. Even the short ones seemed better suited for Bashbathars than for fighting.

"Did he know?"

"Did it work?" Carad had a few questions of her own.

"Yes."

"Did the two of them figure it out?" Carad continued.

"Maybe. Maybe, yes. There's a chance . . . but it's over. It's too late." Maerah turned around to face Carad. "And anyway, both of them will be dead soon. Whatever they figure out about our involvement in the murders will be burnt with their bodies."

"What if she betrayed us to him? She stayed with him an awfully long time. Rumors are she tried to save him on Terra."

"She wouldn't betray us. I made sure of it." Maerah didn't exhibit reluctance or doubt about that statement.

"How?" Carad had seen Maerah through most of her training, but the younger woman's ability to strategize was still impressive.

"I made sure he knew Sarza worked for us. And I made sure *she* knew that *he* knew."

"You . . . you . . ." This was unthinkable. To willingly blow an agent's cover after everything they had done to convince the world SparIntel didn't exist. It was lunacy.

"That's insane! He could have talked and then—"

"But he didn't. He was isolated. They were both isolated. You know that. He knew someone was after him. She knew someone was after her."

"How?"

"I sent two Sparcus agents to warn her that her cover was blown. And two more to try to kill her. They were supposed to only *try* . . . and let her go. That way, both Sarza and Wes were . . ."

Carad finished Maerah's thought, "Utterly isolated from the world . . . but they couldn't trust each other." Carad pondered the brilliance of the plan, but then added, "If you know she didn't betray us, why do you want her dead?"

Maerah started walking toward Carad, who was standing in front of the door. They had to go to the meeting hall. "She might. She *is* involved with the human. One of ours followed them for a few days. She has a soft spot for him, at the very least." Maerah stopped in front of Carad. "And she *did* try to save him on Terra. That's no rumor. They protected each other until the end. I can't have that. I can't have any Sparcus think for one moment that they can truly ally themselves with the humans. Not with what we have in mind." Carad understood. The two women walked silently down a hall. The walls were dark brown, the color of the mud from which they were built. On the floor was a bright red carpet that stretched the entire length of the corridor. Light reflected in from large windows placed at regular intervals.

A few moments later, Maerah sat silently at the front of the room on a raised platform behind an imposing wooden and stone desk. The desk itself was centuries old and dated back to the days that Sparcus was first inhabited by their ancestors. Her blond hair fell luxuriously on her lap and nonchalantly around her. She looked like a goddess or a nymph, but her face was still as serious as during her conversation with Carad. The plan had a lot of moving pieces, most of which she controlled, except for one: Sarza. Although she didn't speak of it, she *was* worried Sarza would try to save the human. Something had happened. A shift in their alliances. It had been evident on Terra, from what she had been told. She couldn't risk Sarza saving him. Both of them had served their purpose, and both of them had to die.

Maerah observed the men and women leaders of SparIntel whispering to each other as they walked around the room, waiting for the meeting to start. This was an epic day. This was the crowning of over three decades of efforts at destabilizing the peace that had been earned at the cost of destroying her people.

The oval-shaped room easily accommodated two hundred people. Formerly it had been the Sparcus Chamber, where leaders governed the two Sparcus planets. But, as the elders died off and nobody replaced them, the Sparcus government had moved to smaller quarters, abandoning these large halls. It made the chamber ideal for SparIntel meetings, since nobody would come looking. It helped that it was also located on Qetesh—the other Sparcus planet—the one that everybody believed had been abandoned.

Maerah shifted in her seat. It too was made of wood and stone, reaching up behind her to the ceiling, encircling her in its armrests, making her look even more imposing through its sheer magnitude. The rest of the hall had long continuous benches that stretched from one end of the room, curving at the back, then coming back in an oval. They were made of the same materials as the desk. The hall was devoid of technology, which also made it harder to detect and harder to monitor. This too was ideal for the SparIntel.

A man broke off from his conversation with two women and walked toward Maerah. He stood in front of her desk and nodded at her.

"Congratulations Maerah! This is your day. Your plan has come to fruition."

Maerah leaned forward, putting her elbows on the table. "It is our day. It is the day of the Sparcus. Congratulations to you too, Malik." She wasn't smiling, but she was glad. She looked forward to explaining to her people exactly how successful they had been. She stood up as Malik went back to the others and took a seat. The room quickly fell silent as people hushed. When she sat back down, everyone sat with her.

Vigor sat in the front row. It had been over two years since he had been allowed to attend a full SparIntel meeting. His position on the IP Council had made him "a liability." This was the first time he would get to hear firsthand what the SparIntel—his people—had been up to. Perhaps he would be able to understand what was happening to Sarza.

Maerah took a moment to think about what was about to happen. She was trying to find the words to report on the recent events. Exhaling and looking up at the room, she began, "Today, IPP agents arrested a human for the murders of beings from every other planet around the system. Our sources tell me that he will be tried, he will be found guilty, and he may well be executed."

A rumble erupted among the audience. This wasn't exactly what they were expecting. An older woman, her brown hair tied up on top of her head, stood up. "Chair, if I may."

Maerah nodded at her. The woman continued, "My understanding was that the planets would *blame* the humans. But if a human was actually arrested and tried, are you not afraid the other planets will be placated? Will they not accept that as justice?"

Maerah nodded. This was a valid concern. The plan to frame a human for the murders that the Sparcus themselves had committed had required tremendous amounts of resources, but its success was largely dependent on how much the other planets would accept law enforcement and human resolution of the murders. If the other planets accepted the IPP's human-led investigation, and its outcome, then their mission would have been for naught. It was imperative that the planets experiencied the upcoming trial as a sham and instead resort to violence to punish Earth as a whole.

Maerah looked at the older woman. "I appreciate your comment. And I understand this is a concern on everybody's minds, but our representative on the IP Council assures me that there is no avenue for peace. The human can be executed, tortured, or set free. It will make no difference." Maerah looked at the back of the room, searching for a face. She scanned the seats, once, twice, trying to see past the sunlight shining into the room from the slits along the top of the walls. Finally, she saw one of the IP Councilmembers, who served as a double for SparIntel standing at the back of the room. The woman understood she was being summoned. She stood up. She too was wearing the tunic and the waist cincher. Her light brown boots rose to just under her knees. Their soles were flat and thick, ready to walk, fight, or run. Her hair was black, shoulder length. Her features were somewhat masculine — with her square and imposing nose. Her green eyes betrayed exhaustion and tension, the result of years living between illegality and the public eye. She had served her people well.

"The IP Council was supposed to meet this morning. They did not. They could not even stand to be in the same room as each other. The arrest came too late to satisfy anybody. And the fact that a human—the human assigned to investigate these same murders—was arrested, has left everyone, the Braxians, the Kerouacs, the Ishtars, the Corsini, the Bar'aats—everybody—with a deep distrust of the humans. There is no turning back."

Vigor nodded. The past few days had consisted of heated discussions by communicator between the various intragalactic representatives. Although all of them were supposed to head to Terra, nobody had done so. It was pointless. The rage among them was unhinged. The humans had been left utterly isolated.

"Will he be found guilty?" asked a voice from the room.

"Yes." Maerah answered without hesitation.

"How can you be so sure?" Murmurs of approval at the question.

"One of our agents seduced the Earth IPP captain. In return for the agent's silence about their affair, the captain gave us unfettered access to the investigation files. We inserted evidence of the human at every crime scene, and nobody but us was given access. So there are no loose ends."

"What about the Sparcus woman? The one who worked with him?"

Maerah gestured to the IP Councilmember and answered the question herself. "She escaped. We issued an execution warrant for her, and there are SparIntel agents trying to find her at this very moment."

A man stood up. "Did she compromise SparIntel?"

"No." Maerah paused. "I know there were concerns about her involvement with the human, but . . ." she was looking for the rights words, "she is a double IPP/SparIntel agent, and there is no evidence that she either betrayed our cause or leaked any information about SparIntel." That was the truth. Her involvement with the human was, in any case, pure rumor and speculation. Nobody had a trace of evidence on her except for the fact that the two of them had been traveling around together. But that was entirely consistent with her cover as an IPP agent.

"Is she still a threat to SparIntel?" said another voice in the audience.

"Possibly." The murmur grew to a hushed indignation among the people in the room. Nobody had expected a Sparcus to be this involved in the investigation. Vigor couldn't stand it anymore. He stood up as his long grey cloak fell behind him. He wore the black outfit of a Sparcus agent. The people in the room turned to look at him.

"The agent you are talking about is no more a threat to SparIntel than I am. She has worked for and dedicated herself to the Sparcus. She has been tireless in her efforts to . . ." he caught himself, "to fulfill her mission." Vigor felt an overwhelming urge to defend Sarza's name, to reverse this course. Maybe he could convince them to withdraw the warrant of execution. "She is *not* compromised. She is not —"

Maerah interrupted him. "Vigor. I understand you have a personal relationship with her, and I understand you trained her, but we have to consider the bigger picture."

Vigor turned to look at their leader. "Yes, but even if you are afraid that the humans know about her role with us, what difference does it make at this point? If war is truly breaking out among the planets —"

Maerah raised her hand. "If a single one of us gets caught, a single one of us talks, a single one of us reveals the existence of this organization, we will lose ears on the ground on every planet, in every government, at every level of government. We cannot allow that."

"But there is no evidence they even *know* for sure about SparIntel." Vigor was standing his ground.

"There's enough for her to be a liability." Maerah held her hand up. Vigor was done talking, and he had been unable to call off the dogs. He felt defeated. He sat down, clenching his jaw.

Maerah continued, "We will soon have the humans at our mercy. They will have nobody to turn to but us. And then we will get anything we want from them."

Vigor looked around the room. He didn't understand what she was talking about, but heads were nodding in approval. Everybody else was on the same page. Malik, seated next to him, leaned over and said, "Project Genesis. We will get Project Genesis from the humans."

"And then what?"

"It will allow us to reverse the sterilization."

"And then what?"

"We slaughter them. We do to them what they did to us." Malik's expression was tense, angry, betraying the resentment of a generation deprived of something as profound as the ability to reproduce itself. "We will break their world like they broke ours. But we will bathe theirs in blood the way they bathed ours in tears." Vigor looked at Malik, and then at the people around him. Maerah's plan had been both brilliant and perfectly orchestrated. No detail had been left up to chance, except for Sarza's serendipitous assignment to the case.

Maerah adjourned the meeting and left through a side door. Vigor followed behind her. He caught up to her in the hall.

"Maerah!"

She turned around. "Vigor. I am glad you were able to rejoin us."

Vigor wasn't interested in banalities. "Call them off, Maerah."

"I can't."

"Of course you can."

"Vigor . . ." She sighed. The two of them went back a long ways. Maerah was approximately ten years older than Sarza and twenty years younger than Vigor. He had trained her the same way he had trained Sarza.

"You *know* Sarza would never betray us." Vigor wasn't going to let this go. Maerah couldn't blame him. "You *know* her. For heaven's sakes. You two know each other. You trained together. You came to SparIntel at the same time."

"Vigor. This has nothing to do with me or Sarza or you. But the fact is that the IPP Earth captain was adamant about their knowledge of Sarza's double agent status."

"What evidence do they have?"

"That's beside the point. And the more time she spends with the human—"

"Don't!" Vigor wouldn't let Maerah sully Sarza's name in front of him, not even as the Chair of SparIntel. She was everybody else's leader, but right now she was still the same girl he had taught to fight, as far he was concerned. "Don't you dare say that about her." Maerah didn't like his tone, but he pushed on. "He's under arrest. She's nowhere to be found, on the run. There is nothing she can do to harm us."

"Vigor. The decision has been made. This conversation is over." Maerah turned around and walked away. Vigor watched her, then a thought occurred to him. "How did you know to assign him? The human? Why was everyone so adamant about assigning *him*?" He remembered the conversations relayed from the IPP Council and summarized for the IP Council. There was an obsession by the humans and Sparcus to assign Agent Wes Venta—and nobody else. No doubt, the humans at the time had also been somehow compromised and were doing the Sparcus's bidding. He hadn't noticed it at the time.

Maerah stopped and shouted down the hall without turning around, "He will make it easier for everyone to believe that Earth and Sparcus were in this together all along. The more they are associated with us, the more likely it is that other civilizations will turn against it."

"How?"

Maerah stopped, turned around and uttered words that seemed surreal, "Agent Venta is a Sparcus that chose to live as a human. Nobody will ever want him as one of their own." She smiled and started walking away from Vigor again. He stood in place, frozen, unable to move. This was utterly unreal. He began running after Maerah, but she had disappeared into one of the many doors lining the halls. He looked behind him and walked back into the meeting room. Most of the people had disappeared. He needed someone who would give him answers. He caught a glimpse of a much older SparIntel woman. Carad! She was one of the oldest SparIntel agents. And she had Maerah's ear. If Maerah knew something, so did Carad. He walked toward her. She turned to watch him and politely excused herself from her conversation.

"Carad."

"Vigor."

They had spent many nights together at Bashbathars. Vigor was surprised they had never Matched. It always had seemed to work so perfectly between them.

"What can I do for you?"

"I need answers."

"I'll see what I can do."

"Why did we pick Agent Wes Venta for the mission?"

"Ah! Maerah didn't tell you?"

"No." He wanted to know what she had to say if she thought he knew nothing.

"Well, he is about to be executed, so I figure it won't make much of a difference. He is a Sparcus. His mother ran away with a human after the First Great Conflict. She defected from the Sparcus people and raised him on Nash'amir."

"How . . .? Why . . ." Vigor didn't know which question to start with.

"She was a Sparcus warrior—special forces—and one of our top scientists. After the Great Conflict, she lost her mind, fell in prem with a human, and ran away to raise a Sparcus child. It sounds outrageous, but it's not very complicated. War can sometimes damage people. It was a pity. She was one of our finest fighters."

"Who was she?"

"Vadama Pax."

"*The* Vadama Pax? Vadama Pax of the million foes?"

"Yes."

"I thought she was childless, and that she had died during the Great Conflict."

"Well," Carad looked at Vigor with a pained expression, "she did, didn't she? She fell in prem with a human—she fell in prem with a monster—and moved away from our homeland to raise a child. One of the last children our people gave birth to. She died when she betrayed us. The Sparcus in her died."

Vigor was trying to make sense of this. He couldn't even feel anger at her. It sounded so tragic, so deeply broken, so damaged of her to do such a thing. "Does . . . does he know?"

"The boy? Wes?" He wasn't a boy anymore. Hadn't been for a long while.

"Yes!" Vigor couldn't tell her that the man had stayed in his house, but it baffled him that he had somehow not noticed a full-blown Sparcus man and instead, he had mistook him for a human. It was even more awe inspiring that he was the son of the great Vadama Pax.

"We aren't sure how much his mother told him. He certainly has never shared this information with anybody as far as we know."

"How do you know? How do we know who his mother is?"

Carad smiled coyly. "The women on Nash'amir talk. He was raised there. It doesn't take much for the word to spread about a Sparcus woman, a human man, and a child living together."

"Why didn't we . . . why didn't we go after her? It was treason. It still is treason!"

Carad looked at the floor, then at the walls around them. She wasn't keen on answering. "If someone was entitled to be left alone, it was Vadama Pax. She did enough for our people while she was still herself. We let her be for some time and let her raise her son. We had moved on."

"Where is she now?"

"Dead."

Vigor breathed in sharply and—unconsciously—held his breath. "Did we . . . did we have anything to do with her death?" Vadama Pax was one of the most revered warriors of all time. He was swallowing, trying to brace for the disclosure that they had killed her.

"We tried." Cadar was nonchalant. Vigor put his hands over his face, closing his eyes. He felt such shame for being part of a group that would do such a thing. Carad continued, "But she died of natural causes."

Vigor exhaled, resuming breathing again. He wasn't sure if Carad was lying to him. But he gave her the benefit of the doubt—she had never been outright dishonest with him.

They paused. Vigor's thoughts went back to Wes. "Except you now throw her son to the lions!" Vigor felt disgust at his people's callousness. "He will be executed. He will be executed by humans, of all things!"

Carad looked at him sternly. "And he will have served his people well. Maybe even better than any of us ever will."

"But why him? Why a Sparcus? Why do you want his blood on our hands?"

"To spite them. To show them that even after they've taken everything from us, we can still make a mess of their world. And besides," Carad quickly added, "it helps the narrative."

"What narrative?"

"That the humans have gone so far left field that they let a Sparcus—not even one of their own—murder members of every other civilization. They covered for a Sparcus. Isn't that disgusting? Would you not be disgusted if a Sparcus agency covered for a human?" Vigor saw the twisted logic. But all of it was still unbelievable.

"What about Sarza?"

"What about her?"

"Why Sarza?"

"She was a bonus. Agent Venta had a history of . . . asking to be paired with Sparcus. Maybe a way to make up for his mother's roots, or a way to connect with her. I don't know. Unresolved mother issues. But he chose her. So we had her assigned to the case. End of story."

Vigor couldn't stop himself. "She can't be just a random victim of this plan!"

"Of course she can. In fact, she is." Carad paused. "I'm sorry for your loss Vigor." Carad turned around and walked away. The finality of her words made Vigor shake.

BOOK I
CHAPTER 11

The judge shushed the audience in the courtroom for the twentieth time that day. Crowds of people attended every day to watch Wes stand trial. It was one of the most entertaining events of all time — to the public at least. Every day Wes looked into the audience, wondering if Sarza would show up, but she didn't. Part of him was relieved, while the other fell utterly abandoned. It would have been nice to have one friendly face who knew he wasn't guilty. Sometimes he wondered if she had been in on this all along. He tried to put the pieces together, and sometimes they fit, sometimes they didn't. For example, he had spent hours figuring out how he had been assigned to this case — given that he had followed Sarza and not the other way around. He had volunteered to be Sarza's handler after her previous one was killed. Was that a setup? Did they know he would do that? Probably not. *She* had been assigned to the case, and he had followed. So maybe she *didn't* know about any of this?

215

He looked up from the witness chair, a plastic armchair with a joke of a pillow on the bottom. His ass could feel the hard, flat surface. He knew these were going to be two painful days. Although not as painful as the last month he had had to endure at the hands of Sparcus guards, conveniently working for IPP Earth, and assigned to "keep an eye on him."

His mind wandered back to the regular, merciless beatings. He had lain on the floor of his cell, wishing for death. The taste of blood in the back of his throat was no longer surprising. He had, at first, refused to comply with their demands. He wasn't going to admit to crimes that he had not committed. The beatings had become increasingly violent. He remembered lying there as the Sparcus guard used a caterpillar prod to hit him in the back, the stomach, the knees, and the elbows. Then his two Sparcus IPP guards had resorted to outright torture. He could still hear his screaming reverberate through the halls as they ran utterly unbearable but completely safe currents through his body. It didn't matter that he knew it wasn't actually damaging him and couldn't kill him. He would have done nearly anything to make it stop. Except confess. The point was to torture him without leaving traces of it, and they had done an admirable job. On the surface, he looked great, but on the inside, his joints barely worked and he could feel every muscle and every bruise on his back and torso.

After weeks of this, he was sitting in his cell once again, waiting for another round to come down on him, when he saw something worse than anything he had experienced up until then. His two guards walked by his cell, without even turning to him, with his father between them. He wasn't sure where he had been all of this time, but his understanding was that he had been released after Wes turned himself in. How they had found out who his father was or where he was living was unclear, but people talked. Maybe someone from Nash'amir had said something? This thought made Wes fear for Nana's safety, wondering whether they had harmed her as well.

It had taken one muffled groan from next door. He wasn't even sure if it came from his father, but it didn't matter. And the guards knew that. Every time he would hear someone in pain, somewhere within earshot, he would think it was him, and that was enough to break him. The next time his Sparcus guards came in, they started their usual routine: "Are you ready to confess?" That time, sitting on the floor, his face looking down, Wes answered, "Yes." They never hit him again.

It was the first time he was in court. Apparently, they didn't need him to sit through his own trial. The government—the people he had worked with for years—argued he was too much of a flight risk, had known allies both on Nash'amir and Astarte, and there was a good chance that someone would attempt to "disrupt the orderly process of justice" if he was allowed to attend every day. But the instinct for purported safety was far weaker than the desire to make a spectacle of his conviction. His willingness to confess had made it all the more interesting that he testify "live" from the courthouse. His counselor, assigned by the government, had kept him apprised of the testimony from a variety of witnesses, some of whom he had never met, some who had processed crime scenes, corroborating his involvement in each crime. He had been made to watch recordings of testimony by other agents, IPP agents, who had investigated the various scenes. He thought back to Velin IPP Agent Brock's testimony.

"Mr. Brock, when did you arrive at the crime scene for Necrological Reviewer Caragan?" The government counselor—Jack Mora—asked, knowing the answer.

"We received a call that there had been a murder so we, my partner and I, went as soon as possible." His voice had the monotone factual timber all police officers were taught to take on the stand.

"What did you find when you arrived?"

"We found the defendant, Mr. Venta, at the scene. He had been there a while." According to his attorney, Mr. Mora purposefully instructed his witnesses to refer to Wes as Mr. Venta, not Agent Venta, to make him sound less official and avoid the natural respect many people felt for figures of authority.

"Objection. Speculation. He doesn't know how long he was there," his counselor objected.

The judge's voice ruled, "Sustained as to the timing. Everything else stays in."

"Was anyone else with him?" Mora continued.

"No. He was the only person at the scene."

"Were there any signs that other people had been at the scene with him?"

"No."

"What was the first thing you noticed about the murder scene?"

"The victim was lying in the bed, in a pool. He had not been dead very long."

"Was a crime scene analysis performed?"

"Yes."

"And what was found?"

"The defendant's palm and finger prints were all over the furniture, the walls, and the bed."

Sitting in the counselor-detainee meeting room of the New York prison, Wes had cringed at that. It now made sense why he couldn't access the crime scene reports. Every one of them had been doctored to make him look as though he was present at the scene. In fact, in this particular case, he *had* been the first on the scene, and he had never admitted to Sarza being with him because of protocol. The whole thing had been beautifully orchestrated to leave him absolutely screwed. Moments like these, he wondered how much Sarza had known. How much she had played him. How much their afternoon on Astarte had been nothing but an elaborate ploy in making him feel like she was being "vulnerable" to him.

Then he remembered her hair—the part of her that couldn't lie—and he found some comfort.

Wes had also watched testimony by a Bar'aat agent, Agent Calax, in charge of reviewing the arms dealer's home. He had an eerily similar description of the evidence: Wes's fingerprints were everywhere, and there was no evidence of anyone else being there, except for Sarza, of course.

"What did you find, Agent Calax?"

"I found traces of a Sparcus and a human."

"Could you identify the Sparcus?"

"Yes."

"Who was she?"

"Sarza Beshemet."

"And the human?"

"The defendant, Agent . . . Mr. Wes Venta."

"What traces did you find?"

"Palm prints and fingerprints. And witnesses said they saw two individuals flying away from the home, which was consistent with the Sparcus and the defendant flying away after the murder."

"Was there anything else?"

"Yes. The timing of the vehicles leaving the scene and the time of the murder were consistent."

Wes remembered Sarza arriving in his apartment with the deskrock. In fact, the Bar'aat who had helped him retrieve information from the deskrock had also testified. It was damning that a day after the Bar'aat being killed, Wes had brought the victim's belongings to Earth. And again, Sarza had been involved. She had handed him the damning evidence. It was hard not to hate her. Some moments, he hated her so much he couldn't breathe, the rage blinding him. He hated her so much that he would have done the Sparcus a favor and killed her on sight—if it was even true there was an execution warrant out for her. That was probably a sham too. But the hatred usually disappeared when he thought about *her*. When her features came into focus. When he remembered her fighting along his side on Terra. When he remembered her getting shot on Nash'amir. When he remembered their afternoon on Astarte. And then, the hatred would evaporate leaving him exhausted and hollow.

But today, today was the climax of the trial. The murderer, the killer, the monster himself was going to make his first appearance. The Sparcus guards had told him exactly what he was supposed to say. He was supposedly in custody of Earth, but the intermingling of Sparcus agents in IPP forces made the distinction non-existent.

Wes's counselor — Anabel Swan — stood up. Wes had told her he was going to confess. He didn't explain why or how. She was a wiry, unattractive, fair-skinned woman with short brown hair that barely reached her cheekbones. When she stood, her stomach protruded outwards like a small balloon. She was fairly smart, knew how to do her job, but understood that she had been presented with an impossible task. Wes had no resentment. She was doing the best she could — like he was. Swan had tried to talk him out of it, tried convincing him not to take the stand, but Wes was steadfast. Swan could do absolutely nothing to dissuade him.

Wes saw his father sitting in the first row of the audience. His heart lifted. He was safe, he was out of jail, and he looked okay. He smiled at him, tears welling up in both their eyes. They hadn't spoken since that day on Terra.

"Mr. Venta, can you please introduce yourself to the court?"

"I am Agent Wes Venta, former IPP Agent from Earth."

"Who is your father?"

"My father is Carl O'Callagan."

"What species is he?"

"Human."

"Where does he live?"

"On the planet Corsini." These questions were supposed to humanize him and his family. Wes wasn't sure it would work.

"What about your mother?"

"She died."

"Yes Agent Venta, but who was she?"

"Vadama Pax."

"What species was she?"

"She was a . . ." Wes looked at his father. "She was a Sparcus." The crowd gasped and groaned. There was more shushing, hissing, and then a voice rose from the audience, "You bastard Sparcus. Kill the Sparcus! Kill the Sparcus!" A woman was quickly ushered out of the courtroom while the judge tried to impose order.

"Mr. Venta, are you trying to say that your parents are a Sparcus and a human?"

"Yes." Wes knew where this was going, and he really didn't want to give anyone the satisfaction of rolling out his personal life for them. But apparently this was something that had to come out. "The man who raised me is not my biological father. But he is my father. He raised me. My mother . . . I was conceived at a . . . the man who made my mother pregnant was a Sparcus. I don't know who he was." There it was: a piece of salacious Earth gossip. Wes thought back to his father, the human, falling in love with an already pregnant Sparcus woman. Wes had grown up knowing he was conceived at a Bashbathar. And he didn't care. On Astarte it would have made absolutely no difference. It was a common occurrence. And communities usually raised the children anyway. On Earth, it was worthy to be introduced at a murder trial. Someone wanted to make this a very interesting event.

"You were raised on Nash'amir?"

"Objection. Leading." Mora stood up briefly.

"Overruled." The judge waved to him to sit down. He turned to Wes. "You may answer."

"Yes."

"Why?"

I don't know why this has anything to do with anything and you can all go fuck yourselves. That would have been Wes's answer. But he swallowed hard and said, "My parents decided to be discrete. And Sparcus . . . it would have been difficult for a human and a Sparcus to raise a child together." He looked at his father again. The man's face was smiling just a little. Wes recognized that look. He was thinking about his mother and their love, and the beauty of what they had had together before she died. Wes felt chills of emotion run down his shoulders.

"Mr. Venta, you are being charged with the murder of a Braxian agent."

"Yes."

"Do you have evidence that you traveled to Hatuu-oh around the time of the murder?"

"No."

"Can you tell us why you killed the Braxian?"

"No." The Sparcus had not even bothered to give him a motive. In fact, he only had "motive" for a few of the murders, according to their story. He looked up at his counselor. She was really doing her best. Working against him *and* the government.

"Mr. Venta, you are being charged with the murder of a Necrological Reviewer on Sulpuro."

"Objection. Leading." The government attorney objected.

"Sustained. I don't see where this is going, counselor," the judge interjected. It made little sense for a defense counselor to go down this route.

Swan tried a different approach. "What happened while you were on Sulpuro?"

"I found the Necrological Reviewer who had investigated the Braxian. I killed him so he wouldn't talk."

"How did you kill him?"

"I used Sparcus Gloves." His counselor, who had been standing at the table, looked up, surprised. That wasn't in the file and wasn't part of what they had discussed. It wasn't even part of what the Sparcus had told him. But Wes knew it was true, so he stuck by it. It was consistent with the cause of death.

"Where did you get Sparcus gloves?"

"From the Bar'aat I killed." Swan was sweating profusely. She was watching a suicide. No—worse—she was assisting a suicide. She gave it one more try.

"Mr. Venta, isn't it true that when you left the human handler on Hatuu-oh, he was still alive?"

"No. I slit his throat on my way out." The lunacy of it was so outrageous that Wes stopped feeling anything when he said the words.

"Mr. Venta!" His counselor's voice trembled.

Wes kept his hands clasped, hanging between his open knees, looking at the floor. Finally, she turned to the judge. "No more questions your honor." She sat down and stared at the papers in front of her.

The government's lawyer stood up. He wore a grey suit. It was antiquated, the type of thing people wore two hundred years ago. For some reason, lawyers had held on to these costumes while the rules of fashion changed around them. He also wore a tie—a totally unnecessary object that did absolutely nothing useful.

"Mr. Venta," he took on a very professional air, as though this was a challenge of some kind. Wes wondered if the prosecutor was in on it too, or if he was just another pawn. "I want to discuss Mr. Mi-it of Nash'amir."

Wes's heart started pounding. He knew this was coming, but admitting to killing children made him sick.

"Do you know who he was?"

"Yes." He was not being flippant this time.

"Who was he?"

"An Ishtar man."

"How do you know him?"

"He was . . . he was married to an Ishtar covert agent." He had not known that until his time in prison. The Sparcus guards had given him this information, made sure it stayed in his head with a few gratuitous beatings, and reminded him—repeatedly—to testify about it when on the stand. At the mention of Nash'amir, Wes thought back to the week he had spent with Sarza. The memory soothed him, and then the anger came back. He had been such an idiot.

"How did you know her?"

His memory failed him for a moment. What had he been told? He breathed out, closed his eyes, and tried to remember the lecture the Sparcus guard had given him. What was it? He looked up at his father. Two IPP agents standing on either side of the room moved a step closer to him as he sat in the audience. Wes's heart started racing. He had to remember. He *had* to remember.

"She . . ." *Shit! Who was she?* "She . . . Oh! Yes." Wes looked up at the two people in the crowd, and then at his father. "She knew about the murder on Hatuu-oh. So I was trying to threaten her. To get her to be silent."

"Can you take us through the events of that day?"

"I arrived on Nash'amir. I found their home. He was there with the young ones. So I killed all of them." Wes thought back to the scene. The young ones were so helpless in the face of their death, and their father had been unable to protect them. Their small bodies were strewn around the tent. Their small hands, small fingers, small feet, small tails all lay there motionless. He felt a wave of nausea sweep over him as he admitted to these crimes. He bent over and threw up between his legs. The audience murmured. He looked up, trembling. He thought the torture had been the hardest part. Now, he wasn't so sure. The government attorney pushed on without missing a beat.

"Why did you kill Samuel Kensington of Brax?"

"We were having an affair with the same woman. I caught them together on Sulpuro."

"Who is the woman?"

"She was a Corsini woman."

"The same Corsini woman you attempted to murder?"

"Yes." He had never even seen her face. He still—to this day—didn't know who she was. But apparently, someone had tried to kill her and she had gotten away. Wes wondered if she would live much longer. He hoped, for her, she had not seen her assailant's face. If she had, whoever was behind this would get back at her and make her disappear.

"Are you aware that the same woman committed suicide last night?"

"No." Wes had his answer. "I was not aware of that." Maybe the first inkling of truth in his whole testimony.

"What about the Kerouac woman? Another mistress?"

"Objection! Argumentative." Wes had to give it to his counselor. She was trying her best in the face of absolute defeat. She kept on doing her job.

"Sustained." The judge showed no emotion.

"Who was the Kerouac woman?"

"A covert IPP agent."

"Who killed her?"

"I did." This must have been the easiest cross-examination in the history of cross-examinations. There wasn't a question he wasn't willing—or obligated—to answer. And every answer was exactly what the counselor wanted to hear.

"Why?"

"She was very close friends with Samuel . . . Samuel . . ." He blanked on the last name. "The Braxian." He was tired, so tired he felt his body was falling apart.

"*He has a name Mr. Venta!*" the counselor bellowed, proud to have caught the vicious murderer acting callous about his victims. "His name was Samuel Kensington, and he had a family Mr. Venta!"

"*Objection*! Argumentative." Swan was none too happy.

"Overruled." Then, to Mora, "Keep the commentary to yourself, Mr. Mora."

The Sparcus had shown Wes photos of the Kerouac, in case it came up. She had, in fact, been very close friends with the Braxian. It was one of those unexpected friendships. The whole thing had been such a perfect fabrication. These people had died simply because they happened to have relationships that made enough sense to create a perfect murder plot.

"That doesn't answer my question. How did her friendship make you want to kill her?"

I don't have a fucking clue you asshole. I don't know. Fuck you! Wes was staring at him. His eyes probably did look murderous at that point. He had done his part, he was doing what he was supposed to, but they were asking him to be part of a farce. A ludicrous, nonsensical farce.

"She was . . ." Wes breathed in deeply, held his breath and exhaled slowly, trying to control his fear and anger. "I . . . she was at the home of the Corsini when I got there. She was asking her about Samuel so . . . she had to go." Just like that. The crime scene photos flashed in his head. The Kerouac's body lay there, her torso blown apart in the middle of the Corsini's living room. Wes wondered how she had gotten there. Why had she gone there in the first place? Maybe she was visiting the Corsini woman to give her condolences. It didn't really matter.

"Did you have an accomplice?" Mora asked.

"No."

"You were the handler for another IPP agent, am I right?"

"Yes."

"What is her name?"

"Sarza Beshemet."

"What was the nature of your relationship?"

"We . . ." This had not been part of the script. "I was her handler and that's it."

"Were you romantically involved?"

"No." *Yes! Kind of. Maybe. I was romantically involved because I'm a dumbass.*

"Was she with you during your investigation?"

"Yes."

"Was she your accomplice in the murders?"

Wes hesitated. He wanted to throw her under the bus so bad. *But what if she had nothing to do with this?* That doubt had kept him sane through some of the darkest times at the hands of the Sparcus. What if she had been exactly like she had appeared? Conflicted, attracted, sometimes protective, and maybe even attached to him?

"No." He wasn't going to lie. "No. She wasn't." Wes glanced at the two IPP figures. They weren't moving closer to his father. Apparently, he was allowed to keep Sarza out of this. Or maybe it didn't matter. Nobody believed him anyway. The government counselor looked dejected. Everything else had panned out so well. But he pressed on, changing topic.

"You are a Sparcus, right?" To damn him, to damn him again, to bring this up in every which way possible. Mr. Mora would do this for hours if he could. Because by just being a Sparcus, he was guilty. And by being a Sparcus who had dared to hide his origins, he deserved to die. Murders be damned, all that mattered was his mother's ancestry.

"Objection! Relevance." Wes had nearly forgotten his counselor sitting at her table.

"Your honor, opposing counselor raised this in direct. I'm entitled to cross on it."

The judge looked at both attorneys. "Ms. Swan, you did talk about this with your witness. You can't object to Mr. Mora discussing the same topics. You know that. Overruled."

"Mr. Venta, you are a Sparcus, right?"

"Yes." There was no reaction from the audience.

"But you have lied about your nature your entire life, correct?"

"My entire adult life." Wes looked at his father. His father, with his grey shoulder-length hair, looked back him. There was so much love and pain in that man's face, Wes felt they were talking to each other rather than to a roomful of strangers.

"You lied about it to get into the IPP, right?"

"Yes."

"Mr. Venta, did the IPP know you were a Sparcus when they hired you?"

"No. I don't think so."

"Did they ever inquire about your past?"

"Yes. I told them I was a human. And my father is a human. So it made sense."

"When you turned eighteen, you asked for your record to be sealed, am I right?"

"Yes."

"Why?"

"To protect my father." He choked on those words, remembering watching his foces to his knees in the middle of the plaza on Corsini and then later escorted to a sordid cell. He had done anything but protect him.

"Why did you join the IPP?"

"To . . . to serve peace." Wes turned his eyes to Mora. This was another piece of truth that nobody gave a shit about, no doubt.

"Isn't it a fact that you joined the IPP to infiltrate us as a Sparcus?"

Wes was about to deny it, but the two IPP agents in the room moved closer to his father, staring directly at Wes. "Yes?" The two people stopped moving, "Yes. Yes!"

"Isn't it true that you were aided in your infiltration efforts by Earth?"

This was ludicrous and unnecessary. He didn't answer, but he once again saw the two figures shift inward.

"Isn't it true that the Captain—conveniently executed by the Sparcus—assisted you in your efforts?"

Wes was utterly confused. Nobody had discussed the Captain. Nobody had discussed his origins. In fact, he didn't know anyone was aware of his mother's race or his ancestry until he was captured on Terra. And the Captain had certainly never known about it. "Yes?" It was a question because he really didn't know what they wanted from him.

"Isn't it true that the Sparcus agent, Sarza Beshemet, was actually helping you?" Wes looked at Mora in disbelief. What was the point of trying to create an alliance that defied all logic, all sense, and that defied thirty years of history? An alliance that didn't exist!

"I don't know." Wes looked at his father, who had been silently asked to stand up by the two agents. They quickly escorted him out of the courtroom, one on each side. Wes didn't know if it was what he had said. "Yes? Maybe. I don't know. She may have been helping me. I don't know. Yes." But apparently it was over. Mora ended, "No further questions," and sat down. The noise in the room became deafening. The two hundred and fifty people were all talking, shouting, and arguing. Some directed their comments at him. The judge pressed a button on his desk, emitting a very loud, painful blare. The room went quiet. Some people were holding their ears.

"Quiet! Do you hear me? Quiet in the courtroom." Wes looked up at the ceiling, then back the floor where his vomit had begun to solidify. It stank. He had not even thought about it up until then, but it really did stink. He shifted his feet away from it to avoid dirtying his prison-issued moccasins. The counselors both stood up. The judge looked at them. "Are you ready for closing?"

"Yes your honor," they answered in unplanned unison.

"Very well. After lunch."

The government counselor stepped forward a little. "What about the prisoner?"

"He is returning to his cell, as agreed." Wes wasn't even listening. He was thinking about his father. He had given them what they had asked for—nearly. He hoped this would work. The Sparcus had not just asked for his admission of guilt. They had asked for a conviction. If he did not get convicted—highly unlikely at this point—they would kill his father. It was a perfect way to obtain absolute compliance.

A court officer was behind him, helping him to his feet. He had trouble walking. His knees gave way. He pushed on them and tried to get up. He sat back down. The officer thought he was faking. "Get up."

"I can't." Wes looked at him straight in the eyes. "I can't." He looked back at the floor. This was humiliating. The officer was of slight build. There was no way he could carry Wes's mass of muscles. Even after weeks in prison, he was still far better built than humans.

The officer waved for a colleague to come over and assist. She was sturdier than her male counterpart. They put their hands under his armpits and lifted him. With a little support from either side, he was able to make it to the courtroom floor. The two attorneys were still standing there, watching him move slowly. He walked by his counselor.

"Your honor. May I have a few moments to talk to my client?"

The judge puckered his mouth. "Sure." The two officers let go of Wes. He strained a little, but caught himself on the table with his hands and was able to stay standing. They stepped back. Swan leaned in. "Why did you do this?"

"Is it over?"

"What?"

"Can you do anything else to fix this?"

"No! I'm done Wes. Evidence is closed. And we are not allowed to re-open. This afternoon is a formality."

"Good."

"Why?"

"Just let me go. I'm tired. Just let me go back to prison."

"Wes!"

Wes shook his head and gestured to the two officers to come get him. They came to him, pulled his arms behind his back, and re-activated his magnetic bracelets. With one on each wrist exerting magnetic attraction to the other, he couldn't move his hands apart unless someone deactivated them. Once they were done, they resumed holding him under the arms and walked out of the courtroom. He was using his legs, which he was surprised he could still do. He had imagined his knees exploding every time they were hit with the tip of a boot. But apparently, they were still there and (of all things) functional. As they passed the doors of the courtroom, reporters and members of the public gathered, waiting for his statement. There was nothing for him to say. His two helpers, to his credit, kept walking, pushing everyone aside. The progress was slow. Wes kept looking at the floor, focusing on his legs and feet. They finally reached the back of the building. Two massive metal doors slid to the sides as one of the officers swiped a badge. The prisoner hovercraft was waiting for them. The rear doors opened. There were two pilots sitting at the front, but Wes could not see them clearly. The prisoner hovercraft was a large white cylinder on its side. On the front was a cone-like cabin that held three guards. The back of the silo was a transparent bubble that lifted itself to let prisoners in and out. The bubble allowed everyone to see what was going on, and was resistant to almost any weapon.

As the bubble lifted and the officers prepared to load Wes onto the transporter, the earth shook with a deafening explosion. Then another one followed. Ten or fifteen fighter planes flew overhead, shooting at buildings, people, and transporters. Everyone looked up. Smoke filled the sky. Wes could hear screams of terror and people running around aimlessly, trying to find cover. Sonic booms reverberated through the buildings. He couldn't tell which booms went with which attack crafts, the sky was so full of them, running amok. A squadron of ten or fifteen Bar'aat attack crafts, Vighnas, flew overhead, slow enough so Wes could identify them, but still so fast they were above him for just a fraction of time. More explosions could be heard at a distance. Then something blew up the building across the street. The earth shook again, and shards of material spread everywhere. They were at the back of the building in an area little bigger than an alley. Wes couldn't see much of what was going on in the streets. But he, instinctively, bent into himself, trying to protect his face. His thoughts were racing. Where was his father? He had hoped his father had been moved out of the courthouse to scare Wes. Now he was hoping that he had actually been transported somewhere. Maybe he was still safe. He saw no other transporters around him.

"What the fuck is going on?" One of the two officers muttered. If Wes had any strength, he would have started running. The two officers were distracted enough to let him get across the *planet* before they realized he was gone. But he had no strength. He heard the front of the prisoner transporter open. He saw the black and brown Sparcus guard boots—the ones that had kicked him so many times—walk toward them. He looked up. These weren't the same legs. Those weren't the same hips. He had his guards' two bodies seared into his mind. His eyes traveled upward searching for the face he hoped—he really hoped—to find. Sarza stood in front of them, her black hair whipping in the wind, her purple eyes glad to see him.

BOOK I
CHAPTER 12

"We'll take it from here." Sarza sounded so self-assured. Wes started shaking in relief. The anger was gone. The resentment against Sarza's imagined betrayals vanished. He knew instantly — he hoped — that she was there to save him. "Please load him." She had all the authority of a woman in charge, but her voice also had a soft edge to it. She was being charming for the two people at his sides. Without a word, they handed him over to her. Wes fell forward, and she caught him.

"The scum can't walk. Good luck with that." The two officers disappeared, trying to look for cover.

"How bad is it?" Sarza whispered, holding Wes up and trying to put him in the back of the prisoner transport.

"Pretty bad. I can barely walk. My arms don't fold well." Sarza didn't answer. She was still trying to help Wes into the back of the transporter. He sat on the edge, pulled his legs up, and moved toward one of the walls. There were no benches.

Prisoners just sat on the floor. As he pushed himself back, he bumped into something.

"Don't mind them. I took care of them for you." Wes turned around as much as he possibly could twist and saw the bodies of four Sparcus guards—the two who "guarded him" and the two who drove there. They were lying in the front of the prisoner transporter, their throats slit from side to side. Their eyes were still open, staring blankly at the roof of the vehicle. Blood covered their necks. Two of them, the two women, had been stripped. This was why he had recognized Sarza's uniform. Wes felt overwhelmed with unprecedented gratitude toward Sarza. Even if he would have preferred being there to watch his tormenters die, he was glad she had taken care of them for him. She had vindicated some of his pain. He looked at her, speechless.

While he reviewed her handiwork, Sarza was busy using the de-activator on her prison guard outfit to release Wes's hands. She used one of the dead guard's fingers for fingertip recognition, and the small grey innocuous looking box lit up. She held it against Wes's wrists. Not only did the bracelets release each other, but they fell on the floor of the transporter in four metallic semi circles. After flinging the prison guard's limp arm back over the dead body, she reached into her own pocket and pulled out an elongated pen-like object with a sucker at the end. She slapped it onto his thigh, and he felt the sting of a shot from the needle inside the sucker. She then pulled out another one from her belt and shot his other leg.

"What are they?"

"A very strong pain killer. And a very, very strong stimulant. Your heart is in for a ride." Sarza smiled at him as the bubble closed down between them, and she was gone. The vehicle started moving. Relief started to wash over him. He dropped his head between his knees, breathing deeper, taking in as much air as he could. He felt his strength come back with every breath. And he didn't know if it was because he was about to be free or because she had come back for him. The explosions outside quickly pulled him out of his thoughts and back into reality. He could hear the sonic booms as planes soared by overhead. The van swerved, throwing him onto one side, then swerved again, throwing him to the other. He let out a groan as his whole body reminded him of the beatings it had survived. As the side of the van took a hit, Wes realized they weren't just avoiding random gunfire. They were avoiding shots fired *at* them. His heart started pounding, and his hands began to shake. The stimulant was taking effect.

Sarza and Sasha, the Ishtar redhead that had saved both of them on Terra, jumped out of their seats at the front of the vehicle and ran to the gaping hole that had just been blasted into the prisoner compartment. Wes hadn't been hit. He reached for them, moving his body as best he could. He expected pain, but was glad to find the medication had taken effect. He could move. They each grabbed one of his hands and pulled him out. As soon as he was out, he pushed on his knees. To his surprise, they held. The destruction and mayhem around them was astounding.

"Are they shooting *at* us?" Wes wasn't quite sure.

"Maybe. You *are* a wanted man, Wes. And not just on Earth. Everyone wants a piece of you." Sarza looked around for a split second, trying to get her bearings. Then, the two women started running, taking cover in an alley. Wes tried to keep up.

"Where are we going? And why *maybe*? What else are they shooting at?" Wes wasn't sure if there was another part to this plan. But his training and instincs were kicking in. He stopped asking questions and concentrated on keeping up with the women, while ducking from debris.

Sarza stopped running abruptly. A blast behind them, on the other side of town had just created a multi-storey high explosion visible fro mwhere they stood. Then she turned her attention to the redhead. "Sasha?"

Sasha tightened her grip on Wes. "I think Mika and Pen are a go. Jenna and Slitter are going to have to pull out on their own. Hopefully Vera can hold onto her position until we all make it there. We need to get out before the blockade."

Sarza didn't miss a beat. "Okay. Mika and Pen are on." She turned to Wes. "They were waiting for us somewhere else in case we couldn't make it this far." Sarza pointed at the storm of dust created by explosion they had just witnessed, indicating their fellow warriors were on that side of town. Wes didn't have time to answer. A fighter craft—Braxian from the symmetrical blue markings on the bottom—flew low overhead, shooting short bursts of lasers into the street, the buildings, and the remains of civilian hovercrafts on the ground. The three of them ducked and the two women began running, nearly carrying Wes's body across the street. He was trying to keep up in vain. Nobody was after them, but it didn't seem to matter. The explosions were continuous, and the destruction stayed constant. Wes watched as the New York buildings he had grown semi-accustomed to over the years crumbled while people ran helplessly around in the conflict.

The adrenaline finally started pumping, overriding the pain and discomfort. He pushed on his legs and started running alone. He felt the two women let go, but they slowed down to let him keep up. They were in an alley. Wes had no idea where they were going, but Sasha and Sarza seemed to be headed somewhere in particular. He kept going, oblivious to everything else, his heart beating through his chest, the strength coming back, and hope filling him. He didn't know how long they had been running. Sarza kept looking back to make sure he was keeping up. They took a quick right, then a left, then another right. They found a Nego-Pod sitting peacefully in a tiny cul de sac. There was barely enough space for it. Sarza pressed her hand on it causing it to open. Before Wes could voice his opinion—demanding to stay by their side, telling them it was lunacy to stay behind—the two women pushed him into it. He was protesting, but the Nego-Pod closing on him, drowning his voice. As he took off, Wes caught a glimpse of his two saviors disappearing back into the alley. Then he was gone.

Moments later, he landed in a desert plane. Wes recognized it. They were in Jornada del Muerto. More specifically, they were using one of the oldest spaceports on Earth, "Spaceport America." There was chaos all around him. Citizens were running to their transporters with bags of belongings, loading up children, pets, and the elderly, and trying to get off the planet as fast as possible. Most of them, he thought, were probably headed for either Earth 2 or the moon. Or—if they could—further. A Sparcus Vex-2 was also parked there. The Vex-2 was the same shape as a Vex but far larger, holding up to eight to ten people. Mika, the pale-skinned blond Sparcus from Terra, was already there. The Nego-Pod opened. Mika reached in and started helping Wes out. Jenna, her ubiquitous sword on her back, was right behind. Wes, signaling he could handle it, pushed out of the gel capsule and stood on his own.

"Hello Jenna." He nodded at one of them, then at the other. "Mika."

"Hello Wes." Mika smiled at him as she helped him out. Without another word, the trio jogged toward the Vex-2, dodging frantic humans. Its door opened toward the outside, revealing a staircase along the inside of the door. Without slowing down, they climbed the stairs and made it into the Vex-2. It was spacious, with four private quarters, each holding two people. A hall connected all four quarters and led to the front cabin, which included a pilot's chair, a co-pilot's chair, and six auxiliary seats—four on each side at the back of the cabin.

"Where is Sarza?" Wes noticed the women preparing for launch.

"She is meeting us somewhere else." Mika was taking the pilot's seat.

"Where?"

"Up there." she pointed up at the sky.

"But where is she now?"

Jenna slid in the seat next to Mika. "She went back to get your father."

Wes inhaled slowly. He didn't like this. Whatever relief he had felt was gone. Leaving Earth not knowing whether Sarza had made it off the planet wasn't reassuring. He also wanted to ask more questions. But that would make him get in the way. So all he could do right now was be quiet and trust them.

Jenna was preparing the vehicle for launch. She sensed the concern. "If we don't get your father, you won't be safe. They can pull you back in any time. So in order to save you, we have to save him." Jenna paused for a beat. "And your mother wouldn't forgive us for leaving him."

Mika turned to look at Wes standing in the cabin. "Go rest. Go lay down in a bed. We got this."

Wes was in no mood to lie down. The stimulant had him wired. He settled for sitting in one of the auxiliary seats, although even sitting seemed very passive. As soon as he sat down, four straps pulled out of the seat, crossed over his chest and each of his legs, holding him perfectly in place. The Vex-2 came to life, rumbling and shaking a little. Then, the g-forces took over and pressed him down while the machine lifted itself into space. The ship made a vertical takeoff until the boosters took over and propelled the craft straight into space, leaving Earth at a ninety-degree angle. He looked at the two women in front of him. His mother had trained them and looked after them. She had actively recruited both Sparcus and Ishtar women, because she believed warriors were warriors, regardless of heritage. And because falling in love in a prem made recruitment by a Sparcus somewhat problematic. They had fought alongside each other, although they had been mere teenagers when his mother was already an adult.

They had been in and out of his home since he was a child, but he knew they had always been there for her and would always be there for him. The bond they had with the great Vadama Pax was unbreakable, despite the fact that she had fallen in prem with a human. They had always cherished and respected her as their leader.

The sky went from light to dark blue, and then to black, as they left Earth behind. Hundreds of thousands of personal transporters dotted the skies, moving upwards, marking the scattering of human beings fleeing to planets other than Earth in search of safety. He looked up ahead and saw two Vexes flying in front of them. A voice came through the in-cabin speaker.

"Medea to Hekate, status?"

"Cax." That was Sarza's voice, confirming receipt of the radio message. "Hekate has Carl. I repeat, Hekate has Carl. He's fine. He was in another transporter, right next to Wes's." Wes leaned back into his seat. "Hello son." Hearing his father's voice was more than Wes could have dreamed of. Whatever doubts he'd had about Sarza, they were all gone. All he wanted to do now was hold her, and then some.

"Medea to Lilith, status?"

"Cax. Lilith to Medea. Ready." That was Slitter, the Ishtar with the scar on her face.

Wes turned to Jenna and asked, "Has she been with you the whole time?"

Jenna didn't need him to explain who "she" was. "Yes." Her blue eyes stayed fixated on the horizon. "We had to upgrade her training. She's got more work to do, but she has potential." Wes smiled. He looked down at his hands on his knees and then back up into space. Mika adjusted the ship's course and Earth became visible on one side of the craft. Wes's eyes widened in disbelief and horror as he saw the blue dot under attack. Large war vessels from every imaginable planet had locked into a geosynchronous orbit around his adopted home. Smaller crafts were going in and coming back, peppering the skies. Large war ships were stationing themselves in low earth orbit, creating a blockade. A few more moments and they probably wouldn't have made it out.

Wes leaned forward. "What is going on?" He had been too busy trying to save himself until now to ask. "What is this?"

"The Second Great Conflict, Wes."

"What? Why?" He couldn't formulate more articulate questions.

Jenna sighed. "The others can explain it better. The politics of this are not my thing." They flew in silence for a while as Wes watched in horror. The planet and its attackers faded from view as the three Sparcus vehicles flew side by side. Mika broke the silence, "Tensions have been high. The trial made everything worse. And war broke out. I really can't explain it more than that. But the other eight are setting up a blockade around Earth. We, literally, got you out just in time."

Jenna muttered, "It actually helped us." She shifted in her seat. She wore a dark grey see-through Sparcus tunic. A black cincher around her waist held a sword across her back. She was trying to readjust to allow the sword to fall more comfortably along her seat.

"True."

Wes thought about that, but he couldn't put it together. "Why? Why did it help us?"

"Everyone is too busy attacking Earth to care about the Sparcus. And Earth wasn't prepared for this. They're always so unprepared . . ." Mika didn't turn around as she said this. "We thought everyone would be coming for you. As it turns out, there were bigger fish to fry today."

Jenna, however, continued, "Getting you out was the most crucial thing. Everyone was heading for the court as soon as your appearance was confirmed. But we got there before the others."

Mika muttered, "Barely."

Wes wasn't quite sure he understood. "Why were they trying to get *me*?"

"Every species wants you tried and executed on their own terms. In prison, you were unreachable. But as soon as you left the gates . . ." Mika was still trying to get them away from Earth as fast as possible.

Wes knew he didn't have to thank any of them. He knew they would be there no matter what. But the debt of gratitude had always, and always would, weigh on him like a tremendous honor he needed to live up to.

Slitter's voice came up on the coms. "Uncloaking Big Tu." A larger craft—a Nash'amir Ambo-42—appeared, floating peacefully in mid-space. "Welcome home ladies." A man's voice crackled on the coms. Wes recognized it but couldn't quite place it. An opening the size of several buildings was sealed with a force field. The field disappeared, allowing the Vex and the two Vex-2s to land in the Ambo's hangar. The force field reactivated as soon as they were in, while panels slid in from the sides, sealing it shut. The green lights on the Vex consoles indicated the presence of adequate ambient pressure and breathable air. All three Vexes opened. Wes stood up and walked out of the Vex-2. Sarza was reaching the bottom of the stairs of the other Vex-2 parked alongside his. Wes stopped a few meters from her. She looked in control and unshakeable. Her hair wasn't changing color. It just stayed there, black, straight, and still.

"Hi Wes." Her voice was gentler than he remembered.

"Hi Sarza."

Pen walked up to them. Her green eyes and blond hair were still as striking as ever against her dark skin. "Sarza, can you take Wes to his cabin. He needs to rest."

Wes turned to her. "And my father?"

"I'm right here." Wes turned around. He threw his arms around the man who had raised him and held him tight. The two of them stood in their embrace a few moments. As they pulled apart, Wes turned toward Sarza.

"Dad, you met Sarza. Sarza, this is Carl, my father."

"Yes. You can dispense with the introductions. She carried me for ten blocks." Sarza smiled at him and then at Wes.

"Did they hurt you?"

"No." Wes wasn't sure if his father was lying or not.

"When I was in jail I heard muffled sounds, groans, like someone was being beaten, and I thought . . ." Wes tried to explain.

"It wasn't me. They sat me in a cell and I waited for days — maybe a week — until they took me to court."

Wes looked at him and then at the floor. "Good," he said, although he felt like a fool. They had gotten everything they wanted from him by tricking him. "Dad, during that trial, I didn't . . ."

"Wes, If you think for a moment I believed any of those things . . ." The old man's eyes were filling with tears.

"I'm sorry you had to see that."

"It wasn't your fault, Wes." They stood there, nodding, letting the silence hang between them, unsure what to say next. Then, both of them turned around, remembering they weren't alone, but Sarza was gone.

"These scenes are probably not her thing." Wes mused, half to himself and half to his father.

"Give her time."

"What?" Wes didn't understand.

"Your mother couldn't stand emotions, but she fell in love with me. She fell in love with a human. It just took some time."

"Oh! We're not . . . I'm not . . . she's not . . ." Wes was scrambling around for an explanation.

"Sure." Wes's father patted him on the shoulder. "Sure. You two are *not*. Totally not." Then, changing the subject, he said, "I have to go rest. We have a long trip ahead of us."

"Do you know where we are going?"

"No."

The two of them started walking out of the hangar and into the living quarters of the ship. As they walked through a hall, Wes saw Sax walking out of a room. He put two and two together: that was the voice on the coms when they were flying in. Sax looked serious, maybe even a little irritated. Wes hesitated for a moment. "Sax." The Sparcus man stopped and turned around to face them both. He walked toward them.

"Hello, Wes."

"Hi."

"Welcome back."

"Thank you." There was an awkward silence. Then Sax continued, "I'm needed at commands." And he walked past them toward the flight room.

"You know him?" Wes's father inquired.

"Yes. Sort of. We met on Astarte."

"You were on Astarte?" Carl was very surprised.

"Yes." Wes thought back to Astarte and to what had happened with Sarza. "Yes, I was."

They fell silent. Although he would have done anything to protect him, Wes had not seen his father in years. And it was hard to restart something that had been kept voluntarily dormant for so long. "I should go sleep." Wes—the excitement of the escape over—could feel the pain reappearing everywhere. It occurred to him that sleeping in a bed was about the best thing he could think of.

The two men parted, and Wes started walking down the hall. He wasn't sure where he was supposed to go, but he figured nobody would object if he found an empty cabin and stayed there. As he walked past the cabin Sax had exited, it opened. The doors were old-fashioned—metal slabs that slid upward. Sarza was sitting on her bed. Wes stopped. Jealousy—and there was no other word to call this—was suddenly gnawing at him. Why had Sax been in Sarza's room? It really wasn't his business. She had saved his life. That should have been enough from a human-hating Sparcus. But then it occurred to him: did she know he was a Sparcus? Maybe. News of the trial was everywhere. Then his fogged up mind cleared and it hit him. She *had* to know. She'd spent the last few weeks with his mother's protégés. They would have told her, for sure. They had probably told her everything they knew.

"Hi." She purred. This was the first time he had heard Sarza use that tone.

"Hi." His body was reacting to her voice a lot faster than his head.

"Come in." She wasn't asking. Wes did as he was told. The door closed behind him. He didn't even notice. He was entirely focused on Sarza. "What are we doing?" A rhetorical question if there ever was one.

"You are a Sparcus. I am a Sparcus. After pain, pleasure." She savored the moment, smiled, her eyes flirting with him. "Take your clothes off." Her hair was turning blue, lifting itself off her head, and brushing her shoulders as it waved sensuously in the air. For the first time since she met him, this felt right. This felt so right she could taste linking with him before it began. Wes pulled the clothes off, slowly, heeding his painful joints. She didn't rush him. She just watched.

"Come here." He approached the bed and bent down to kiss her. As he took her mouth onto his, he felt a rush, but the stimulant had nothing to do with it. This was the effect she had on him. He pushed her onto the bed and climbed on top of her. He didn't have to fake the Velcra hurting him. He wasn't going to fake anything anymore. Her legs were around his waist, were pulling him in. She inhaled, "You smell like a Sparcus. That familiar smell, it was yours. All along . . ." He smiled and kissed her again. "Shut up."

His hands ran down over her breasts and onto her hips. He found where her corset closed and started taking her clothes off as fast he could. Her corset came off first, then her boots, and then her leggings, followed by her turtleneck. Soon she was naked under him. He was still devouring her mouth with his. He moved down to her breasts, across her stomach, and between her legs, repeating what he had done on Astarte. She arched her back as his mouth came down on her. And although he knew he should probably spend more time there, he was done. He had wanted her for so long he thought he was going to turn as blue as her hair. He got back on top of her, pulling her violently down on the bed, ignoring the jolt of pain coming from his arms, and he was inside her.

She responded in kind, gripping his shoulders with her fingers and pulling him deeper. He made love to her with everything he had, discharging the frustration, pain, and misery of the past few months. He noticed how she ran her nails on her thighs, before she let her fingers drip between their stomachs, found herself and complemented what he was doing. She guided his rhythm with her other hand on his hip. Finally, when she was ready, she lifted herself and effortlessly turned him onto his back to ride him. She wasn't slowing down though. Her hips grinding against his. He felt so alive. Her fingers hadn't left her mound, but Wes — remembering Astarte and observing her in action now — gently pushed her fingers aside and took over the rhythmic rubbing from her, watching her reactions. They took their time, following each other's invitations, responding to desire. She guided his free hand onto her breast and her hair started turning green at the tips. He didn't let up, following her whispered requests, remembering what she had liked, watching as the color moved upward toward the roots until Sarza, finally, let out a groan followed by the most satisfying moan. Her green hair whipped wildly around her head. She pressed her hands into his chest. Wes wanted to be on top again now that she was done. He put her on her back, and looked at her half-closed purple eyes, her face still flush from climaxing. She kissed him, lightly, on the lips. Then, pushing against his chest, made him lift himself just enough so she could turn onto her stomach.

Her body was so inviting he wondered how he would ever get enough of her. He laid his chest against her back, and was back inside her, pinning her into the bed. He wanted her to be his. He wanted to possess her so thoroughly that she would never go to another Bashbathar in her life. He slowed down his pace. She grabbed his hand and slid it underneath her, leading his fingers back to work. As he traced light circles, he whispered in her ear, "Why was Sax here?"

Sarza relaxed, looked at him, he cheek on the bed, and smiled wickedly, "That is none of your concern." She closed her eyes again, melting in his hand.

"I don't want him to ever touch you again." It was a plea more than an order.

Sarza smiled, a nearly cruel smile this time. "Who touches me is none of your concern Wes." She moaned.

He grabbed her hair with his free hand, hard enough to sting, but not hard enough to hurt. "I want you to be mine." He couldn't believe he was saying that. He didn't understand how he could want this. He barely even knew this Sparcus.

"That's very *human* of you Wes, but Sparcus women don't belong to anyone. They belong to themselves." There was no anger in her. Her hair stayed blue, green, and shades in between. This was a game she was happy to play. Part flirt, part conversation, and part sex game, all rolled into one. Wes's mouth came down on hers. His fingers weren't letting up, applying a little more pressure. She moaned. He was a quick study and he listened. He was figuring out what she liked.

Sarza's hair started to turning green again. And, as an act of kindness, she quickly delivered the truth, "I told him I wasn't interested in his services . . ." She didn't finish her sentence as her hair flew up around Wes's face in a green glow. She groaned and mewled into the bed. Her behind came up to press against Wes's pelvis. He let go of her hair and buried his face in the bed, right above her shoulders. She reached around to run her hand through his hair. With a few hard, rhythmic thrusts, he finished himself inside her. After the final tremor subsided, he lay there on top of her, his chest on her back, their torsos moving in unison as they panted, reeling from afterglow. Wes finally rolled off and onto his back. He turned to look at Sarza. Her eyes were closed. Her face had the strongest, most fascinating features. And he loved her. It hit him like a ton of bricks. There was no doubt about it. He was in love with this creature. As he watched the emerald color disappear from her locks, he noticed it wasn't going back to its normal black. The green was turning darker and darker hues of green and then . . .

"Sarza."

"Hm-mm." She didn't open her eyes.

"Sarza . . ."

"Yeah." Her eyes were still closed and her face relaxed.

"What does brown mean?"

"What?" Sarza's eyes opened lazily.

"What does brown hair mean?"

"What? Why?" Sarza sat up and looked down at her now-brown mane. Her eyes widened. She looked at Wes, then at her hair, then at Wes again. She stood up. She swallowed. Then started walking away from him, backward, as though he had just turned into a monster.

"What's wrong?"

"Wes . . ." She paused. "Wes . . ."

"What?" He had no idea what was going on, and today had been stressful enough. Between confessing to multiple murders that he didn't commit, witnessing the start of an interplanetary war, being rescued from torturers, and having sex with a Sparcus—there was only so much he could take.

Sarza finally blurted it out, "We Matched, Wes. Brown hair means a Match. My hair will never change again. We Matched." She was holding up her hair and looking at it.

Wes was happy. He smiled a big goofy smile. "Okay! Congratulations to us then."

"No, no, no, no. You don't understand. Nobody has ever matched since the Great Slaughter."

"Okay . . ." Wes wondered how much his mother had *not* taught him growing up.

"You're a Sparcus male . . ."

"Yes."

"We just Matched."

"Yes Sarza. I think we've been over this." Wes was still confused.

"You don't understand. Matches only happen between partners who can produce offspring. Who can *actually* produce *excellent* offspring." Sarza was still standing across the cabin from him. She was staring at him, trying to explain herself. She put her hands on her face. He had no idea where she was going with this. Then, finally, she found the words, "You're a Sparcus male and you're *not* sterile." Wes was about to answer when the ship's comms came alive.

"Sarza! On deck!" That was Slitter. There was tension in her voice. This wasn't a social call. Sarza didn't hesitate. She rushed to gather her clothes and hurriedly dressed while Wes did the same. A minute or so later, they were both barreling down the hall to the flight room. They had to go up two flights of stairs. The flight room perched on the top of the ship, a large hemisphere of transparent material that gave whoever was at the controls perfect visibility. The hard shell was virtually unbreakable. Even direct hits would take a while to make a crack. Because the walls were all glass, and the controls were in small islands around the room. Each island had two chairs bolted to the floor. They were curved, with no sharp edges, in case people were thrown about the room. Mika, Pen, Jenna, Slitter, Sasha, Sax, and Carl O'Callagan were all there. The moment Sarza walked in, she realized what the problem was. A few fleeting glances her way triggered murmurs. The brown hair didn't go unnoticed, but there were more pressing matters to tend to.

A fleet of Sparcus SI-2200 war ships was pointing at them, lined up, ready to fire. The Sparcus war ships had not been flying — and supposedly not been built — since the end of the Conflict. They were dark red. Each of them had a control room much like the one she was standing on. They were a little larger than the Ambo-42. The number of visible weapons was impressive. But even more impressive was the sheer firepower of the SI-2200. They were also tremendously fast, able to produce a little anti matter around the tip and push the boundaries of speed. It had been one of the reasons the Sparcus had gained the upper hand thirty years ago. Sarza's stomach sank. They were dead in space.

The windows around Sarza also served as screens. She looked to the left and saw Maerah's face.

"Is she there?" Maerah asked.

"Yes." There was hesitation in Jenna's voice.

"Sarza. Turn yourself over and we will let the others go free." Maerah jumped straight to business. Wes walked up to Sarza's side in a futile attempt to protect her.

Sarza stayed silent. Either she died alone or they all died with her. This wasn't really giving her an option. Sarza walked over to the coms where Jenna sat. Jenna shifted to let Sarza take over.

"You don't want to do that Maerah."

"Why not?" Maerah was amused.

"I have Project Genesis." Sarza lied. Maerah laughed. She wasn't buying the bluff. Not even for a moment.

"No you don't, my dear."

"I have Project Genesis, and if you kill anyone on this ship, I will take it with me to my death."

Maerah was smiling. She leaned forward, her image getting a little bigger in the cabin. "Project Genesis doesn't exist Maerah. We just asked Earth to give it to us in exchange for protection from the other planets. And the fact is," she paused, serious now, still irritated at the news, "there never was a

Project Genesis. It's a myth!" The laughter had given way to anger. Now came the fury she had buried. Her cropped hair, what was left of it after she cut it off, turned a bright, fire red. The blond only made the bright red more like the color of blood. Her plan had failed. After all that effort, it had still failed.

Carl stepped to the coms. Everyone in the room looked at him, not understanding what he was doing. "Project Genesis exists, Maerah."

"Who are you?"

"Carl O'Callagan, Earth defector, collaborator on Project Genesis, and the only remaining person of the twenty who worked on it." The people in the flight room were baffled. Wes stared at his father in disbelief. He walked toward him. "What are you doing?" he whispered. "Are you out of your mind?"

Sarza was speechless. Her faced registered shock.

Maerah leaned forward. "That's impossible."

"Project Genesis was a Sparcus project. You really think Earth would try to find a way to reverse the sterilization? For what purpose? To have something to hold over you?" Maerah's expression betrayed her agreement with that hypothesis.

"Earth never gave a shit about you after you were done." Carl's words were brutal, venomous. Sarza didn't know if he hated Earth or Sparcus more at that moment. "They used science to destroy a civilization, and they washed their hands of it." He was definitely more angry at Earth!

"Prove it. Prove you have Project Genesis."

Carl turned off the coms and looked at Wes, who stood by his side. "If this can harm you, if what I am about to do can harm you, is it worth doing?"

"I don't know what you're talking about dad."

Carl breathed in then exhaled slowly through his nose. "Wes . . . I can't explain right now. But . . . you are Project Genesis." Across the room, Sarza felt her knees give way.

To stop herself from falling, she tensed and managed to stay standing—barely. She was having trouble breathing. She put her hand on the console next to her for support. Her eyes darted from Wes to his father and back again. This was incomprehensible. Carl continued, dropping his voice, "And I'm your father. I'm really your father. I conceived you with your mother." Sarza had her hand over her mouth. If what Carl was saying was true—true like a terrible nightmare that nobody thought could actually take place—then Wes was a half-blood. An abomination. The mixing of Sparcus genetic material with inferior human DNA. But, worst of all right now, she was Matched with a half-blood: an impossible, scientifically inconceivable, never-done-before, monstrosity.

Wes tried to ignore Sarza's reaction and without hesitation told his father, "Tell her. Tell her now. I have no idea what's going on, but they will kill all of us if you don't buy us time. Just tell her." He looked at Sarza. She was regaining her composure but they were each as baffled as the other.

Carl turned to Mika. "Give her a visual of this room."

Mika turned to her console, placed her hand on a glass plate, and a live feed of the flight deck appeared on another window that was then broadcast to Maerah's ship.

"Sarza, come here." Carl asked softly. Sarza stood up and walked toward him, slowly.

"Maerah, can you see Sarza?"

"Yes."

"Can you see the color of her hair?"

Maerah's expression changed. Her eyes widened as her eyebrows darted up, her mouth opened in a quiet gasp.

"When did it happen?"

Sarza was putting the pieces together. "Ten minutes ago."

"With whom?"

Carl jumped in, "No! I want safe passage. I want everyone on this ship to be safe. And I want Sparcus to ally itself with

Earth." He punctuated each part of his sentence by pressing the tip of his index finger against the console in front of him.

Maerah didn't answer.

Carl continued. "If you kill us all, you kill the chance of getting to Project Genesis. If at any moment you try something, I will kill myself. I'm an old man. I don't care. And . . ." he glanced at Wes, "Nobody else knows. Nobody else on any planet knows what I know about it. So." He left a pause after every word, "I demand a Sparcus alliance with Earth. And safety for everyone aboard this ship."

Maerah leaned back into her chair, still looking at Sarza's hair. She pressed two fingers to her lips, thinking about it. This was her basic plan all along. There was no downside. They would have a promised alliance with Earth—although now she actually had to make good on that promise. But the possibility of reversing Project Geno would make a short-lived alliance well worth it. If they could have children again, the Sparcus would be invincible once more.

"Deal."

Carl turned to Sarza. "You can answer her question. With who did this happen?"

Sarza clenched her teeth and silently pointed at Wes. Carl leaned on the console, the weight of his words making it difficult to keep going. "That's my son, Maerah." Then, looking up at her so that he was staring right at her through the screen, "That's Project Genesis."

Book II

Sparcus: Resurrection, is scheduled for
publication in **Spring 2014.**

For more information on the author, reviews, and Book II of
the Sparcus Series, visit us at www.TheSparcusSeries.com

www.ingramcontent.com/pod-product-compliance
Lightning Source LLC
Chambersburg PA
CBHW072226190626
46809CB00017B/684